UNCAGING THE SILENT SONGBIRD

THE SILVER LEAF SEDUCTIONS: BOOK 3

AVA DEVLIN

Uncaging the Silent Songbird

The Silver Leaf Seductions - Book 3

Ava Devlin

Copyright © 2021 by Ava Devlin

All rights reserved. This book or any portion thereof may not be reproduced or used in any manner whatsoever without the express written permission of the publisher except for the use of brief quotations in a book review.

Printed in the United States of America

First Printing, 2021

http://avadevlin.com

Contact the author at ava@avadevlin.com

Cover art by BZN Studio Designs

http://covers.bzndesignstudios.com

Copyediting by Claudette Cruz

https://www.theeditingsweetheart.com/

 Created with Vellum

For Marietta, who rescued and loved a little bird named Pip.

CHAPTER 1

Gigi Dempierre had always loved weddings.

Which was to say, she had always loved the *idea* of weddings.

She was certain she would love the real thing, too, if ever she were invited to attend one.

From a young age, she had imagined herself in flower-soaked meadows wrapped in bright sunshine or seated in a marble pew under the dome of a spectacular cathedral, watching rapt as a bride and groom exchanged vows.

Perhaps, to some, it was strange that Gigi did not place herself as the bride in these fantasies, but such a thing had never occurred to her younger self. After all, one only marries once or twice in a lifetime, but a person might attend an infinite amount of weddings as a guest.

Think of all that cake! The flowers! The gowns and hats and smiles and chatter! It was her perfect paradise, simply being allowed to experience it all, over and over in the way of childhood fancy. One wedding would be on a snowy morning, with crocus flowers down the aisle, and another in the blazing heat of summer, under the canopy of an enchanted forest, with the chatter of foxes and squirrels as an orchestra.

In any event, it came as no surprise to anyone that the morning of Gigi's first wedding attendance was a giddy affair, some twenty-three years into her sheltered existence.

Her mother, of course, had many opinions about what Gigi should wear, how she should style her hair, and what she would say and to whom, upon leaving the little Rococo castle perched on the white cliffs of Dover. This was, after all, a very rare (and much-anticipated!) social event amongst the British.

"Of course, most of the attendees are already aware of who we are and what we do," Therese Dempierre said with a crease in her brow, tapping her manicured fingernail to her chin as her daughter flitted about the bedroom, comparing this dress to that one, already corseted into her underthings. "You'll need to watch your words, of course, but I think a degree of comfort is not inappropriate, especially as you are such intimates with Mrs. Atlas."

Gigi rolled her eyes, keeping her back to her mother, and settling on a confection of pale pink streaked with white. "*Maman*, I do not know why you think me so indiscreet. I have never given you cause to worry."

To that, Therese Dempierre gave a delicate snort. "You only believe that because your brother's recklessness so frequently eclipses your own."

"So perhaps you should go scold him instead?" Gigi

suggested with a sniff. She strode over to her vanity mirror, plucking two white feathers from a silk cloth, and held them up to the dress she'd chosen to ensure the shade matched. Yes, this would do very nicely. She would make a fitting guest in the presence of the bride.

She blinked her eyes, inviting in sunlight to compare the moss green of her irises to the pale pink of the frock. Yes, she thought it would look well. It was still summer, after all, even if only barely. She spread the winning dress over her bed and tucked her hair behind her ears, signaling to her maid that she was ready for her attentions.

"I saw Isabelle's bridal gown while Mme. Bisset was still working on it," she said to her mother, sighing wistfully as she sank into the chair opposite her mirror. "It is absolutely divine. Sea foam green with little daisies on the neckline."

"She is a dear girl," Therese replied, seeming to measure her words, "though only passingly familiar with the scope of the Silver Leaf Society. I, of course, encourage your friendship, but do mind your tongue."

"I always do," Gigi replied, with only a tiny drop of acid to her words.

It was true, after all, and the bride, Isabelle Monetier, had spent several months aboard her brother's boat without him having to put lock and key on every word he said to her. Isabelle was already embroiled, neck-deep in the Silver Leaf whether she liked it or not, and so was her husband-to-be.

Gigi resisted the urge to sigh again at her mother's senseless concern. Whatever Isabelle did not know already, she would surely learn in the days to come, whether or not Gigi was present for those revelations. Such was the burden of her birth and her choice in spouse.

Meanwhile, Gigi's brother, Mathias, was already docked outside of Meridian House, likely enjoying early-morning libations with the groom and other gentlemen, thinking not at all about any of the words he might say from one moment to the next.

Sometimes she hated Mathias a little bit for the freedom he had, though she knew it was not his fault she had been born a girl, nor was it his choice to have all the privileges that came with being a man.

She loved her brother, of course, but they bickered the way siblings are wont to do. Even at this stage of their ever-mentioned maturity, there would always be a streak of ribbing and rivalry between them.

The fact that he would be officiating the wedding today, for example, had given Gigi endless hours of entertainment, many of which had been spent acting as though this made Mathias a man of the cloth—which meant he would need to embrace all the piousness and restraint that goes along with such a noble designation.

It was, she knew, a particularly grating suggestion for her rakish brother, whose carefully cultivated image as the swaggering sea captain brought him great pleasure and pride.

She chuckled to herself, letting her eyes flicker shut as her maid began to comb through her hair, and imagined what Mathias would look like in a vicar's vestments, all buttoned up to the throat. She could only picture him thus with a big frown on his face, his dimples drooping down into his chin.

"Did you assemble the documents for Zelda?" her mother interrupted, already wearing her customary mask of concern as Gigi readied herself for any outing beyond the walls of *La Falaise*. "If not, I will finish them now. I would rather be done with any direct contact with that particular woman as quickly as possible."

"Hm, is that true?" Gigi replied blandly, if only for a jolt of silent amusement at the way her mother's eyes narrowed. "Yes, the packet is assembled. I also took the liberty of binding it up in an envelope for increased security. It is all rather exciting, isn't it? We could turn the tide of the war!"

"I very much hope we do not," her mother confessed, a frown turning the corners of her lips. "Our mission has always been about individuals on both sides of the conflict and reuniting them with their families. It is politically neutral and far more palatable to me than favoring one nation or the other. Zelda agreeing to such a high-profile exchange without consulting the rest of us makes me very nervous, especially considering the way these ambitious undertakings have harmed us in the past."

Gigi knew better than to respond, lowering her eyes and pressing her lips shut as her maid twisted and pinned tresses of her golden-blonde hair to her head. It had been a very long war, and one that had displaced her family from France to England, leaving them somewhat suspended between loyalty to both nations.

Her mother was one of five founding members of the Silver Leaf Society, though only two remained today to share the burdens of operating the cause. One had died, one had been caught, and one had been missing for some months now, having escaped the Silver Leaf's only French headquarters and vanished into the shadows with her husband. Her disappearance was the other matter that would need to be discussed today.

"Has there been any news of the Oliviers?" Gigi asked, though she knew very well there hadn't. "I confess I have had nightmares about what may have befallen them."

Therese shook her head, looking unsettled as well. "Pauline is very canny, and Gerard is wise and cautious. I have no doubt they have landed on their feet. I simply cannot fathom why they would do so without making contact, if only to assure us that the two of them are safe and well."

"Perhaps Zelda will have news," Gigi said optimistically. "She always seems to have the best information."

"Yes, for all her bile, I'll give her that," her mother said with a shrug. "Zelda is very effective, and she cares for Pauline and Gerard Olivier. We will discuss it after the wedding, when we go over the documents you assembled. You have been doing very good work lately, my love, and it is much appreciated."

"There has been much to do," Gigi said with a grin. "Thank goodness for new discoveries of old ledgers, hm? Sometimes I feel as though I can see the distant shores when I'm reading those entries."

"I hope that you can," her mother replied with a sentimental little smile. "I wish I could pluck my memories of home from behind my eyes and give them to you, wrapped in ribbons and bows. Someday, little bird, we will go home."

Gigi had never been to France, but a Frenchwoman was all she had ever been.

At home, where grand parties were hosted for other exiles, only French was spoken, and the manners of their ancestral home were expected. On days she walked the streets of Dover, familiar to her as anything could possibly be, she was a foreigner, French to her bones.

Despite being born and bred on English soil, despite knowing their names and their families and their wares, the people of Kent would never see Gigi Dempierre as anything but a French girl, far from home.

It was a strange creature to be, she thought, though her mother had always disagreed. It was yet another thing to envy about her brother, for Mathias had visited France so many times, she had lost count. She felt that this meant he knew who he was, better than she ever might hope to match.

Today, when she boarded the *Harpy* for the first time, to sail out onto the Channel for the wedding vows, she would be closer to that storied nation than ever before, even if it was still nothing more than a line on the horizon.

It was one of many exciting and promising changes that had entered her life over this last year. It seemed to her that a gear had finally fallen into place, and allowed the clockworks of her life to experience motion for the very first time. She did not dare speak it aloud, but she fervently hoped that these changes were only the beginning of a future full of surprises.

After all, having been born and raised in the thick of a secret society should have been a great deal more exciting than it had been. For Gigi, all it had meant was a keener eye on her studies and how they might benefit the Silver Leaf

Society, and a tighter rein on her words, lest she accidentally release a secret in mixed company.

She knew it was important, yes, and she was glad to be a part of it. Proud, even. It was just that it had been so dreadfully boring, and often quite lonesome.

Outside of the Silver Leaf, it was only the other French that her parents kept on a close social tether. There were only so many maudlin gatherings of fellow exiles a girl could attend before it all became repetitive. Even the guests that were no older than Gigi herself seemed to endlessly mourn for a world that was long gone, and would certainly never return.

Of course, every servant at *La Falaise* had dealings with her mother's secret society in one way or another. Many of them, like the maid dressing Gigi's hair this morning, had been smuggled over borders and reunited with either loved ones or the embrace of safe harbor in a time of war.

For all the days of her life, Gigi Dempierre had been clutched close to the bosom of those invested in her family's secrets, and as such, she could never escape the aura of strangeness that settled over her, simply due to proximity.

Privately, in the most secret part of her soul, Gigi thought that she would choose to stay in England, if ever the opportunity arose to return. It was something she could never say aloud, even in the safety of her home, and so perhaps all of those years of learning to bite her tongue had been worthwhile after all.

A cooing chatter from the window drew her thoughts back to the present and put a smile on her face. Her two favorite parakeets were rising from their down-tucked slumber, greeting this new day with their customary gentle enthusiasm. They stretched their elegant necks, stuck out their twiggy legs, and twitched their wings as they hopped about on their perches, enjoying the early rays of sunlight streaming in from outside.

The female was reserved, chiming sparingly as she spread her vibrant green wings and used her beak to fluff them. The male, powder blue and smaller than his mate, had chosen to strut back and forth on the longest perch, crooning at the sun as though he had missed it terribly through the night. They suited one another well.

"*Mademoiselle Dempierre!*" the maid tutted, losing her grip on one of the tendrils of hair she was weaving into place. "You must stay still!"

"*Désolée, désolée,*" Gigi apologized, but so cheerfully that the maid could not repress a returning smile. "Is Pip's morning song not a joy to us all?"

"He sings beautifully, of course," the maid admitted, "though I rather think he ought to let his lady love have the aria once in a while. I would be very cross if my husband always outshone me."

"Husband," Therese Dempierre repeated with a dry laugh. "Have the birds entered legal union?"

"Of course they are married, *Maman*," Gigi told her with a grin. "Pip would not dishonor Emerald in such a profligate fashion! Besides, she prefers to sing at night. They support one another when it is time to sing."

"Married your parakeets, did you?" Therese asked, breaking into a dimpled smile. "Are both of my children officiators?"

"I consider myself more of a facilitator," Gigi replied, indicating to her maid the feathers she wished to have woven into her curls, her eyes sparkling with happiness. "I'm sure one of the other birds saw to the legalities."

"Oh, naturally," her mother replied with faux seriousness. "Speaking of which, I had best ensure your father is dressed. There is a jest implied at this juncture about feather-brained husbands, but I shan't make it. Meet us at the coach in no more than twenty minutes, *d'accord?*"

Gigi nodded, her fingers twitching and feet burning to leap up and be away immediately, though she had manners enough to allow her maid to complete the work on her hair. The pink dress was swept up with appropriate haste, and as Gigi stepped into it, she stole a glance at her reflection, feeling anticipation gather up in her chest like champagne bubbles free of their cork.

"I am so excited," she said to herself, to the maid, to the birds, to the universe at large. "It is going to be a spectacular day!"

CHAPTER 2

*K*it Cooper had not attended many weddings in his life, but he was fairly certain that today's was the strangest he had ever come across.

Perhaps its strangeness was intentional. It was certainly fitting.

After all, the bride and groom were unconventional, as was the hosting family, the venue, and the guests besides. All things considered, maybe it was far more mundane than it should have been?

In Kit's experience, these events were usually already partially underway by the time guests arrived, with a harried vicar and his underlings ushering people into seats and plying them with refreshment. Not so this morning at Meridian, where Kit had simply found a place to stand that felt appropriately out of the way, and watched a ballet of curious to and fro unfold around him on the green, unburdened with biscuits or wine, and uncertain when or how the actual wedding would start.

There was no church to gather in and wait for things to kick off. Kit wasn't even certain how formal his attire should have been, though he'd erred on the side of caution and worn his finest waistcoat. Any effort he'd put into taming his sandy blond mop had already been destroyed by the late-summer breeze that was raking over the wedding party in one direction, then another, then back again, as though it, too, were impatient for the main event to commence.

He realized that he did not recognize a single person on the green just now. From here, the white-blond hair of a man in the distance might have been the bride's adoptive father, though it was impossible to be certain through the trees. He had only met the man once before, anyhow.

He certainly had never seen any of these children before. They ranged in age from what appeared to be mid-adolescence to those who still needed help pulling on their knee socks, each one with dark brown hair and rosy-cheeked enthusiasm. He wondered how so many nearly identical-looking little people kept each other straight. He also wondered how many of the squeals they made as they ran in merry chaos across the lawn were glee or distress. With children, it was hard to say.

Had Nell, his cousin's wife, and her twin, the groom Peter, grown up in this gaggle of adolescent chaos? If so, they had come out the other end remarkably well composed. He winced as one child began to wail and another demonstrated just how amusing he found this development. Were children always so exhausting? It was a wonder anyone had them apurpose.

What a blessing to have been an only child, hm? Or was this not the usual way of siblings?

He decided to ask the opinion of the guest nearest to him, but when he turned to see what polite and silent guest was creating the shadow to his left, he found next to him a rather dignified-looking donkey, staring out at the ocean waves with a determination that Kit thought was singularly devoted to not acknowledging the children in question.

For all that she was a donkey, his companion looked rather festive for the wedding day, wearing a garland of daisies atop her head and a loose-knit white blanket over her back. She swung her head over to meet his eye and blinked at him expectantly, as though she would hear what he was going to say, even if she was not the companion he might have been expecting.

"Lovely weather we're having," he said, winning a rather encouraging flutter of the lashes from the daisy-topped donkey. He chuckled, sinking his hands into his pockets, and craned his neck around to take in the rest of the lawn, hoping for a familiar face.

His mother had vanished almost the instant they had arrived this morning. She had spent the last week beside herself with a very particularly focused excitement, talking frequently of how much she was looking forward to attending the bride. Kit wasn't entirely certain what type of assistance a woman needed on the morning of her wedding, but it must be a very demanding affair, for Isabelle's chambers today were no less than a gravitational force that had absorbed every woman who had yet arrived to this affair with alarming and precise consistency.

He chuckled, picturing the bride's distress at all these women packed into her chambers, each one hoping to be the next to help her button a cuff or find an earring. She had not grown up with attendants or any of this fanfare. He imagined she would have much preferred to dress on her own today and was, at this very moment, considering escaping out the window while her coterie of attendants were distracted by their next task.

Isabelle was rather more like Kit himself than her brother, he thought with no small degree of pleasure. He looked forward to coaxing an honest accounting of her morning from her once she'd had a glass or three of the fine French wine waiting for them on the banquet table.

Isabelle. His cousin. The bride.

It was a strange collection of thoughts still, though he had now known her for over a month. How odd it was to successfully find a missing person, someone that has already been grieved and folded into the domain of the past! He could barely remember a time before when he had thought her dead and gone, and now suddenly here she was, as vibrant as the blazing sun.

Whatever he could recall of her from those long-ago years was no longer relevant in the least. She had still been just a baby in swaddling the last time he'd seen her, her only actions either screaming or snoring. And here he was, in the blink of an eye, ready to watch her walk down the aisle and bind herself to a husband.

She looked like her mother. Everyone said so.

Kit only remembered Aunt Mary in passing, a shadow that had lurked behind his father's eyes and spoken through his mother's stories. He was still coming to know Isabelle, just as her brother, Nathaniel was, and what an odd thing, when

Kit and Nathaniel had spent every day of their early lives together, as familiar to one another as can be.

People often thought them brothers, with looks similar enough that no one could mistake the relation, even if their temperaments were frequently at odds. Would Kit and Nate have grown up the way they had, forging a bond as tight as it was, if Isabelle had not been spirited away to flourish elsewhere? Or would she be the one Nathaniel considered his closest bond, leaving Kit alone to find companionship elsewhere?

It was an uncomfortable question, and Kit shook it off, reminding himself that the domain of brooding belonged to Nate and Nate alone. Today was to be a joyous day. She was home now, and that was all that mattered, even if he was not invited to fawn and fuss over her as she readied herself for matrimony.

The absence of the ladies did raise the question of where the devil all the men had gotten off to, though, and he swung around, scanning the sparse population of people on the Meridian green, looking for someone to whom he could attach himself until such a time as he was given a place to sit and a scene to view. No offense to the donkey, of course. She was welcome to come along.

He confirmed yet again that he did not recognize a single person on this lawn. His cousin, Nathaniel, whose home served as their current venue, was nowhere to be found, nor was Peter Applegate, the groom, or, as a last resort, Mathias Dempierre, the ship's captain who would be marrying the happy couple.

The man who might have been the father of the bride had found conversation elsewhere, likely with the father of the groom, and they had paired off to talk amongst themselves near a cluster of fruit trees, leaving the gaggle of unmonitored children to run willy-nilly with Isabelle's little dog in the middle of the fray.

This left Kit and his unexpected companion alone near the cliff face, watching the lazy roll of the Channel waves as all the matters that made weddings happen were apparently being attended to by people far more capable than either of them.

"It's no matter," he said to the donkey, who was a very good listener. "There could be far worse company than just myself. And you, of course, mysterious lady."

"I believe her name is Hortensia," came a posh and somewhat chilly female voice from behind. "Rather grand for such a creature, but eye of the beholder, I suppose."

He turned to find a tall, slender woman of middling age had approached, evidently with impressive stealth. She was dressed for the occasion, in a smartly cut blue gown with a pile of stark white hair gathered atop her head in a style he recognized as fashionable, but managed somehow to look severe.

She had handsome features, high cheekbones, and eyes of flashing pale gray, and when she smiled at him, Kit rather got the impression it was the way a panther smiles at her prey. He immediately knew who she was, and evidently the recognition was mutual.

"You must be the Cooper boy," she said to him. "Christopher, is it?"

"Kit," he said genially, extending a hand. "No one calls me Christopher."

She arched a brow, apparently pleased at the offer of a handshake rather than some form of foppish gender play, and returned the gesture with a firm and assured grip. "Zelda Smith," she told him. "I am aunt to Peter and Nell."

"Ah, yes!" he said, cracking a smile. "Nathaniel has mentioned his wife's fearsome aunt. Steel and silver, he calls you, though only in the most respectful tones."

The woman's lips curled up on one side, the faintest impression of amusement as she rested a gloved hand on the donkey's back.

Hortensia stilled at the touch, evidently humbled by this gracious acknowledgement, her daisy crown fluttering in the light summer breeze.

"Nathaniel's tone is rarely indicative of his true feelings," said Zelda Smith. "You are not with the groomsmen?"

"I'm afraid I am quite taken with Lady Hortensia here," he said somberly. "And to be honest, I am only casually acquainted with both bride and groom, despite the relation. I've never known what to do with myself at events like this, anyhow."

"I tend to seek out the spirits at my earliest convenience," Zelda Smith told him, as though imparting a sacred wisdom rather than cracking a jest. "I am rather fond of gin, in fact, if you've knowledge of its current whereabouts."

"Gin!" he replied in surprise. "I would have predicted a fortified wine or perhaps an aged whiskey for a lady such as yourself."

She motioned that he should offer her his arm and wove a firm hand through it, patting the donkey on the rump as a means of good-bye. "Perhaps do not mention my fondness for gin to my sister or my niece," she said, after giving it a moment of thought. "I'm sure they'd wonder where I picked up such a questionable habit."

They walked toward the house, his cousin's ancestral manor, warm and welcoming on the hill in a way he had still not entirely become accustomed to. The place had sat derelict and abandoned for so long that for a moment, every time Kit glanced at the old house, it seemed to flash in time, uncertain which version of itself it should be before his eyes.

The woman at his side invoked a similar phenomenon. Such tales he'd heard of this woman, many later recanted as misunderstanding. Yet she did seem to him to be wrought of the same pure and polished alloy that made up the most fearsome of weapons. Some women were flowers, delicate and sweet. This one was a sword.

He had made her smile, he reminded himself, even if only just a little. He imagined it was an honor he did not share with many men.

"Whose donkey is it, by the by?" he asked, opening the door of Meridian House for the lady and leading her in the direction of the most thorough collection of spirits, held in the drawing room. "I cannot imagine it belonging to Nathaniel and Nell."

Mrs. Smith gave a dry chuckle, releasing his arm and passing over to the drink cart, tapping her fingers on the bottle tops until she found the one she wanted. "The answer to that question is a matter of some contention," she said wryly. "What will you drink, Mr. Cooper?"

"Gin sounds just the thing," he replied, if only for the novelty of it. "I'm sure there will be plenty of champagne after the vows, should anyone suspect our pedestrian indulgence."

"Right-o," Mrs. Smith clipped, pouring two glasses with smart precision. "We shall be lowbrow in solidarity."

Kit clinked his glass against hers as she passed it to him. "I don't suppose you know when the wedding is supposed to commence?" he asked, settling himself onto the settee. "I feel as though I arrived hours too early."

She gave a brief cast of her eyes heavenward. "I quite agree," she said, tipping the clear liquid into her mouth. "The boat is docked below, so I'm certain we could make our way down there at any time and await the others, but I rather prefer the ground under my feet to remain stationary. Perhaps I will go hasten things along after our little tipple. We have quite a lot more than just an exchange of vows to get through today, after all."

Kit raised his eyebrows but did not reply. If there was more to weddings than vows and the food that followed, that was news to him, and as far as he was concerned, ignorance was as good a reason as any to escape before he could be asked to participate in any assortment of other wedding-related rituals.

Suddenly he felt as though the formidable woman across the room was studying him, taking his measure over the rim of her glass of gin. She opened her mouth as though to spin the first silken thread of a web he would never escape, and by all the mercy of heaven above, the wedding appeared to begin in earnest before she could say a thing.

CHAPTER 3

The vows had been beautiful enough that Gigi was only passingly concerned with her current state of being—which was drenched in salt water in the wake of a particularly enthusiastic wave.

Mathias had warned her, of course, that her perch on the railing may come with consequences, but it had been the ideal view of the ceremony, unimpeded by the other guests.

She doubted anyone in the wedding party had noticed a girl in pink, clinging to the ship's railing in their periphery, because they were all (rightfully!) entranced by the spectacle of true love unfolding before them. And, because they hadn't known she was there in the first place, they had all been delightfully oblivious to the moment in which she was accosted by a lunging wave of ocean spray.

Honestly, despite the sudden slap of cold, the brief moment of absolute terror that she was about to go overboard, and the persistent sting of salt in her eyes in the aftermath, Gigi had no regrets.

Her mother, however, appeared to have several regrets, primary among them the decision to birth such an embarrassing daughter into this world. She had found Gigi mere minutes after the conclusion of the vows, sodden and entrenched in hiccups alternating with laughter.

Even keeping herself hidden near the bend of the captain's quarters, Gigi could not evade her mother.

The fluffy white feathers that had been woven into her hair that morning were now sad, limp things, clinging to Gigi's wet cheeks. Gigi suspected her mother could see the amusement in the whole affair, but was just too stubborn to show it.

"Oh, Gigi, *quelle catastrophe!*," she had moaned, gripping two handfuls of water-logged silk from Gigi's pink skirt in her hands and attempting to wring them dry. "What a lovely dress, too! I'm certain this is quite ruined!"

"Nonsen—" Here Gigi hiccupped, bunching her fingers to her mouth to stop another gurgle of laughter from escaping her lips. She cleared her throat, her eyes watering with the effort of keeping her giggles contained, and spoke again with as much calm as she could muster. "Nonsense, *Maman*. We will simply stretch it out in the sun and have the salt brushed away once it is dry."

"And until then?" her mother demanded, her eyes locking onto Gigi's with a sarcastic widening of would-be trust. "Will you eat the wedding breakfast in a puddle of brine?"

"I will borrow a dress from Nell," Gigi assured her, though she knew very damn well that Nell's clothes would never fit her without hours of alteration.

Another gust of summer wind came curling over the bow, dragging the wet feathers so far down her cheek that she had to bat them away before they attempted to enter her mouth. This, of course, prompted another fit of giggles, which inspired her mother to finally wash her hands of Gigi entirely and stalk off back into the crowd as the *Harpy* made its way back to the shore.

It was Mathias who found her next, stopping dead in his tracks en route to his quarters. He'd found her leaned over the railing, attempting to squeeze the water from her hair, all the pins and feathers that had bound it into respectable fashion now discarded in a soggy pile at her feet.

Quite the opposite of *Maman*, Mathias immediately grinned, dimples popping into both of his cheeks, and then indulged in an episode of hearty laughter at her expense.

"The sea is a cruel mistress," he told her after he'd had his fill, wicking a tear from the corner of his eye. "And it's made a sorry consort out of you, I'm afraid."

"I can't think what you mean," Gigi replied, returning his dimpled smile in a mirror of familiar ribbing and tossing her wet rope of hair over her shoulder. "I feel quite refreshed."

This sparked another round of laughter, which caught from brother to sister, until both were pink-faced and weak from the force of it. Mathias slid into a deck chair and motioned that his sister should take the other, propping his boots up on the edge with his customary *laissez-faire*.

"Ahh, this is why *Maman* is stalking around the deck, brandishing her champagne flute like a club," he realized, shaking his head. "We'll spirit you into the house to change without anyone noticing, I promise. I daresay Nell is pregnant enough now that some of her things might actually fit you."

Gigi threw the nearest object at his head, rather than responding—in this case, a ball of twine a crewman had left near her chair.

"I imagine it would be very roomy to my hips and then end entirely," she mused, picturing the much slighter, much shorter Eleanor Atlas standing alongside her. "For as much as I pester her to borrow her things, I'm fairly certain the only thing I could wear is her jewelry."

"I'll ask Isabelle," he said with a touch more sincerity. "She's much closer to your shape and always eager to aid unfortunates."

"Yes, it's clear you're very fond of bride and groom both," Gigi said, turning onto her hip to study her brother. "I thought, at first, that you might be jealous that Applegate won the hand of the fair maiden, rather than yourself."

"No." He shook his head with an affectionate twist of his lips. "They were marked for one another from the first. You should have seen it."

They looked in unison across the deck, to where the auburn-haired bride whispered secrets to her bespectacled groom, their hands intertwined as the ocean glittered around them. They made a handsome couple indeed, Gigi thought, but was still surprised by her brother's selflessness in the affair. After all, he had always prided himself on the attentions of ladies, and had never had to try very hard to win them, besides.

"You didn't even *attempt* to woo her?" Gigi asked skeptically, watching as he turned back to her with a look of exasperation in his amber eyes.

"No! Is it so difficult to think I might simply have made a couple of friends?"

"Yes," Gigi replied earnestly, which got the ball of twine tossed back directly at her nose, where it painlessly bounced back toward her brother and came to land on the deck.

"You've got Nell," he pointed out. "And that seems rather a new frontier of companionship for you. Would you say that, before she arrived, freshly married and alone in a new place, that you had anyone you'd call a friend?"

She narrowed her eyes and opened her mouth to say of course she had, but something about the way he was looking at her made her pause and consider the question. "I've been friendly with many people over the years," she said after a moment, thinking of the banquets and balls held at *La Falaise* and the townspeople in Dover.

"And it is the same? Those people from parties and marketplace are equal to your intimacy with Nell?"

"Well, no," she confessed with a little frown, "but that's to do with business, isn't it? When I am with Nell, I don't have to mind my tongue or dissect every word she says. Those I can talk freely around tend to be much older than us, don't they? Madame Bisset and so on. Of course, Nell is special to me."

"Yes, exactly," he agreed. "Peter and Isabelle are the same. The two of them were tossed into a mission with me as equals. They weren't members of my crew to require authority, nor were they Silver Leaf smugglers with questionable values and secret motives for their own involvement. There were no secrets to keep or ambitions at odds with one another between the three of us. It was ... nice. Honest. I wouldn't change a single moment of it."

"The ceremony was lovely," Gigi told him, oddly touched by this confession from her notoriously flippant sibling. "You did a wonderful job. The *Harpy* has never looked so fine, even when she was new."

He rolled his eyes at her, but she thought she detected a slight swell of pride in his chest at the observation. If asked, Mathias would insist that the only woman for him was his ship, and while such a thing was among the more stupid refrains that lined his verbal arsenal, she knew that he did love this boat dearly, almost as though it had a spirit of its own.

The snap of the sails being brought down and the creaking of the wooden beams above them signaled that they had returned to shore. Mathias suggested she hide in his quarters until the ship had emptied, and promised he would return for her once the shore had emptied of anyone whose judgement might send their mother into further dramatics.

KIT HAD EXPECTED to have a fairly straightforward day. The attendance of a wedding comes with a certain litany of events to which one might reasonably taper his expectations. He had thought he'd arrive, chat a bit with his cousin, watch the vows, and gorge himself on some wedding cake.

The day, thus far, was proving significantly more complicated than that.

If the surprises had remained in the vein of polite chatter with a donkey, he would have been perfectly amenable to that. Kit wasn't an unreasonable bloke, and when necessary, was happy to adapt to new and surprising scenarios. That's what had kept him alive in the war, after all.

Those battle instincts he'd honed on faraway shores had begun to tingle before they'd even embarked for the ceremony. That woman, Zelda Smith, had an unsettling canniness about her. As charming as it was to drink gin with a woman of breeding, he had begun to get a rather persistent feeling that he had wandered into a trap.

She hadn't asked anything of him, at least not yet, but she had been whispering with others in the wedding party, casting glances his way as though she were consulting on plans for his imminent future. He found that he did not enjoy this turn of events even a little.

To make matters worse, he had located his mother. It wasn't the finding her that was discomfiting, but the state of her when he had, giggling behind her gloves at the very direct charms of that Frenchman Yves Monetier, Isabelle's adoptive father. Kit did not begrudge his mother, who had been a widow for some time, a spot of flirtation. He simply wished never to have to witness it personally, nor think about it, or know it was possible.

He found himself keenly distrusting of the sparkle in Monetier's eyes, and had positioned his body during the vows in such a way that interrupted his mother's repeated attempts to glance at the man during the ceremony. At least, for this part of the ordeal, Monetier had been singularly focused on his daughter in her wedding dress, her hands clasped with Peter Applegate's and vowing to be his forevermore.

If Susan Cooper had been enjoying a clear view of this fellow, weeping openly over his love for a little girl that he had raised from naught but the goodness of his heart, Kit was fairly certain she would swoon or do some other uncomfortable nonsense for which he was in no way prepared. He would perhaps warm to the idea over time, though the impulse to remind his mother that she had always fostered a long and hearty distrust of the French was a difficult one to shake.

Then, of course, there had been the patch of waves they'd hit during their return to shore. Great walls of water had splashed up over the bow of the ship, rocking them to and fro in such a way that made Kit wonder if that gin he'd enjoyed before was about to make an encore appearance. Mercifully, they docked before any untoward body functions could humiliate him in front of an audience.

He resolved to spend at least a quarter hour cloistered in Meridian House, hiding from all of them. He just needed a second to breathe without that silver-haired matron plotting his demise or his mother flirting with men or the ground conspiring beneath his feet to make him ill. Yes, just a few moments to breathe, and he would be right as rain.

It wasn't that Kit hated surprises. He just preferred predictability. And, mercifully, he was familiar enough with Meridian and its secrets to be able to slip into the solace of the house's embrace quickly and discreetly. He suffered a small pang of guilt as he passed by dear, dignified Hortensia, currently suffering the attentions of a plump-legged child who wished to crawl onto her back.

"Sorry, old girl," he muttered to himself as he hurried past. "I'll save you next time."

He took the stairs two at a time, aiming for the guest bedroom he had used once or twice during the early days when they were renovating the manor. It was Isabelle's room right now, and as she was firmly occupied with her wedding party downstairs, he was confident that she would not mind if he took a moment to enjoy her view of the cliffs and catch his breath.

He eased the door open and slipped in, careful not to draw the attention of any maids or footmen who were wandering about the second floor. He turned and inhaled deeply, immediately beset by an improved feeling of peace. He crossed the room and dropped himself onto the fainting couch opposite the window, flinging one heavy arm up over his eyes. Perhaps he would doze for just a moment, he thought, and simply start the day anew when he woke.

"That was fast!" came a female voice seemingly originating in the walls.

Kit's eyes snapped open, his body tensed to leap from the chaise once he determined its source, but the invisible lady was chattering away, evidently unconcerned.

"I was hoping you could take this outside and stretch it out in the sun to dry. Was Isabelle wi..." She stopped speaking on a startled gasp, the wet *plop* of her bundle of fabric smacking onto the floor as she emerged from behind a privacy screen that blended quite seamlessly into the wall.

She was wearing nothing but wet undergarments, ropes of messy blonde hair hanging over her bare arms. The white fabric clung to her pink skin, her legs plastered tightly against her chemise and her bosom swelling up over stays that were still cinched tight, despite their current state of damp. The lashes around her moss-green eyes were spiky with water, a few droplets of sea spray still beading on her shoulders and throat.

They stared at one another in wide-eyed horror for what Kit was certain was the longest second that had ever passed on this or any other plane of existence, before Kit scrambled to his feet, shielding his eyes, and immediately mumbling apologies while the mysterious, scantily clad, *beautiful* young woman he'd barged in on simply stood frozen in place with her mouth open.

He fumbled forward, reaching for the door, and shot out into the hallway as fast as he could manage, gripping the wooden railing in his hands as he dragged several breaths into his lungs.

Apparently, a moment of reprieve was not destined for him today.

In front of him was the expectant wedding party and behind him was a young miss he had very likely just traumatized beyond repair. If anyone found out what had just happened, he felt certain he'd be shuffled back out onto that damned boat and married off as well, and this time he *would* lose the contents of his stomach all over those freshly scrubbed decks.

He wanted to curse, but couldn't quite find an expletive that was suitable for all that had happened in such a short span of time.

He briefly wondered if he ought to just flee and never return, or perhaps fling himself down the stairs and hope for the sweet embrace of unconsciousness. But alas, this damnable day was not done with Kit Cooper.

Not yet.

Not by half.

CHAPTER 4

"*A*re you *quite sure* you're well?" Mathias asked for the third time, his flaxen brows pulled together in concern as the pair of them descended the stairs exiting Meridian house and walked out onto the green. "You didn't catch a chill, did you? *Maman* will blame the boat if you caught a chill, and we both know it. I do not need more fussing about the dangers of the sea from her."

"I'm fine, Mathias," Gigi lied, her voice struggling to escape against the lump of mortification that was still thoroughly lodged in her throat.

Obviously she was not fine.

She had never been a very good liar. That's why she had been taught to simply not speak at all, and in most circumstances, silence might have worked in her favor, but with her brother, she knew it would only concern him further.

"You look perfectly well in that borrowed frock," he said, frowning. "Is it because your hair is a bit damp? I think it tames your waves rather nicely."

Instinctively, Gigi raised a hand to touch her hair, which felt odd as the salt dried between the strands. It had been a great deal fluffier than she was accustomed to, and after several failed and remarkably lumpy efforts to twist it back into a chignon, she had pinned the sides behind her ears and hoped for the best. Now, on top of everything, she must also fret over frizz!

She forced herself to swallow down the lump in her throat, curving her lips into a mild affectation of happiness once they drew close enough to be observed, and tugged Mathias along at a faster clip, eager to get to the table so that she would not have to evade his concerns any longer.

A wedding feast had been prepared on several long tables on the Meridian green. Framed by the distant sparkle of the ocean and the elegant frame of a freshly painted gazebo, it presented a charming and welcoming image that Gigi hoped was far more interesting than her disarray. There was already a buzz of happy conversation as guests chose seats and admired the food, and it only took a brief sweeping glance along the table to locate the man who had seen her looking like a particularly promiscuous drowned squirrel just a little while ago.

He was pointedly not looking at her, instead making what appeared to be very forced conversation with a woman seated to his side who shared his coloring. She knew who he was, of course, even if they had never met.

It occurred to her that while she had heard a great deal about him, he had likely never heard her name, much less gleaned enough from stories to have recognized her straight away.

That was a good thing, she told herself, even if it did not feel particularly flattering.

Yes, she knew exactly who he was. He looked enough like his cousin that for the briefest moment, back in the guest room, she had thought he *was* Nathaniel.

Nell spoke often of her husband's family, so though Gigi had never been offered an introduction, she knew quite a lot about them already.

This man's name was Kit Cooper, and the woman next to him must be his mother, Susan.

With Nathaniel only a few feet away, their differences were much clearer to Gigi's eye. Mr. Cooper lacked Nate's practiced elegance and tapered figure, instead wearing the heavier muscle of a man who was no stranger to labor. He was fairer, too, his hair more of a sandy hue than his cousin's glossy mahogany. His eyes, she had noted in that brief, frozen moment of shared horror, were a clear and vibrant blue. She would never in her life forget the color of those eyes—the centerpiece of a moment of sheer shock, a frozen breath of time that would stay lodged in her memory until she was old and gray.

Hopefully, by then, she'd be able to giggle over the whole affair, though she found it rather easy to picture herself a wizened grandmother in too much lace, sinking deep into her armchair with a groan of remembered embarrassment at this memory she'd made today. Remarkable eyes, though, she thought. At least there was something pleasant about the recollection. He had beautiful eyes.

She was certain that if she continued to gape at him as she was presently, she could find many more features to admire in the man. However, he had now caught her in the act of staring, those blue eyes meeting hers across the table, and she was forced to make a hasty transition to admiring the grass between her borrowed shoes, her cheeks flaming with heat.

Mercifully, Mathias had already lost interest in her and did not observe this latest display. She found the nearest empty seat and dropped herself into it, certain that she was blushing severely enough in this moment that she must be glowing, a pink beacon of a girl whose lighthouse of a face could keep the feast illuminated well into the night.

The tapping of a glass to indicate that speeches were about to begin rattled her bones, but did give her the courage to glance up from her empty plate and assure herself that no one had noticed her awkward entry to the group, nor was anyone particularly interested in continuing to observe her —including Kit Cooper, whose attention was rather aggressively fixated on his cousin as Nathaniel led the toast.

This went on for some time, enough for some of the tension to melt from her shoulders and for a glass of bubbly courage to be passed into her hand. The bride and groom were the focus of the day, and that was exactly as it should have been, after all. Yes, the only eye she met once the eating had begun was her mother's, who frowned at her borrowed dress and fussed with her napkin, casting meaningful glances down the table at Zelda Smith, to whom Gigi must report once the merrymaking had concluded.

She gritted her teeth and looked around for something else to fixate upon, landing on Nell Atlas, whose dainty hand rested on the huge swell of her belly, her round spectacles catching colors of the sky. She was in remarkably good spirits, Gigi thought, considering the state of her pregnancy. Honestly, once one caught sight of her in this condition, it was hard to look away again.

"Any day now," Nell said to every guest who inquired, and to some who were too shy to do much more than eyeball the size of her belly. "You would think it had been twenty months instead of nine!"

She had pressed Gigi's hand into the swell of her stomach many times, allowing her to experience the way the child within tumbled and kicked as it grew.

They had spent the spring together in London, where Gigi walked those famous cobbled boulevards for the first time in her life, arm in arm with her friend. They had talked of pleasing names to give the child, speculated about the differences between raising little girls and little boys, and indulged in all manner of sweets and delicacies at the behest of Nell's cravings.

It had been a magical time.

Mathias was right. Having a true friend was new and thrilling, and perhaps even more precious than another conquest to feed her brother's swaggering pride. Though, she wondered if it was odd, that one of his newfound friends was of the opposite sex. Did he treat Isabelle the same as Peter, and if so, did she mind?

Gigi had met some gentlemen in the Spring, when she'd gone to London with the Atlases, but not a one of them felt as though they could ever become *friends*. There was always a decorum there, a wall between them, imposed on both sides for the sake of propriety. She supposed that unless those walls were dashed to dust by circumstance right at the start, there was no way a real friendship could blossom between a man and a woman.

Unbidden, she was reminded of just how improper the encounter she'd had with Kit Cooper had been, not an hour ago. She turned her head to look at him again, surprised to find that his eyes were already on her. This time it was he who dropped his gaze and reddened at the cheeks, likely caught in the same bone-deep fluster that Gigi herself was experiencing.

She let herself look at him for a moment longer, considering their unconventional beginning and the matter of how friendship could *only* flourish in the ruins of propriety. Why, without the demolition of Society's carefully constructed walls, one could never truly get to know another person at all, could she? Besides, Gigi rather liked the mental image of picking her way through brick-like rubble that murmured niceties under her feet in the search for something more substantial.

Perhaps this wasn't a disaster after all, she thought, tucking a smile away and returning her gaze to her hands. Perhaps it was simply an opportunity to make a new friend?

∼

DAMMIT.

She had caught him staring.

More than once, too, he'd wager. Now the question was whether apologizing would make things better or substantially more awkward.

Perhaps if he asked nicely, the donkey would run away with

him, never to be seen by any of these people again. They could start anew somewhere nice and remote and never speak of this day. He was certain the donkey would appreciate it too, banishing from her memory all the indignities of being climbed upon by an endless rotation of rambunctious children.

He considered seeking out Nathaniel for advice on the matter, but once the party had moved indoors, his cousin was nowhere to be found. That left him with the options of his mother or Nell. Obviously, he sought out Nell.

"Who is that girl?" he asked, after an appropriate amount of meaningless observation about the wedding itself, gesturing to the dimpled blonde with the infectious smile who was currently having an animated chat with a bemused but tolerant Zelda Smith. "I do not believe I've seen her before."

He thought his voice sounded reasonably convincing, though the question in and of itself caused his cousin's wife to raise her eyebrows, turning to him with a blink of surprise. "You certainly have seen her before," she corrected, turning to face him. "How could you not, when she and I spend so much time together? That is Gigi Dempierre. Surely you see her resemblance to her brother?"

"I barely know Mathias," he pointed out. "I believe we've only ever actually spoken to one another one time. But yes, now that you mention it, the relation is obvious."

He trailed off, distracted by the way the girl flipped an errant curl of her hair over her shoulder. She was wearing it loose down her back, a bold choice for a woman grown. Now that she was in dry and modest attire, her figure seemed somehow less outrageous, the deep curve of her waist looking more in proportion to her ... well, her other parts.

He cleared his throat, forcing himself to take a deep swig of his wine, and pointedly avoided Nell's curious gaze. He was certain she had already drawn several conclusions, at least half of which were likely true. She was too sharp by half, and those wide, gray eyes of hers were so guileless that one often felt compelled to simply confess all manner of humiliating things when looking into them.

Surely there was nothing amiss about his interest in a pretty young woman. Surely not. Yet, there Nell was at his side, the wheels in her mind turning loudly enough that he swore he could hear them. It was only the reentry of her husband that distracted her from whatever deductions she was making, her face lighting up in a bright smile the instant Nathaniel appeared, striding across the room with a singular intent to join her at once.

"Apologies, my dear," he said, pressing a kiss to her temple and sliding an arm around her shoulders. "I got rather caught up chatting with Yves. He's a good fellow, isn't he?"

Kit bit down the urge to respond that his mother certainly seemed to agree, instead listening politely as Nell agreed and mentioned a few other matters relating to the wedding party thus far to her husband. She had proven herself an accomplished hostess.

"Once everyone is settled for the evening, we will have our meeting," Nell said, lowering her voice so as to not be overheard. "The paperwork has been prepared, and I believe things should progress smoothly without any further involvement on our end. However, Aunt Zelda mentioned that there was another matter, one recently come to light, that we all must urgently discuss."

Nate tossed a glance at Kit, cagey as ever about his business with the Silver Leaf Society, even after having roped Kit himself into their scheme to retrieve Isabelle this year.

"Shall I make myself scarce then?" Kit suggested, tipping more wine into his mouth.

"No," Nate replied immediately, a grim weight playing around his lips. "I was rather hoping you would join us this evening instead. Your assistance earlier this year was instrumental to our success with Isabelle and ... well, I'm afraid you've made rather a good impression upon Mrs. Smith."

"I've done what, you say?" Kit demanded, snapping around to look for the gin-loving spinster that he might immediately confront her. "I have done no such thing."

"I'm afraid you have," Nell said apologetically. "We did not expect for her to have any immediate interest in recruiting you, however, and Nathaniel thought he could dissuade her from the idea."

"Yes, it seems whatever new piece of information has arisen will require someone from the innermost circle of the Silver Leaf Society, and with Nell so close to birth, neither of us may commit to such an obligation."

"Oh, can't you?" Kit replied with no small amount of snark. "I'm not part of the inner circle or any such nonsense. I'm not even a member! I didn't even believe this ridiculous secret club of yours existed until a year ago, did I?"

Nell frowned, her face such a picture of injured innocence that Kit wanted to immediately take it all back.

"We are terribly sorry to spring this upon you, Kit," she implored. "It is only that there is a sense of urgency at this particular moment and we already know that you are trustworthy."

"Oh, flattery, is it?" he said weakly.

"Will you just meet us in the sitting room once the port is served?" Nate asked impatiently, glancing over his shoulder at the guests milling about his house. "I really must see to other arrangements now."

"Oh, blast it all, Nathaniel, don't you try and slither away!" Kit barked, but it was too late; his cousin had slipped through the crowd with all the oozing elegance of the accomplished statesman he was before Kit had even finished speaking.

Nell sighed, flicking an apologetic grimace at Kit. "I find it unsettling when he does that."

"I find it all too familiar," he returned, rubbing the back of his neck with a resigned sigh. "I suppose I'd better just submit to whatever is going on, before he starts to become actively manipulative."

She pressed her lips together, suppressing what Kit suspected was an urge to laugh.

At his quizzical reaction she held up a hand and shook her head. "I am not laughing at you," she assured him. "I am laughing at myself. You grew up with Nathaniel and I with Zelda, and now here we are, stuck with them both."

"Lord grant us mercy," Kit replied dryly.

And at that, she did laugh.

CHAPTER 5

She had decided to undertake the introduction herself. It was only fair, as he could have no way of knowing if she wished to speak to him or not, following such a shocking encounter.

Yes, Gigi would march right up to him, extend her hand, and make herself known. If nothing else, it would diffuse the tension of what had happened earlier, and absolve the poor man of any guilt about an honest mistake. It would be easy as pie. Just as soon as all the Silver Leaf business had concluded.

She swatted at her mother's hand again as Therese frowned and picked at the stray strands of blonde hair that had begun to go awry on her salt-tinged mane, which had now dried completely and taken on the appearance of wildly untamed waves.

The meeting had initiated with only Zelda, Therese, and Gigi, going over the finances and addresses that she had spent the last few weeks pulling from Mary Atlas's old ledger. These resources would be central to the success of the large mission that was being undertaken, and Gigi was rather proud of her part in making it possible. The smuggling of a central player in the ongoing hostilities between England and France would have been exciting even from a distance, especially as their work generally involved common people who simply had the misfortune of being caught in the crosshairs of matters beyond their control.

It took Gigi by significant surprise when other members of the Silver Leaf began to slip into the room, apparently gathering for a much larger meeting than she had expected at this stage in the affair. Her brother arrived, both of the Atlases, and most surprising of all, a recalcitrant-looking Kit Cooper, who shuffled in with all the enthusiasm of a man en route to the gallows.

Her heart gave a little lurch. Why, this was looking more promising by the instant! If Kit was a member of the Silver Leaf, and he *must be* if he was in this room, then the prospect of courting his friendship was even more realistic. She caught his eye and gave him a bright smile, which was received with an expression of deep confusion.

No matter. She would clear things up once she could speak to him.

Did one speak to male friends the same as the female ones? Would Kit perhaps enjoy meeting her songbirds? Surely there would be some differences to how she would speak with Nell, but what on earth would they be?

It was hard to say for certain, but if Mathias could cultivate such a friendship, surely she could too!

As Nathaniel Atlas moved to secure the room for a private

meeting, there was a brief and hushed argument at the door, culminating in the bride and groom gaining entry into the meeting and refusing to hear any arguments otherwise.

"It is our fault they were compromised," Isabelle said to her brother, her hands planted firmly on her hips. "If there is news, we want to hear it."

"And help," Peter added.

"Yes, of course, and help however we can," his bride agreed.

Nate sighed and gestured to the couches in defeat, muttering about how conspicuous their absence would be now that the guests of honor were also missing, but doing nothing meaningful to rectify the issue. He gave a whispered command to the footman at the door and closed them into the sitting room with enough finality that Gigi could swear some of the air in the room had stilled in preparation.

Zelda Smith stood and handed a set of documents to Mathias, who flipped through them curiously while she took her position in the center of the room, like a queen settling in for court. She narrowed her eyes at the bride and groom, giving a look of prim disapproval specifically to her nephew. "I will allow you two to be present for the sharing of information," she said tartly, "but you will not interrupt your honeymoon to participate in this any farther than a set of ears. If the matter is not resolved by the time you return, then you may participate as you see fit."

The couple exchanged a look and a set of nods.

"All right," said Peter Applegate, and took his wife's hand. "That sounds fair."

Zelda exhaled sharply through her nose in a way that suggested she didn't give a toss whether she was being fair or not, and returned her attention to the rest of the room. "There are a few matters to discuss, and I will try to be brief. First, regarding the extraction of the admiral, which is the largest undertaking we have ever attempted, the final pieces of preparation have been sorted today. Mathias will depart for Lisbon in three days' time to begin the process. With Nell so close to giving birth, Therese and I have agreed to split the remaining tasks between us to allow the Atlases a reprieve from additional stressors."

"Which we appreciate," Nell said softly, planting a delicate elbow in her husband's rib cage when he rolled his eyes.

"Yes, fine," Zelda said, already looking back down at her notes. "There is another matter that has arisen with some urgency relating to the disappearance of Pauline and Gerard Olivier from their home in Marseille some months past. While I have heard only vague and unreliable reports of possible sightings of them, a rather significant action has been taken that could only have been Pauline's work. This means that she is most certainly in England and she has, intentionally or not, put the Silver Leaf in great peril of being discovered at a rather critical time."

Gigi glanced at her mother, who had gone very still. "What has she done?" she asked, in a tone that suggested she was afraid of the answer.

Zelda turned to look Therese directly in the eyes, a slight frown playing about her lips. "Randall Ferris has escaped from prison."

This won a gasp of shock from Gigi's mother, but only silence from everyone else, who had no idea who the devil Randall Ferris was.

"Have you contacted Diane?" Therese demanded, panic in her voice. "She will surely be next!"

"No. It would have been too obvious a connection to those watching her, who are now surely on high alert." Zelda sighed and turned to the rest of the group, clearly annoyed that she had to bring everyone up to speed. "There were five founding members of the Silver Leaf Society," she explained, "myself, Lady Dempierre here, the late Mary Atlas, the missing Pauline Olivier, and one Mrs. Diane Ferris. Out of necessity, Diane has been inactive in Silver Leaf affairs since shortly before Mary died. A mission undertaken by her and her husband was compromised by a set of loose lips and it landed them in a great deal of trouble."

"They have been kept apart all these years," Therese said. "Randall was sent to prison, while the status of Diane's parents and her condition at the time reduced her own punishment to house arrest. To my knowledge, she is *still* under house arrest, at the behest of the Crown. We had to sever communication with her to protect ourselves."

"Why would Mme. Olivier act against the interests of the Silver Leaf?" Nell asked, frowning. "Why would she remain hidden?"

"She is not allowed on English shores, strictly speaking ... legally," Therese answered with an awkward grimace. "She was caught up in the same exposure as the Ferrisses but was able to return to France before facing any consequences, and will continue to evade them as long as she never shows her face here again."

"Which she has," Zelda added. "Even if she has thus far remained undetected."

Nathaniel was absorbing this, fingers laced in front of him. "It seems odd to me that she would risk committing such a bold crime if she is attempting to remain anonymous."

"You must understand," Therese replied. "Pauline has always been rather adamant that we find a way to free them."

Zelda nodded, closing her eyes for a brief moment in exhaustion. "Pauline has never acknowledged how much we would be risking if we took action to liberate Diane and Randall. She has insisted that she could give them safe harbor in Marseille, but all that would have done is reveal yet more of our operation to those who have been looking for us, as Nathaniel was doing to a concerning degree of effectiveness before being brought into the fold. It is for the good of the cause that we have stayed our hand, but Pauline sees it as abandonment and betrayal of our friend."

"And I suppose she is right," Therese muttered. "In her own way. I expect that is why she has not contacted us since arriving back in Britain. She knows we would stop her from this fool's errand."

Zelda waved her hand, shooting a disapproving glare at the other woman. "None of that matters. We must find a way to speak to Diane before Pauline attempts to contact her or, God forbid, takes steps to liberate her. Tracing Randall's escape might be the quickest and most effective route to finding the Oliviers before they can inadvertently do any more damage."

"Is that even possible?" Nathaniel asked with a furrow in his brow. "If the authorities can't track the escape, how on earth are we supposed to?"

"There are a great number of people who will talk to us, but would never assist the authorities," Mathias answered, turning to meet Nathaniel's eye. "I could arrange useful meetings with my network immediately, sending out missives tonight, but it will be impossible for me to personally execute those meetings until I return from Lisbon."

"Yes. Ideally, I would undertake this issue personally with Mathias in tow," Zelda said. "Many of our contacts work best with one of their own countrymen, and so for this task I require both an English and a French agent.

"However, with marriages and babies and all manner of inconveniences relating to our current primary task, none of the obvious choices are available. That is why I asked you to join us, Mr. Cooper. I believe you are uniquely positioned to request an audience with Diane Ferris without raising any suspicions, and you are well enough known for your business dealings for your orchards that you may move freely between tea rooms and flop houses in London, if needed."

"I haven't the foggiest idea who this woman is," Kit Cooper replied, looking legitimately befuddled. "And I'm not particularly well versed in flop houses either, for that matter."

"She knows who you are," Therese said gently. "The loose

lips that got the Ferrises caught belonged to your late father."

There was a moment of stunned silence, in which the room seemed to mutually share the ricocheting effects of discomfort.

"You have a reputation for attempting to right your father's wrongs," Zelda commented, crisp and businesslike. "No one would find it amiss if you sought out an alleged criminal connection in search of answers about his involvement and perhaps to extend an apology on his behalf."

Kit looked entirely drained of color, unable for the moment to respond in a meaningful way.

"Well, that sorts the English, then, if he accepts," said Mathias with a wince of sympathy. "What of the French side?"

"Giselle will go," said Zelda breezily with a shrug, as though this were an obvious conclusion with which everyone should be comfortable.

It took a moment to register, for no one but Zelda called Gigi by her full name.

Once this statement had permeated their audience, however, it was clear that this was not a welcome suggestion by any stretch of the imagination.

Both Mathias and Therese began to protest in loud unison, while Gigi herself experienced a mirror reaction to Kit Cooper's, drained of color and frozen in shock.

"She stayed with me after Nell returned to Kent in the mid-

Season," Zelda said loudly, holding up a hand to silence the Dempierre arguments. "Giselle has been working as an agent of the Silver Leaf since she was a girl. I will home and chaperone her and ensure she is in good care, but I see no other option."

"What about Yves Monetier?" Therese asked, a ragged sort of desperation in her voice as she looked at the daughter she had spent nearly a quarter of a century protecting.

"He knows too little and has given too much," Zelda said, winning a nod of agreement from Isabelle. "Your daughter is already a valuable member of the Silver Leaf Society, and she is a woman grown besides. She will be doing little more than having conversations with her countrymen, Therese. She will be fine."

"She hasn't said a word on the matter!" Therese shot back, placing a protective hand on her daughter's shoulder. "What if she doesn't wish to go?"

"I will go," Gigi said immediately. Her voice came out in a thin, reedy croak, but in her soul, she was shouting it as loud as she could. "I want to go."

"No. I cannot allow it," Therese cried, looking desperately around from face to face. "She is still a child. She belongs here with us."

"She is not a girl any longer," Nell Atlas said, her tone gentle but firm. "I saw for myself how Gigi managed herself amidst the chaos of the Season and the challenges of the *ton*, and I have every confidence that she can manage this task."

"And you, Mr. Cooper?" Zelda said, before anything else

could be said on the matter of Gigi's participation. "You will be compensated for your time, of course."

"Compensated?" he repeated, turning a hollow look of helplessness to his cousin. "Did you know about this?"

"Some," Nathaniel admitted. "If you had found out about Mrs. Ferris tonight and Uncle Archie's part in her plight, I daresay you'd wish to speak to her anyhow. Why not do some good in the process?"

Gigi watched him with her breath held. It seemed fated, didn't it? What a perfect opportunity to pursue this idea of friendship that had formed in her mind. What an exciting and thrilling and singular opportunity! *He must say yes*, she thought. *He must!*

"Take a day to pack your things and sort your affairs," Zelda Smith said, coming to her feet without waiting for a final answer. "We will depart for London the morning after next, from Meridian House. Giselle, you may bring *one* pair of your birds and no more. I will not negotiate."

"Yes, ma'am," Gigi said breathlessly, a burst of warm and sparkling anticipation beginning to build in her lungs.

She looked around the room at the other faces, none of whom were smiling, and some of whom had begun to mutter amongst themselves. Kit Cooper was staring at the floor, his blue eyes wide and fixed on nothing at all. She imagined he had quite a lot to think about.

Gigi, of course, knew that she should not make a great show of her joy, for this was all very serious and somber, but privately, in her heart, she was dancing. It was not complete freedom, nor was it permanent, and perhaps it only counted as half of an adventure, but it was magnificent all the same.

No *Maman*, no Kent, no Mathias, and no need to hold her tongue. It was freedom of a sort she had rarely even dared to imagine, and she intended to embrace it with both hands for as long as she was able.

It had been a truly spectacular day, after all.

CHAPTER 6

*K*it disliked packing as a concept, but he was finding it far more irritating than usual under the scrutiny of his cousin, who had apparently arrived with no purpose other than to sit and stare. Nate had settled himself in on the wooden shaving chair Kit kept in the corner of his bedroom, had steepled his fingers under his chin, and hadn't moved for the last twenty minutes, evidently transfixed by how many pairs of breeches Kit intended to bring to London.

"Is there something you wanted?" Kit asked, his words punctuated by the curt snap of a shirt as he shook it loose from his wardrobe. "You know I hate it when you *watch* me like that."

"Hm? Oh," Nate said, shaking his head as though to break a spell. He blinked his hazel eyes a few times, scrunching his brows together, and sighed. "I'm sorry, I've a lot on my mind at the moment. You know, I am starting to worry that Nell will simply be pregnant for the rest of our lives."

"She might well be, the way you two get on," Kit agreed with a grin.

"You know what I meant," Nate snapped, making Kit laugh. "I expected this child to show its face weeks ago. What on earth is the delay, you reckon?"

"Maybe it's been listening through Nell's belly to all your scheming and is having serious reservations about getting involved with you lot as parents. Smart child. Must take after me."

"You are hilarious," Nate said flatly. "I sent word ahead to have the house in Marylebone prepared for you. Quite a few of my servants now move between the properties with Mrs. Atlas and I depending on our current location. I have been told this is bizarre, but I find it damned convenient."

"Sounds sensible enough to me." Kit sighed, taking a step back from his valise and examining its contents, certain he'd forget something in the end. "I admit I've a fondness for your London townhouse and those mattresses you spend a fortune on. That part of this venture, at least, will be pleasant."

"I rather thought you'd enjoy the company of Lady Giselle as well," Nate said in that wry, noncommittal way of his. "You certainly seemed to enjoy looking at her during the wedding."

"Lady Giselle, is it?" Kit mumbled, turning back to his wardrobe to hide the color in his cheeks. "She introduced herself as Miss Dempierre and gave me a rather firm handshake, then her mother said she was *Lady* Dempierre. It's bloody confusing trying to keep status and rank straight with these exiles. Can one be a noble with no seat? Now I've no idea what to call her."

"Call her Gigi," Nate suggested. "It avoids the problem entirely."

"Rather familiar isn't it?" Kit said, his voice strained to near silence at the memory of just how familiar he already was with said lady. It was not gentlemanly in the least how frequently he had dwelled upon the memory of her in her soaking-wet underthings, startled like a fawn in the center of that guest room. He cleared his throat, refusing to give his overly observant cousin the satisfaction of deducing his secret. He must change the subject.

"And what of Mrs. Smith?" he asked quickly, snatching a roll of socks from their drawer. "Formidable as a scowling headmaster, isn't she? Do you trust her?"

"Absolutely not," Nate replied, chuckling to himself. "And you shouldn't either. She isn't out to harm you, but she loves to gather information to use for her scandal sheets, many of which are not flatteringly rendered illustrations of said subjects."

"Ah, yes, I saw the one depicting your wedding! Nell keeps it in a frame."

"Yes, she does," Nate replied with amusement.

The print in question featured Nell herself as a mystery woman wearing several veils as Nate whisked her to the altar with what appeared to be desperate urgency. Spiky print below it read: *MP Marries Mystery Maiden*.

The depiction of Nathaniel was caricatured but impressively accurate, managing to make him look both lovestruck and conniving at once. Nell had purchased it from her aunt as a Christmas gift for Nathaniel last year.

At the time, Kit had thought it was to prevent it from circulating amongst Nate's political rivals, but now it sat on a mantlepiece in their parlor so anyone who might want a laugh might see it.

"She might put you to the pen and ink, for certain," Nate continued, "but I am more concerned with the information that she has decided to retain about the mission you are to be pursuing. It is clear to me that there is something important remaining unsaid."

Kit paused, drawing in a fortifying breath of air, and turned to his cousin. "Please enlighten me," he said, dropping himself onto the corner of his bed to face his cousin. "Because I am apparently not slippery enough to commune between you and Mrs. Smith, and I do not enjoy being so out of my element."

Nate pushed himself to his feet, which rather defeated the purpose of Kit sitting down, and began to pace about the room. "Our missing founder has successfully broken a man out of prison, yes? So, why would they doubt her ability to remove a woman from simple house arrest? The entire explanation for this mission hinges first and foremost on the assumption of failure, when the Oliviers have already proven themselves more than capable."

Kit considered this, resting his elbows on his knees. "Perhaps, but it seems any risk at all in being discovered is the primary concern to them, while they're undertaking their larger mission."

"Even so, they could simply pull strings to have Mrs. Ferris moved to a more secure location so that the Oliviers could not reach her. I know for a certainty that Mrs. Smith has enough sway with people in power to ask such a favor. No, she wants Mrs. Ferris there as bait. The goal here is not to prevent a second jailbreak, it is to find the Oliviers directly. Why?"

"Personal concern?" Kit suggested, though even to his own ear that sounded weak and unlikely. "It sounds like Pauline was the wild card of the founders. Maybe Mrs. Smith wishes to keep her on a shorter leash."

"She would only shorten the leash if there was something at the end of it she wanted," Nate replied. "We could speculate all day, but I know from experience that the only way to get the truth out of Zelda Smith is to have the thing she's after. Obviously, I am not going to obligate you to probe deeper into this matter than you wish to do, as your participation already comes with clear reluctance, but I do advise you to keep your senses alert, lest you find yourself at a disadvantage at any point."

"Noted," Kit said grimly, just as a knock sounded on his bedroom door. "Enter!"

"Oh, Kit, you're already packed," his mother said as she poked her head in. "Are you leaving already?"

"In the morning," he answered, gesturing for her to come all the way into the room.

As far as his mother was concerned, Kit was attending to urgent business on Nate's behalf, so that Nate would not have to leave his wife behind. It was true enough, and she had no reason to pry for particulars.

She was massaging her hands, likely stepping away from a long session at her loom, and frowning at the valise, as though she had somehow failed in her motherly duties by allowing Kit to pack it himself.

"Do you know how long this business will keep you away?" she asked, reaching out to adjust the stacking of some of his items, which opened up rather a lot of new space for more things inside the case. This apparently gave her a sliver of satisfaction and her frown eased, her pale blue eyes rising to meet his.

"Hopefully not long," Kit answered. "It is the very tail end of the London Season, so I imagine I will have to conduct any business with the *ton* quickly, before they all flee back to their country estates."

He did not mention flop houses or their potential necessity to his mother.

"Well, that's all right then." She gave an encouraging smile, evidently more at ease with his departure than he had expected. "I imagine it shall be busy here in Kent, with a new baby soon arrived and visitors to entertain."

"Visitors?" Kit asked. "Have you invited someone to stay?"

"Oh, no, no," she said quickly, waving her hand over a faint blush. "I meant Mr. Monetier, only just come to England as a proper guest. It is rather novel to meet someone to whom everything mundane is brand new. And autumn is always so beautiful here, as you know."

Nate, who was stood behind Susan Cooper, put his hands in his pockets and grinned widely at Kit, an antagonistic smile if he had ever seen one. They both knew that Susan

Cooper did not fuss over social visits or new acquaintances, and what it must mean that she was doing so now.

"Well, he *is* French," Kit reminded his mother, hoping to tug at the threads of her prejudices. "I think they have autumn in France."

"Isabelle is French as well, isn't she? After a fashion," Susan said defensively, crossing her arms over her chest. "It is our duty to make Mr. Monetier feel welcome here. His daughter is your cousin, after all."

"Adoptive daughter," Kit reminded her. "Her father was Walter Atlas."

"You are just being contrary for the sake of it," Susan huffed, her color rising.

"He is," Nate agreed with a sympathetic murmur, arranging his face into a mask of saccharine compassion as his aunt turned to face him. "I think it's lovely and kind that you've been so welcoming to our guest. He has certainly been very appreciative."

"Well, thank you!" she said, tossing a pointed glare over her shoulder at Kit. "Thank you for saying so, Nathaniel. Will you stay for supper?"

"I wish I could," Nate said regretfully. "But I am unwilling to be too long away from Meridian until the child arrives."

"Yes, of course, of course." Susan took a wistful breath of air and smiled at Nathaniel. "You will be a wonderful father."

"I certainly hope so!" he replied, managing to steer her back out of the room as though it were her idea to leave. "I will say good-bye before I depart," he told her, and somehow, a few seconds later, the door had clipped shut again and she was gone.

"Don't you ever herd me out of a room like that," Kit told him.

"I would never!" Nate lied, returning to his seat. "You know, your mother has been widowed for some years now, and was alone for a lot longer than that. A courtship with a man we know to be honorable and good would not be the worst thing."

Kit grimaced. "No, but I would still prefer to not think of it. And besides, he is here quite illegally, so I am unclear on how any relationship could proceed, even if an attachment is formed."

"That is a problem for another day," Nate said, "and one I would be happy to handle myself, if it came to it."

"Yes, yes, you and your almighty power," Kit muttered. "You really have been insufferable since you won that office."

"I find that rather offensive," Nate said with a sniff. "I believe you have *always* found me insufferable, and it is a point of pride so far as I am concerned."

Kit shrugged, acknowledging that this was a fair enough point. He and Nate had grown up like brothers after Mary and Walter Atlas had met their untimely ends. Bickering was part and parcel of their relationship, and perhaps it always would be. And he was right, as it happened. He had been the same charismatic little snake since he was ten, and no one but Kit ever seemed to take notice of his puppetry with the people around him. It was as amusing as it was infuriating.

Yes, his cousin was insufferable. And he loved him dearly.

"I do have to leave soon," Nate said, glancing at the lowering light beyond Kit's window. "We ought to discuss what we can about your mission, before you set off."

"Gladly," Kit agreed, shutting his valise and latching it shut. "For a start, why don't you tell me everything you know about the Silver Leaf Society?"

CHAPTER 7

It was Mathias that finally chased *Maman* away from the coach, insisting that she was needed urgently by Mrs. Atlas within Meridian. For this, Gigi gave him a fleeting embrace of gratitude and a hefty sigh of relief.

"I will not be surprised if she crawls into one of the trunks and pops out once I am arrived in London," Gigi told her brother. "This is even more dramatic than when I left the first time with Nell and Nathaniel."

"Well, I think Mother is rather more fond of the Atlases than of Zelda Smith, especially in the care of her only daughter. I confess, watching them circle each other like a pair of vipers has always amused me greatly."

"But if you suggest they are not the best of friends, both will rather aggressively correct you," Gigi agreed with a roll of the eyes. "What a strange duo they are."

"Effective, though, as partners," he noted, which was certainly true. "I have a list of contacts for you that might be helpful, though one of them is rather insistent on speaking to Lady Silver and Lady Silver only in my absence. I would still strongly suggest you speak to him, however. He was the smuggler who got Pauline and Gerard out of England under the noses of the authorities. His name is Richards. Rather cagey fellow, but I've always had clean dealings with him. I've already arranged a meeting. You will just need to convince Zelda to come along."

"I think I can do that," Gigi said uncertainly. "Who else?"

"A few names that are better for Mr. Cooper than for you, I think. Richards is the most promising lead, and you might also find some information from an actress who works as a courier for us from time to time. I've included her information, as I do not know how to contact her directly."

"You don't?" Gigi asked in a flat and skeptical tone.

"I don't," he agreed with a cheeky little smirk. "Rather deliberately on her end, I suspect. It's all written down in the envelope in your trunk. I did not want to hand it to you directly lest it be snatched by *Maman*. I think the less she knows about your doings, the better. Poor thing is acting like she's going to drown the instant you go past the county line."

Gigi rolled her eyes rather than respond, straightening her posture again as her mother and Zelda Smith exited the Meridian estate, a hushed argument apparently in progress between them. They argued the way Gigi had always heard married couples do, which was odd, because *Maman* barely talked to Papa, and when she did, it was beyond dispassionate.

She only ever seemed to truly come to life when bickering with Mrs. Smith, and just now, with their heads bent together and their voices in quite loud whispers, Gigi thought her mother looked very well. It was a strange friendship indeed.

She glanced over her shoulder again at the main road, hoping to see Mr. Cooper making his approach. She was anxious to be off and excited to pursue her goal of friendship.

Pip and Emerald were quiet in their covered cage, but Gigi checked them again and again, just to be sure. Traveling with her birds was a new endeavor, and she dearly hoped it did not upset them, but she was beyond pleased that she would not be away from all of them this time, while in London. The others, of course, she would miss, but a pair to keep her company was generous indeed, especially as Mrs. Smith did not seem to take much to animals.

Beneath the sheet, in their little cage, her parakeets were snuggled close to one another and had apparently dozed off. Gigi hoped their serenity was a good omen of the task to come, and when she looked up at the horizon again, there was Mr. Cooper, arriving to set them off on the adventure that awaited them.

~

Gigi was rather disappointed with the first leg of their journey. Mrs. Smith had delved immediately into a series of newspaper articles she clearly had amassed while at Meridian, while Kit Cooper had leaned back in his seat, pulled his hat down over his eyes, and apparently fallen immediately into a snooze.

It was rather a waste of all the topics she had prepared in anticipation for this trip. Was it to be two days of silence, then? If so, she dearly wished she had fished Mathias's envelope out of her trunk before they'd set off, or at least brought along a novel or some such to keep her mind occupied.

She had spent quite enough of her life bored senseless in rooms where she couldn't speak, thank you, and she refused to allow this newest venture to unfurl the same way. If her companions were to be stubborn, she would talk to her birds. They enjoyed her conversation anyhow, at least as far as she could tell.

In the end, all of her thoughts of how best to rebel against the stifling atmosphere of propriety lulled her to sleep as well. She woke rather abruptly as the carriage took a bumpy turn through the northern hills of Kent County, slowing as it neared a waypoint where they could all grab a bite to eat and take a moment to stretch their legs.

She rubbed her eyelids with the bases of her hands, stifling a large yawn that had begun to bubble up behind her nose. She didn't know where they were, exactly, but if they were traveling the same roads that she'd taken with the Atlases some months past, it would be tomorrow before they passed from Kent into Middlesex en route to the city of London.

She had memorized the cities and shires of this nation as a girl, tutored by her mother rather than the traditional governess. And now, years later, it was just a little thrilling to recognize sign posts and city markers. She knew in the grand scheme of things that London was not so terribly far from Dover, and yet it was another world entirely, one made of brass and marble, with the grumble of a mighty river tied 'round its waist rather than the sea lapping at its coast.

"I do hope this place serves something palatable," Zelda

Smith said, flipping down the top of her newspaper to look across the seat at Gigi. She had donned a pair of half-moon reading spectacles, which left a little red dent on her nose when she took them off, and stowed them in a rather gaudy bejeweled case. She turned to Kit with a wrinkled brow, extended one sharp finger, and jabbed him in the ribs. "Mr. Cooper, rouse yourself. It is time to eat."

He startled so violently that Gigi thought he was apt to shatter and then tumble out of the carriage window. "I am awake!" he slurred unconvincingly. He cleared his throat, blinking his vision back into the waking world, and asked, "Erm, what time is it?"

"Half two or thereabouts, if we are keeping to schedule," Mrs. Smith answered, nodding in approval as her door was popped open by the driver. "And I believe we must be, for there have been no unforeseen obstacles. Fairchild?"

"Yes, ma'am," the driver answered cheerfully. "We're making very good time."

"Excellent, excellent," Mrs. Smith said with a tight little smile tossed over her shoulder at Kit and Gigi. "We shall stop for the night near the border of Sussex."

Gigi reached out to take the driver's hand, stepping carefully out of the carriage chamber and onto the soft grass in front of the little inn. She stretched her arms over her head, indulging in her yawn while her back was turned to the others. It felt good to be upright again, even if only for a moment.

When she turned back, Zelda had already charged forward to arrange their fare and seating, leaving Gigi and Kit to walk into the venue together.

He cast a wary eye at her and gave a respectful nod. Evidently, her enthusiastic introduction to Mr. Cooper the other day had not relieved his concerns over their rather unfortunate first encounter. He still seemed uncertain of her and embarrassed.

"Going by way of Sussex seems rather odd," Gigi said conversationally. "Admittedly I am no navigator, but I think we will be making a U shape rather than a straight line if we do that."

"The roads are likely better," he answered quickly, with something in his voice that might have been relief at such a mild topic. "Especially this late into summer, with all the rain. Do you not travel to London for the Season?"

"Oh, no, I do not," Gigi answered with a humorless little laugh. "In a shockingly late debut, I have only just this year experienced my first social Season in London, at the charity of Mrs. Atlas. My mother was less than pleased that I insisted upon going, and so I suspect it might also be my last."

He glanced at her with a raise of his eyebrows, clearly taken aback by this honest and informative answer. In reply, he only said, "Oh."

Well, this was going poorly.

Gigi pressed her lips together and allowed him to hold the door for her as she stepped into the inn, which already smelled wonderfully fragrant for luncheon. She took a bracing little breath and told herself not to give up. She would attempt conversation again over lunch and again in London and so on, if she must.

She stole a glance at Mr. Cooper as he took his seat, removing the hat from his mop of sandy blond hair, which was disheveled in a rather fetching way. He looked in good spirits. His color was high and his smile at the ready for the barmaid who appeared with their food. So why could he not speak to her?

She frowned, studying him as though she might find the secret written in very tiny print, just below his ear. He was not a traditional man of the *ton,* though she imagined he moved within its circles easily enough. He had the build of a fellow who participated in work rather than simply delegating it. His skin had a golden hue, likely from walking in the orchards he owned, and of course there were those eyes, the pale, clear blue that she had remembered so clearly from the startled moment at the wedding.

Now she must simply figure out how to turn those eyes onto her.

The thought gave a little jolt in her belly, which she promptly squashed beneath a mental boot heel.

No, she scolded herself internally. *There are plenty of men to flirt with. Plenty of beautiful men who fancy you. Try to make this one your* friend. *Friendship is the goal. Nothing else.*

But then those eyes did turn across the table for a moment, locking with her own, and she felt that scolded, unwelcome crackle of attraction wiggle out from under her mental squashing and drop into the pit of her stomach. She must have looked stricken, for he spoke to her of his own volition, asking her if she was well.

"Oh, yes, I believe so," she said, reaching for her glass of water to quench a throat that was suddenly dry. "I was simply ... planning for the journey ahead."

"Ah," he replied, gracing her with the same kind smile he'd given the barmaid, unaware of the encouragement it was giving to her rebellious inner workings. "It is a good habit, to plan, so long as you are prepared for the unexpected."

"Yes," she said weakly, managing a nod as she lifted the water to her lips. "Quite."

CHAPTER 8

*H*e knew he was being rude.

It was not his intent, of course. But he was not completely oblivious. He could hear himself speaking, sounding as crisp and distant as Nate did when he wanted someone to go away.

He could attempt to apologize or explain, but of course that just created other issues.

How do you tell a woman that you are struggling with conversation because every time you look at her, you remember how she looked in a soaking-wet chemise, clinging to every curve and swell of her delicious little body?

You don't. That's how.

He wasn't sure what would be worse in the carriage, sitting next to her or across from her. Both had significant disadvantages when speaking to his more primal nature, which, he was beginning to realize, he probably should not have been neglecting for such a long time. Honestly, he had bedded women in the past and been able to speak to them without constantly thinking of their naked forms afterward. Perhaps it was because he was absolutely *not* supposed to have seen what he'd seen that was making it linger so in his mind.

She very clearly wished to move past it. It was obvious in the way she'd introduced herself to him at the wedding party, forthright and firm, that she had decided to forget the event entirely and move forward as new. She spoke to him as though they were old friends, dimpling at him any time he managed to catch her eye, with a bright enthusiasm that seemed entirely at odds with the way she behaved when he observed her with anyone else.

At the inn, she seemed to retreat into the fine manners of her upbringing, commenting sparsely and allowing others to guide the direction of the conversation. She moved like a cat, either snatching things from her eye line with impressive precision, or lingering in a single movement for so long that one began to wonder if she would ever complete it. Perhaps her feline nature was what attracted her to those birds in the carriage, perhaps the strangest companions on a journey to the capital he'd ever encountered.

He wanted to study her at length, just as much as he wanted to cart her upstairs, strip her to her shift, and dump water on her for the pleasure of revisiting that accidental encounter.

He knew he was being boorish and distasteful, and forced himself to polite conversation for the second leg of their journey. Initially, he had attempted to include Zelda Smith, but she clearly was not interested in chatter, and had answered in crisp monosyllables that discouraged further engagement.

Gigi, for her part, was a ready partner for any topic he touched upon, and so it was rather a simple matter to steer her to the most mundane, polite things he could imagine, to serve as a buffer for his lingering thoughts and all the places his eyes wished to travel.

It wasn't a perfect strategy by any stretch. Every time she giggled or reached up to tuck a curl of golden blonde hair behind her dainty ears, he felt his blood stir. But it was the best he could manage just now. Once they got to London, he'd be several neighborhoods away and likely working on his own toward their mutual goal. He just had to arrive there without doing anything stupid.

To his immense relief, Zelda and Gigi would share a room at the inn they had booked for the night. It wasn't that he thought he'd go knock on her door otherwise. Of course he'd never be so bold! *But* the knowledge that such a thing wasn't even possible would make sleeping far more likely.

In fact, the imminent end to this journey cheered him enough to regain some of his customary charm over dinner, drawing out at least one laugh from the formidable Mrs. Smith and several stifled giggles from the lovely Gigi.

She had spent the meal savoring the rustic food served by the inn. She took each moment, each little bite, with such lingering devotion that he was rather amazed he hadn't lapsed into mute panic again.

He had managed to retain his head. At least for the moment.

But only because he knew he could think about it later.

∼

KIT AWOKE the next morning feeling surprisingly refreshed. He hadn't struggled to sleep at all, it turned out. Perhaps he was simply exhausted from his mental trials from the day before.

He whistled to himself as he bathed and dressed, stopping once to poke his head outside and sniff the air as the scent of bacon began to beckon him down to the dining room. He wanted a strong cup of coffee too. He pulled on clean clothes and combed his hair into some semblance of respectability and then took the stairs two at a time, anticipating the day ahead of him.

He strode over to where the two ladies had already seated themselves at the table and gave them a bright "Good morning," which apparently startled them both.

Gigi was frowning, refusing to take a folded sheet of paper that Mrs. Smith was proffering at her, he realized, though now their attention had turned to him.

"Good morning, Mr. Cooper," Mrs. Smith said with her usual air of briskness. "I am glad you are arrived, as this concerns you too. I have written detailed instructions on your first actions once you reach London, but I suppose if you have any questions about your tasks, it is good to have breakfast to discuss them before I must be off."

"Off?" Kit repeated, his brow wrinkled in confusion. "Off to where?"

"Guildford, if you must know," Mrs. Smith replied,

extending her arm so that he might take the list she'd written, if Gigi would not. "It makes little sense for me to go in a circle when I can complete this business now and meet you in London in a few days' time. My driver knows where to take you both, and you will have all of my resources at your disposal."

Gigi was clearly fuming, her cheeks bright pink with the effort it must have taken her not to explode. "Am I meant to stay at your flat by myself?" she asked incredulously.

"Of course not." Zelda sniffed, reaching for another cube of sugar for coffee. "Harriet will be there when you arrive and throughout your stay, as she manages the shop. I also have a small staff, of course, but you know all of this already. I fail to see the reason for your outrage."

Gigi let her eyes fall shut for a moment, her lips pressed into a line as she weighed her next thoughts. "What about the meeting with Mr. Richards?" she pressed. "Mathias made it very clear that he would only speak to Lady Silver. That's you!"

"Oh, nonsense. Lady Silver is whomever is wearing the costume. I believe the last Lady Silver that man met with was Mary, and obviously she won't be joining you in Seven Dials. Simply wear the veil and meet with him yourself."

"Seven Dials!" Kit exclaimed. "You cannot expect Miss Dempierre to go into such a neighborhood on her own. Even if she were familiar with London, it would be dangerous!"

"Why on earth would she go alone?" Zelda answered in a slow cadence that she likely reserved for use on children. "You will accompany her and watch from a distance to ensure her safety. Even I never go into Seven Dials completely alone, but it is far safer than meeting in Mayfair."

Kit blinked at her in astonishment, certain that he must still be asleep and dreaming. "Where in Seven Dials do you meet your contacts?" he asked, still grappling with disbelief.

"A public house called the Swan's Tooth," she answered with clear impatience. "Harriet and my driver both have all of this information, *and* it is included in my instructions there. If you two would be so kind as to *read* what I've put together for you, we may have a quick, congenial discussion before I depart."

Gigi opened her mouth and shut it a few times, clearly just as blindsided by this turn of events as he was. "You were meant to chaperone me," she said faintly, turning to gaze at the other woman.

"Do you require a chaperone, Giselle?" Zelda sighed. "You know very well how to behave, and you needn't worry about gossipmongers following your every move, as you never officially debuted. I trust that Mr. Cooper here is not a lecherous predator, waiting for his first and most opportune moment to strike."

Kit gaped at her, completely distracted from the arrival of his much-anticipated plate of bacon.

"Christopher!" Mrs. Smith snapped. "Do reassure Giselle here of her safety."

"Y-Yes. I mean, n-no. Of course she is safe with me," he stammered, glancing down at the sheet of paper in his hand as though it might suddenly rear back and sink fangs into him.

"Excellent."

She resumed her breakfast as though it had been a perfectly normal conversation, while Kit and Gigi both sat in their places, processing that they were now entering this new and strange world alone.

He had never been anyone's bodyguard! How the hell was he supposed to protect someone as tempting and wide-eyed as Gigi Dempierre in a place like Seven Dials? That was not what he had agreed to do for this mission.

"What of Mrs. Ferris?" he asked. "I've no idea where to find her."

Zelda released a long exhalation of breath, pressing her fingers into the space between her eyebrows. "The address and information is in your hand, Mr. Cooper," she said in that same, overly slow and simplified tone. "Anything else? I really must be off soon."

He exchanged glances with Gigi Dempierre, who gave him a flabbergasted shrug in response. He was certain there were many, many questions that they should both be asking right now, but damned if he could think of even one.

"Very well," said Zelda Smith with a little smirk. "I am certain you both have the wherewithal to overcome any obstacles you encounter on your way. As I said, I shan't be long. Only a couple of days."

She said this last thing in a way Kit could have sworn was almost smug. Was she amusing herself with them?

Further, was there anything they could do about it if she was?

He gazed down at his breakfast, amazed that it had somehow managed to appear as expected, ready to be eaten as though the morning were just the same right this moment as it had been an hour ago, when he was in the bath. He decided there was nothing for it but to eat said breakfast, and take note if any questions arose that he might launch at Mrs. Smith before she vanished.

Of course, under that sort of pressure, no questions made themselves known.

She barely muttered a farewell to them, already occupied with the tasks ahead of her as she bustled out the door to catch a communal stagecoach headed west. All the two of them could do was helplessly watch her go. There was no stopping her, this aging slip of a spinster who had somehow managed to get her way no matter the circumstances.

The list she'd written was open on the table now, but neither of them touched it. The notes were neat and precise and thorough, written with exacting slanted script, razor sharp at the tip of every letter. They now had several tasks to complete that, to Mrs. Smith's credit, were clearly defined and should occupy the whole of their time in her absence.

"It is like you said, isn't it, Mr. Cooper?" Gigi said softly, blinking those big green eyes at him. "Prepare, but be ready for the unexpected."

It startled him enough that he gave a short laugh, the spell of shock momentarily broken. He shook his head and took up the paper, folding it into his pocket. "I suspect I cursed us when I said that," he confessed. "The world is always aching to prove such observations correct."

"Perhaps so," she replied. "Though, if the world is listening so closely to our conversations, that bodes well for the challenges to come."

"I hope it does," he said with sincerity. "I truly hope it does."

Their challenges to come were myriad, of course, even before Zelda had taken her leave. Now, Kit simply needed to decide how he was going to navigate a significant amount of time alone with Gigi Dempierre.

CHAPTER 9

The rest of the morning felt strange, as though something had taken over Gigi's body and was behaving methodically and rationally toward the goal of returning to the road. She seemed to observe herself from a distance, with at least a little bit of pride, as she directed the luggage from the rooms and spoke with the driver about the day ahead.

Kit Cooper had stood at the ready, offering his help once or twice, but otherwise allowing himself to be pulled into Gigi's current as they coped with the strange new scenario facing them.

She dug Mathias's envelope out of her trunk, and holding it tight to her chest along with the letter Mrs. Smith had apparently penned while Gigi slept, she climbed into the carriage and summoned her usual self back to the reins of her sensibility. She blinked several times, reminding herself that this was all real and happening right now, and she glanced crosswise to Mr. Cooper, who had chosen to seat himself as far as possible from her on the opposite side of the opposite bench.

He was watching her warily, as though at any moment she might throw a fishing net over his head and commence some dastardly plot. It was funny, but Gigi knew she should not laugh.

Once the carriage jerked back to life, the plod of the horses taking them from soft grass to the hard dirt road, she met his eye and gave him what she hoped was an encouraging smile. "Well, it's been a devil of a morning, hasn't it?" she said, perhaps a little too brightly.

She thought she saw his lips twitch, likely in reaction to her tone. It made her blush.

"It has been at that," he agreed, his shoulders seeming to relax a little at the exchange. "Mrs. Smith isn't an easy woman to be around, but I feel suddenly like a child without supervision now that she's gone."

"Oh, well, I'm a rather talented mimic," Gigi said with half a smile. "I can impersonate her if it would soothe you."

"Can you really?" He leaned forward, clearly intrigued by this suggestion, those blue eyes sparkling despite the shade of the carriage interior. "Go on, then."

Gigi straightened her shoulders, assuming Mrs. Smith's particular correctness with her posture, and narrowed her eyes, lifting her chin a few notches. "Mr. Cooper," she said with a brisk Wessex clip, "you are perfectly capable of executing these tasks without my assistance. It is why I chose you, after all. Now, come, let us all be silent so that I may ignore you both in peace until we reach London."

"Ha!" said Mr. Cooper, clapping his hands together in amusement. "Brava! That was uncanny."

"Naturally, naturally," she answered in her Zelda voice before relaxing back into the cushions again and allowing herself a giggle. "Don't tell her, though, hm?"

"I would never." He shook his head, running a hand through his hair with a chuckle. "That is a terrifying talent, truth be told. Can you impersonate anyone?"

"A few people," she confessed. "It used to get me in terrible trouble as a child, when I'd petulantly parrot back rebukes to my mother. Of course, my brother encouraged me to hone the skill behind closed doors for our own personal amusement, so I'm afraid it rather took root. Mrs. Smith is an easy subject, though she is quite ... singular."

"She is a distinct character, that is for certain," he agreed. His gaze dropped to her lap, where she was still holding the envelope from Mathias and Mrs. Smith's letter in her hands. "I suppose I should take the time to actually read that letter she wrote, now that the shock has worn off. What else have you got there?"

"Oh. My brother assembled some items for us, including what appears to be a promising lead with a contact by the name of Mr. Richards. He has worked exclusively with Mathias over the last several years, and I'm afraid he is rather jumpy at the prospect of speaking to anyone new, so if Mathias is unavailable, he will meet only with Lady Silver in his stead. An impending meeting with Mr. Richards is what I was referring to this morning with Mrs. Smith. If we are to get information from this fellow, I'm afraid we will have to do as she said over breakfast, and delve into what I assume is a fairly dangerous neighborhood with myself in the role of Lady Silver."

"Seven Dials," he replied grimly, accepting the documents as she held them out to him. "My first instinct is to discourage you from taking this meeting."

She shook her head, twisting her fingers through one another in her lap. "If my brother says he is our best chance at good information, then we must brave the Seven Dials, Mr. Cooper."

He sighed, leaning to the side to lay out some of the documents on the bench next to him. "I cannot imagine why she chose such a notorious slum for her meetings," he muttered. "If we aren't assaulted outright by the residents, we're sure to catch some foul ailment instead."

"Why is it called that?" she asked, tilting her head at him. "Some architectural fancy?"

"I haven't a clue," he said with an absent chuckle. "It's part of St. Giles. The worst part, from what I understand. I've never been there, but it is close enough to Covent Garden that I'm not concerned about navigation."

"Another odd name," Gigi said, turning to glance at her birds, who were currently preening. She reached through the bars to stroke the pale blue feathers on Pip's little head, smiling at the way he leaned into the caress. "Was St. Giles not the saint of hermits? It sounds as though this place is very populous indeed."

Her companion laughed outright at that, raising his eyes from the documents to consider her. "You are not at all what I expected, Miss Dempierre."

"Oh?"

That was a curious thing to say. What had he expected, she wondered? Someone more ... French? Or had he thought she'd be a traditional English miss, and was finding that she was not? It could easily be either. She hoped he was not disappointed.

He considered her for a moment, scratching at his chin, and appeared to think through his next words carefully before allowing them out into the universe. "I feel we should address the ... well, the circumstances of our first encounter. I feel that if we do not, it shall be hanging between us forevermore and make this whole business of sleuthing together damned difficult."

She felt herself color. She had expected never to speak of it. Not ever. He had seen her at a particularly vulnerable moment, with none of the armor of beauty or poise usually allowed to women when confronted with the unexpected.

"Is it really necessary?" she asked weakly. "It was an honest mistake; an accident. I hold nothing against you, Mr. Cooper."

"Please call me Kit," he said with a sheepish half smile.

"If I'm still imitating Mrs. Smith, I shall have to call you Christopher instead," Gigi replied immediately, followed by a nervous laugh. "Kit, then. I suppose it's proper if we are to be partners in ... well, in stopping crime, at least temporarily, whilst also facilitating it? It is a moral quagmire we find ourselves in."

He raised his eyebrows, inclining his head to her in acknowledgement of that fact. "We do not have to talk at length about the awkwardness of our first meeting, of course, I simply wished to say I am sorry for startling you as I did and for invading your privacy, however unwittingly. It is a shame you only ever get one first impression on a person, isn't it?" He cleared his throat, adjusting his collar with a click of his tongue. "I am making it worse, aren't I?"

"I honestly do not know," Gigi replied, eyes wide. "I have never been alone with a gentleman before, much less discussed said gentleman stumbling upon me in my underthings. On the hopeful assumption that this is also alien to you, Mr. Cooper, I think we are handling ourselves rather well."

He gave a little snort of laughter, his cheeks appearing to color a bit, though Gigi was unsure if men ever blushed. "I assure you, it is new territory for me as well."

"I had thought," she said after a moment, "that in light of such an unconventional event, there would no longer be any ice between us requiring breaking, should we make acquaintance. After all, it is hard to remain aloof with someone you've shared mutual humiliation and horror with, is it not? Unfortunate as it may have been, perhaps it has given us a sturdier foundation for the endeavor we must now embark upon?" She hesitated, biting her lip. "What I mean to say is that we already share a secret between us, so a few more will be no bother."

"Hm, that is a positive way to look at it," he said, brightening. "And I think you may be onto something. I interpreted it exactly the opposite way, and while you were being friendly and assertive, I couldn't get out more than one syllable at a time. Brava, Miss Dempierre. I shall defer to you in all future matters of conduct."

She giggled, scooting herself down the bench so that she might be closer to sitting just opposite him. She leaned over to sort the papers he had laid out, her fingers briefly brushing against his, and swallowed down the tiny jolt of excitement it awoke in her. She found Zelda's quickly drawn map of Seven Dials and passed it into Kit's hands. "Our contact, Mr. Richards, is an undertaker," she said, returning to the pile of papers to retrieve the relevant one from Mathias's stack. "He lives on the outskirts of London proper, and services the prison where Mr. Ferris was being held."

"An undertaker," Kit repeated, obviously intrigued. "I wonder what service he provides in the way of spycraft. You say your brother sent word ahead of us to this gentleman?"

"Unfortunately, yes," Gigi confirmed, uncertain if she was happy or angry with Mathias just now. "Which means we only have the remainder of our journey to prepare and we must immediately be off to meet him. Mrs. Goode, who manages Mrs. Smith's print shop in her absence, will apparently show me where the Lady Silver costuming is kept. I suggest we set off at the earliest possible time and arrive well in advance to Mr. Richards in Seven Dials."

Kit nodded, but also sighed. "It is not how I generally prefer to end a two-day journey. Tell me, how did our little liberation front become involved with a grave digger?"

"According to Mathias, the Silver Leaf Society liberated Mr. Richards from a French prison some twenty years ago, when he was an enlisted soldier, and assisted him in returning to London and starting life anew. It is the typical story of Silver Leaf operations. In gratitude, Mr. Richards has been amenable to assisting in transports of both people and goods under the protective guise of his funerary business. However, he has worked almost exclusively with and for Mathias for some years now and is wary of new contacts."

Kit nodded, lifting the sheet of paper with Mathias's loopy scrawl covering the page, and took a moment to scan it. "It seems to me that if anyone could smuggle a man out of a prison, it would be someone like Mr. Richards. Perhaps two bodies to a coffin or some such thing?"

"We will have to ask him," Gigi said with a shudder, mentally batting away the unpleasant scenario it had formed in her mind. In truth, she had pictured Mr. Richards with caskets full of wine or gems or other contraband, but she supposed Kit was right and that anything spirited away convincingly likely shared quarters with the deceased.

Kit looked thoughtful. "If it is as Mrs. Smith says, and Lady Silver has been a guise for all of the founders of the Silver Leaf Society, it is possible that Pauline Olivier wore a silver veil and approached Mr. Richards herself with this task."

"Yes, I suppose that could be so," Gigi said with a small note of surprise. "Until Zelda recently said otherwise, I never knew that anyone but she assumed the Lady Silver persona. It is a good theory, though I suppose it is just as likely that our undertaker friend knows nothing at all. Regardless, I think Mathias is correct that he is the most likely source of information if we are to unravel this mystery. It is only unfortunate that he sent instructions for the meeting ahead of us without knowing that Mrs. Smith was going to leave us in the lurch."

Kit considered this, reading over both Mathias's notes and the curt, spiky instructions left by Mrs. Smith this morning at breakfast. When he wrinkled his brow in concentration, it made him look so serious, older even. It was only natural to wonder what he was thinking.

She sat politely with her hands crossed in her lap, stifling the internal urge to spout off the collection of theories and thoughts she had amassed about this situation in the last few days. For being so practiced in the art of stifling herself, Gigi was finding it increasingly difficult to maintain her usual composure in the presence of Mr. Cooper. She felt driven to engage him, just so that he might look at her and speak back.

It was silly.

"You could always impersonate her voice, if you feel it necessary," Kit suggested, though Gigi could not be sure whether he was in earnest or teasing her. "We can practice a bit if you like."

"Oh, that sounds like a good idea!" she breathed, breathless already at the prospect of what she must do. "Will you pretend to be Mr. Richards, then? Oh, I shall die of nerves for certain and muck up this entire investigation."

"You will be splendid," he assured her. "After all, I've seen you recover from shocking things before."

She gave a little hiccup, swallowing her urge to laugh. "Thank you, Mr. Coo... Kit."

"You're welcome," he said, "Gigi."

CHAPTER 10

The sun had been setting earlier by the day, but Kit was still startled by how few chimes the clock sounded as their carriage trundled its way into Central London around dusk. Summer was very nearly done, he thought, and the days would only get shorter from here. He imagined he would be missing the busiest days of the harvest back in Kent, and though he'd never tell any of his foremen, he rather felt like he was the one who had managed a well-timed jail break rather than this mysterious Randall Ferris fellow—an appropriately dashing name for a faceless fugitive.

After all, it was spectacular luck that he was spending the hours with the enchanting and lovely Gigi Dempierre, his arse on a cushioned bench in a luxurious coach, rather than slaving away, snatching fruits off the vine under the beating heat of the late-summer sun.

They had combed through the documents left for them by both Mrs. Smith and Gigi's brother, Mathias, until they both felt they had absorbed every piece of information provided. Their attempts at practicing the imminent meeting with the undertaker, Mr. Richards, had been more fun than it rightfully should have, with Kit being granted the opportunity to flex his most outrageous cockney growl, which was rewarded with a series of giggles from his charming companion.

She was rightfully nervous.

From what she'd told him, Gigi had rarely been allowed outside of the little castle she'd been raised in, perched on the cliff face just outside Dover. It was certainly a large leap from such a sheltered existence to the task she would have to undertake tonight. For his part, Kit hoped he was up to the task of serving as her protector. He did his best to exude confidence in the endeavor, but the truth was that he'd been long out of practice in using his battle instincts, and serving as a bodyguard was a far, far cry from his time as a soldier.

"Ah, at last," Gigi said with a heavy sigh, her gaze locked on the carriage window. "We are here."

"You needn't sound so very relieved," he teased, winning a flash of dimpled amusement from her.

The carriage rolled to a halt outside of Mrs. Smith's print shop, announced with brash red letters on a glossy wooden sign over the door. Its beveled ground floor window was plastered with examples of the various illustrations one could find therein, all featuring cutting political commentary or scandalous insinuations about the gentry. Kit assumed that Zelda herself had avoided retaliation by the powerful people she mocked with a combination of righteous fear of her as a person and enough amusement at the others who were caught in her crossfires to allow the slight.

Perhaps there was even a queer sort of honor in being featured in one of her prints, he thought as they alighted from the carriage onto the damp cobbles of the street. He pulled his hat lower on his brow to obscure the drizzle, and followed Miss Dempierre as she frolicked in light-footed anticipation toward the entrance and swung the door open.

Though he was only a few steps behind her, he felt as though he had missed a large chunk of time as he entered the shop, for Gigi herself was already wrapped in the embrace of a plump, brassy-haired woman and the two were chattering at one another so quickly that he couldn't for the life of him discern what was being said on either end. He waited a moment, and then, upon realizing he had been utterly forgotten, he cleared his throat, hoping to attract their attention.

They parted, the other woman's face pink and enthusiastic, and Gigi motioned for him to join them where they stood near the till. "Kit, this is Mrs. Harriet Goode," she said happily, "she is Mrs. Smith's shopkeeper and a thoroughly delightful woman of her own accord. Harriet, this is Mr. Kit Cooper, Nathaniel's cousin."

"Pleased to meet you, Mr. Cooper," said Mrs. Goode, extending a hand for an exuberant shake. "I can see your likeness to Nathaniel for certain. You are very handsome lads, both. Won't you please come in? Would you like tea? Pastries? It's a bit early for supper, but I could arrange for an early one!"

"Oh, just something small is fine," Gigi assured her. "We

must depart for a meeting on Zelda's behalf soon. I was hoping you might direct me to her ... erm, favorite veils," Gigi said, lowering her voice and casting a nervous glance at a pair of gentlemen customers who were paying them not the slightest amount of attention.

"Ah," said Mrs. Goode, nodding. "Why don't the two of you head upstairs and I shall meet you presently, once I've assisted our customers. Have some tea and pastries if you like. You will find Zelda's *collection* in the linen closet near your bedroom, my dear. You can't miss it."

Gigi flushed in pleasure at the suggestion that she had established her own bedroom in this place, and practically dragged Kit himself up the narrow staircase in the rear of the store with her hand in the crook of his elbow. If anyone questioned the propriety of such a thing, they did not make it known. For his part, he rather enjoyed the sensation of the warmth of her grip soaking through the sleeve of his jacket.

The flat above the shop was quite a bit nicer than he had anticipated, well outfitted in beautiful furnishings and decor, with a cozy little nook for entertaining guests right near the entrance. Gigi practically flung him into one of the cushioned chairs in said nook and set about finding the aforementioned tea and pastries with the confidence of someone who knew this space intimately. Before he could blink, it seemed, there was a plate of croissants in front of him, and the sound of a kettle being put on somewhere to the left of his position on the settee.

The croissant was cold, but otherwise absolute perfection.

He could hear Gigi begin to hum as she arranged a platter for their tea, a task he admittedly had never performed himself before. He could hear the clink of ceramics knocking together over the sweet melody of her voice. It was all rather surreal, he thought. Even more so than being abandoned back at that inn, expected to travel the rest of the way to London, unchaperoned with an unmarried woman of breeding.

It was as though all of the rules that had made up his understanding of how to navigate day-to-day life were suddenly void, and here he was on a flowery, purple loveseat, attempting to figure out how in the hell he was supposed to behave moving forward. It almost made his head hurt, attempting to puzzle out what was allowed now and what wasn't. He glanced anxiously toward the doorway where Gigi Dempierre's shadow swayed in time to her humming.

It would not do to wonder what he could get away with, and that was exactly where his thoughts were headed at that moment. He liked her quite a lot, but it was hard to keep a friendly tone and a professional distance when those dimples flashed out at him and that musical little giggle encouraged him to believe he could win more smiles, if only he continued to charm. Would she let him kiss her? He wondered just how French her upbringing had been, regarding such things.

He would very much like to find out.

Almost on cue the kettle began to scream, as though the universe itself were scolding him for such thoughts. It made him straighten his posture and force his mind onto the task ahead of them, a businesslike wrinkle coming onto his brow as he conjured up the details of tonight's endeavor and forced them to the forefront of his mind.

She reentered the room with a tray, steam rising from the tea in curling clouds that seemed to wrap around her as she walked. She set it down in front of him, innocently unaware of the view she briefly provided of her décolletage, and let out a satisfied little huff at her success in this matter of serving tea.

Kit furrowed his brow farther, reminding himself to think of undertakers and seedy pubs, not Miss Dempierre's extremely tempting cleavage. "I am surprised there aren't servants to make the tea," he found himself saying, just for want of saying anything at all.

She stood back, her lips pursing. "Does it smell poorly, Mr. Cooper? I've only just been taught to make it myself, last I was here. If it is spoiled, I'm certain Mrs. Goode will make a fresh pot."

"No, no, it smells fine," he said, the tops of his ears reddening as he immediately leaned forward to pour himself a cup. "That was not what I meant to imply. I only expected someone of Mrs. Smith's particular demeanor and reputation to have a staff milling about up here, seeing to her whims and needs."

"Oh!" She seemed to relax, her expression softening into its customary dimpled charm as she swept into a chair and shook her head at her own silliness. "There is a staff, of course, but they do not live here. The maids come in the morning and the cook in the evening, while the driver has a room nearby, where the horses and carriage are housed. It was all rather foreign to me, too, when first I arrived, but I have come to understand that space is rather a commodity here in London, and things cannot operate in the same ways they do at home."

"Yes, of course," he managed to say, feeling rather idiotic when he knew very well how different London could be to the country. He took a conservative sip of the steaming liquid in his hands and gave what he hoped was a reassuring nod to the woman across from him. "The tea is very good."

"Oh, I'm so pleased to hear you say so!" She beamed, clasping her hands together at her chest. "Even if you are just being kind."

"I am certainly not. Have some yourself!" He had intended to gesture with his own cup to the pot, but instead he had held it forward in such a way that he could not blame Miss Dempierre for misinterpreting the motion. By the time she reached forward to take it, it was too late to correct the error.

A tentative smile trembled on the corners of her lips as her fingers brushed his, taking hold of the delicate porcelain from which he had sipped. She tilted the cup and brought it to her own lips, with that careful, thoughtful mindfulness he had noted in her behavior on the road.

He was frozen in place, watching the painted lip of the teacup press into the soft wealth of her mouth, the sweetened, amber liquid spilling prettily over her tongue. He wondered, with the slightest flash of heat, if she had chosen to sip from the very same spot as he, and in that roundabout way, had shared a small touch, a proxy of a kiss by way of a gilt-lined teacup.

She licked a droplet from her bottom lip and handed the cup back, looking faintly amused. "You enjoy quite a lot of sugar in your tea, it seems," she teased. "I did not notice you dispensing half the container into your cup."

"Three cubes," he confirmed with a chuckle, making a point

of rotating the cup and sipping from the same place she had, his eyes fixed on hers. "I confess I have a weakness for sweet things."

She watched him do so with an expression like a startled doe in a glade, those wide green eyes blinking at him across the table.

So her little provocation hadn't been intentional, then. Pity.

She opened her mouth to say something, but was interrupted by the arrival of Mrs. Goode from belowstairs. She bustled into the room, all charm and warmth, and shattered the delicate hold that had been weaving around them, all alone in this room for an utterly wasted moment of stolen time.

"Those patrons headed off almost the instant you vanished," the brassy-haired woman said brightly. "Perhaps they knew I was anxious for your company. Did you find Zelda's things?"

"Oh. Oh, no, I'm sorry," Gigi said, turning her attention to the other woman with a wan smile. "I will need assistance putting it all on, anyhow, I'm certain. And, of course, any advice you might have would be welcome."

"Advice?" the woman repeated delightedly. "Well, I can certainly repeat things Zelda has said to me about her dealings in Seven Dials. Anything at all I can do to help, I am happy to!"

"Then let us not dawdle," Gigi said, standing immediately and smoothing down the lines of her travel-rumpled skirts. "I am most anxious to have this first order of business done with. Perhaps afterward, the next tasks will no longer seem so fearsome."

"Oh, my darling girl, you've nothing to fear," Mrs. Goode assured her, placing a maternal hand on the small of her back as she led her toward the curved hallway that split the sitting room from the kitchen. "Mr. Cooper, we will not be long. Please make yourself at home!" she called back over her shoulder.

He had never felt less at home than he did in this shrine of feminine sensibility, he thought, thumbing an embroidered flower on the arm of the sofa. Harriet Goode was not at all what he had imagined as a companion for Mrs. Smith. He supposed he was expecting a whetstone, heavy and dark and foreboding opposite Mrs. Smith's well-honed steel.

Instead, he had found a sugared dumpling of a woman, whose disposition seemed permanently glowing with cheer.

It solved one mystery, at least. Now he understood how a shop owned by someone like Zelda Smith had accomplished the unlikely feat of making sales. He chuckled to himself, taking another sip of his overly sweetened tea as he listened to the muffled sounds of female voices through the walls and the ruffling and rummaging of pulling a great many boxes out of storage.

Asking for advice had been a wise move on Gigi's part, he thought. Here he had been, losing his mind with distraction over her many, many charms instead of considering the task ahead of them and the unknown darkness they were about to descend into. He would need to keep a keen eye and a steady head tonight to prevent Gigi from encountering danger, and he would need to be clear-minded enough to retain the information imparted upon them by the mysterious undertaker, Mr. Richards.

Yes, he would need to master his weaknesses, no matter how little he wished to do so.

It was true what he'd told Miss Dempierre, after all. He was simply helpless when it came to the sweet things in life.

CHAPTER 11

Of the collection, there were two gowns that fit well. One was well over twenty years out of date, but as fine as if it were new. The bodice and skirts were done in a stunning brocade of silver-spun threads on dove gray silk, but cut in a way that was distinctly Georgian and would require padding on the hips. The other was fur-lined and velvet, meant for the winter, and far too warm for the late-summer balm.

Of the two, Gigi thought the former was the better option. Its design would lend to the mystique of the character she must play, and would suggest she had quite a few more years on her than she truly did.

"I think you look very well in it." Mrs. Goode sniffed, using the flats of her hands to bat down the fabric of the skirt into smooth panels. "It's a far touch more glamorous than the plainness and slink of today's gowns. I should like to put you in a powdered wig too, and imagine the glory of days past."

"I already feel quite ornamented enough," Gigi replied,

looking down at the miles of fabric that appeared to spill forth from the pins on her hips, seeming to spill like waterfalls to her feet.

"Oh, nonsense, you have to wear the choker as well, and choose a veil. Oh, you are a sight, on my word." Mrs. Goode looked near tears, pressing her fingertips to her lips and reaching forward only to adjust the fall of the silk or to brush away imagined specks of dust. "You must enjoy your beauty, Gigi, for not all women are blessed with such things."

"Did you really dress like this every day?" Gigi said with no small amount of balking, twisting this way and that to take in her reflection. "I've barely confidence in where my own legs are beneath me!"

It made Mrs. Goode laugh, her cheer an ever-present lightness in the air. "I did, and I liked it," she said with gusto. "You ought to have seen me swishing my way around ballrooms in my youth. I wasn't a beauty. Too much 'round the waist for that, but oh, I was full of life while I could be."

"You still are and still can," Gigi assured her, the words registering like a little thump between her ribs.

Was she full of life? How long would she be considered worthy of being full of life, for that matter? Surely the mission at hand qualified as truly living, yes? Especially at the side of someone like Kit Cooper.

She felt her skin warm at the memory of him turning that teacup to sip where her lips had been, those powder blue eyes turned up at her as though he were doing nothing amiss at all! Perhaps he hadn't realized …

She swallowed, forcing herself to smile at Mrs. Goode, who was proffering a selection of veils at her from a dusty closet. "I think this is the only one that matches, my dear," she said, thrusting forward a rigid metal band with a shimmering layer of silver-gray silk attached to it. "The lace would give too much away, I'm afraid. You'll need gloves too."

"Gloves?" Gigi reached out to take the headpiece, thumbing the little faux pearls embedded along the front ridge. "Whatever for?"

"Your hands are the hands of a young woman," Mrs. Goode said, her generous bottom swishing this way and that as she dug into the closet, her entire top half lost into the void. "If you wish to fool Mr. Richards into thinking you are the same Lady Silver he met with over twenty years ago, you cannot be so obviously youthful."

Gigi looked down at her hands, spreading her fingers to inspect the skin there. They did not look particularly singular in her estimation, though to be honest she had never made a great study of the hands of others.

When Mrs. Goode emerged from the closet, her brassy hair was in disarray and her cap was now entirely missing, likely wrenched off by some mysterious force hiding in the closet. However, she had found a pair of gloves, short gray ones with little white bows at the wrist.

"Here we are! Perfect! Finish your tea and discuss final details with your young man, hm? And if you change your mind about that wig, I do have a few somewhere in the back …"

"No wig," Gigi said quickly, coughing to stifle her giggle.

"My hair is light enough in a dark room to pass for silver, besides."

"Mm, I suppose so," Mrs. Goode relented, puffing out her cheeks with the force of her sigh. "There's nothing to be done for today's sense of fashion, my dear. One can only hope that Society returns to good sense in our lifetime."

"I shall pray for it every night," Gigi said solemnly, winning a guffaw from Mrs. Goode, and a light shove back in the direction of the parlor, where the last of Gigi's luggage and her cooing birds were waiting in a stack in the hall.

They were both grinning when Kit came back into view, looking up with a little jolt of surprise from his overly sweet tea and a half-eaten scone. He shot to his feet, dusting the crumbs off his trousers, and gestured wordlessly at Gigi in her out-of-date gown. He began to speak once or twice, but evidently decided against whatever words he might have chosen to use, instead landing only the words, "Good God."

"Oh, I know it's quite old fashioned," she said hurriedly, bracing her hands against the stiff brocade at her ribs and giving a self-deprecating shrug of her shoulders, "but it will make me a more mysterious figure opposite our discerning Mr. Richards."

"It is certainly striking," he said, still eyeing the dress. "How are we meant to slip out of Bond Street without someone spotting Lady Silver emerging from this shop?"

"Oh, a bright shawl or pelisse usually does the job, and can be left in the carriage," Mrs. Goode said, already crossing the room to pour her own cup of tea. She wiggled comfortably into the cushion next to Kit's on the sofa, and applied a generous dollop of cream, first thing, into her teacup. "Sometimes Zelda will even add a bright hat or garish jewelry so that she looks entirely different on the other side of the carriage ride. We always use our hansom cab for trips to Seven Dials."

"You own a hansom cab?" Kit asked, clearly in awe of everything happening around him.

He seemed to be waiting for Gigi to seat herself before he returned to his own place on the sofa, so she crossed the room, careful of her flouncy skirts, and pulled them far to the side to settle herself into the armchair she had been using before.

"We have a carriage that resembles a hansom cab, I should say," Mrs. Goode corrected, plucking her own scone from the box of this morning's pastry remnants. "I thought it a silly purchase at the time, requiring quite a bit of repair, but Zelda has proven her instincts correct, as she so often does."

"It is a smart ploy," Kit allowed. "I have wondered if I ought to change into something clean, but I suppose the more rumpled and road-weary I look, the less I will draw attention to myself in a neighborhood like Seven Dials."

"I think that's likely true," Mrs. Goode agreed, leaning back to examine him. "I'd keep a cap low on your brow and hide that golden hair of yours. It's far too clean and bright."

"We could always rub some dirt into his scalp," Gigi said sweetly, casting a wink of amusement at Kit when his head came up with indignation. "I jest, of course. We haven't time to do such things anyway. We must be off in the next hour."

"Right you are," Mrs. Goode agreed with a bob of her head.

"I'll call the coach 'round and have some dinner set aside for you both for when you return."

"Thank you, Mrs. Goode," Gigi said, folding her hands over her heart. "And wish us luck."

This made the lady snort with a shake of her head as she turned to leave. "I'd never imply you need it, my dear."

◊

KIT WAS IMPRESSED with how well the ploy of a colorful shawl worked to distract from the fact that Gigi was wearing silver from tip to toe. She was holding the headdress in her hand, wrapped in its veil so that it appeared some manner of reticule. Anyone who saw them depart from Bond Street would likely have thought her a well-bred lady off for a night of revelry with her beau, and nothing more.

Once they were in the coach, however, she flung the multi-colored drapery off her bare shoulders, and heaved in several deep breaths, unaware of the way it made her breasts press alarmingly over the cusp of the neckline. "I feel like I'm wearing an entire textile mill," she complained, fanning herself with her hand.

"You look..." he started, tilting his head to take in her strangely old-fashioned attire, glowing opposite him in the cool blue light of dusk.

"Ridiculous? I know."

"No, no," he chuckled, adjusting in his seat. "You look like some foreign queen, come to ogle the peasants."

"I suppose I am rather that, aren't I?" she snipped back with a curl of her lips. "At least for those who speculate that Lady Silver is French."

"And so she is," he replied. "At least for tonight."

She lapsed into a thoughtful silence, pulling back the window coverings with her gloved hand to watch the city go by, the clop of horse hooves echoing between the buildings on either side of empty streets. She seemed either oblivious or amenable to his eyes on her, and so he took full advantage of the opportunity to study the cherubic lines of her profile.

"Do you know," she said without turning, "the thing that surprised me the most when I came here for the first time was how close together all the houses were, and now, as we head into a poorer borough, I realize that what I thought was crowded in Mayfair was in fact luxuriously spacious."

He nodded, following her gaze to the stone bend that led to Covent Garden. "When I was abroad, the Londoner boys seemed to revel in only having three to a tent. It is my understanding that in some parts of the city, where homes are most convenient to industry, sometimes several families will share a space of only two or three rooms."

"I imagine it's preferable to a long walk to and from a slavish vocation," she said with a twist of the curtain in her hand. "Do you think our Mr. Richards is one of these people, living shoulder to shoulder with others?"

"He might be, though if his mortuary is up in Hackney, he likely has a bit more room to breathe."

"I wonder if he lives in the same building where he prepares the dead," she said with a little shudder. "Perhaps I'd prefer the other families if those were my only options."

"I dunno about that," Kit said, nudging her foot with his own until she looked at him. "The dead are far less likely to nick the last of the Christmas pudding or snore like a forest ogre."

It made her smile a little, rolling her eyes heavenward and shaking her head. "You are irreverent, Kit Cooper."

"Oh, I try to be," he told her cheerfully, "but truth be told I often fail miserably. Perhaps I ought to keep you close to spin ghastly perspectives of all my daily tasks, so that I may rebut you with a cheerier alternative."

"Perhaps you should," she replied, her eyes glittering in the low light of the coach. "I shouldn't mind that at all."

CHAPTER 12

*E*ventually, she had adjusted to the lower light in the alleys here, with the sheen of silver netting hiding her face. But, by the time that had happened, she had already requisitioned the firm and muscular arm of Mr. Cooper to guide her like a blind beggar. She simply saw no need to enlighten him of the change in her circumstances.

After all, it would only rob him of a feeling of usefulness. Never mind how warm and strong he felt at her side. This was something a friend would do, wasn't it? Yes, of course it was. If Nell lost her spectacles on a dark night, Gigi would have been happy to guide her about the way Kit was doing for her now. She only suspected Nell might not get quite as much of a thrill out of requiring the assistance.

"Zelda mentioned that she always brings a bodyguard along when she comes to Seven Dials," he was saying at her side, seemingly oblivious to the enchanting aura he was giving off. "So, I reckon it won't seem amiss if I sit with you at the table when you meet Mr. Richards. I would prefer not to be very far away from you, lest something does go amiss."

"Mathias said that Mr. Richards wished to meet Lady Silver directly," Gigi replied, doing her best to swing her haphazard skirt clear of the uneven bricks jutting out every so often on the path. "One may assume that Lady Silver being present will be enough to put him at ease."

Kit made a grumbling noise of agreement, reaching across with his free arm to lightly touch her fingers, a signal that they were stopping for a moment.

"I think I see it," he said, his fingers lingering over hers, with only the gray gloves between them. "The Swan's Tooth, yes?"

"Yes," she agreed, her heart giving a sudden lurch at the sudden realization that the critical moment was near. "It's silly, isn't it? Swan's don't have teeth."

Kit chuckled next to her, his fingers slipping away as they made to cross the street. "Can you imagine the havoc if they did? Long-necked bastards are already menace enough to put a grown man to the chase."

Gigi giggled, wondering if Kit was speaking from personal experience. She rather liked the idea that something so graceful and pretty could also be ferocious. Perhaps that was why Zelda had chosen this pub. Liking its name was as good a reason as any, wasn't it?

She glanced up as they passed under the wooden sign above the threshold of the Swan's Tooth, though its planks were weather-beaten and colorless, especially in the dark. She rather hoped there was an artistic rendering of a fanged swan up there, even if it did need a fresh coat of paint.

A hush fell over the din of revelry as they entered, though

only nods of respect were tossed their way. Lady Silver was apparently a familiar enough sight in this place to raise no questions, but enough of a novelty to draw stares. Gigi suspected it also had to do with the glow of finery she was wearing, and simply the oddity of a woman of means appearing in such a venue.

She noted that there was a faint stickiness to the floor. She couldn't hear the sound of her shoes peeling off the planks of wood, but she could feel it happening. She clutched a bit tighter to Kit's arm and found he was only too happy to draw her nearer.

"Do we sit?" she whispered to him as the patrons began to resume their chatter.

He was looking away from her, at the man behind the bar, who had watched them enter with a grim expression of familiarity. Kit nodded to the man, and the man nodded back, then gestured toward a secluded booth at the far end of the large common room. As they made their way toward the booth, Gigi noted that it had a curtain pulled to the side over the enclave in which it sat, presumably to give its occupants privacy.

For some reason that sent a curl of anxious uncertainty into her belly. Was she really about to do this? Was the mysterious undertaker already awaiting them, obscured by the curve of the curtain that clung to one side of the table?

"It's all right," she heard Kit murmur to her, low enough that no one else would hear. "Everything is all right."

She gave a jerky nod, forcing herself to release the clench of her fingers from about his arm, where her fingernails had begun to dig into the flesh beneath his shirt. "Everything is all right," she repeated to herself under her breath, stepping into the little enclave to take her seat facing the door.

Once she'd relinquished her grip on him, Kit moved away from her, and slid into the bench opposite her own. Though he could not see her face, he evidently intuited her surprise, and leaned forward, explaining, "It will be much safer if I box Mr. Richards into this seat, with good access to both our company and the pub without."

The table, mercifully, was not sticky. It might very well have been the only space in the entire pub that was clean, though still in need of a good dusting.

They fell silent for a moment as the bartender appeared, setting a refreshing glass of cool, clear water in front of Gigi and looking expectantly at Kit, who simply said, "Ale."

Gigi thought it might give her hands something to do rather than shake, so she reached for the glass, slipping it delicately under the veil to take a sip and perhaps clear some of the dry-mouthed anxiety from her bones. She took a deep swallow, determined to get a hold of herself.

Two things became immediately apparent: First, that the liquid in this glass was not water. Secondly, that it was possibly not liquid at all, but fire posing as liquid. Pine sap and fire. She thought she deserved some sort of commendation from the Queen for not dropping the glass and shattering it and all its dishonest contents onto the table. In fact, she did not even make any embarrassing noises, and because her face was covered, Kit could not see her watering, red eyes, or the expression of horror on her face as she went to resolutely set the glass back onto the table with a thump.

Kit's eyes were on the glass, and though she was certain he

could not see her reactions to what had just occurred, he appeared to be fighting very hard to withhold laughter.

"Gin," he said finally, after taking a sharp, fortifying breath through his nose so that he might speak without obvious amusement tinting his words. "Mrs. Smith has a fondness for it."

"It's perfectly fine," Gigi lied, with a voice that had gone reedy in the wake of having all its edges charred.

Kit scratched at the corner of his mouth, clearly exercising great self-control, and nodded as though he believed her.

To be honest, now that the stuff had made its way down her chest and into her belly, it was giving her a strange and not altogether unpleasant sense of calm. She took a shaky breath, brushing the glass with her fingers, and considered that perhaps Zelda chose this drink for its effects rather than its questionable flavor.

"It has a very strong smell," he said, carefully avoiding her eye.

"I can't smell anything but lavender oil," she snapped, giving a shake to her veil. "That whole closet may as well be an apothecary for it. Harriet says it repels moths, who would otherwise feast upon all their old gowns."

"Ah, I thought that was your perfume," he replied, his eyes twinkling a bit with amusement as he peered through her veil. "I did notice the floral scent when we were in the carriage."

"I would never wear quite so much scent," she said with a little sniff, "and I prefer lilies to lavender, as it happens."

"Noted," he replied, only then indulging in a light chuckle, as the barman returned with a foaming glass of ale.

"Your guest is here, Lady Silver," the bartender grumbled in a low voice, casting a sideways look at Gigi. "Rather anxious, this one. Shall I send him to?"

She was startled to be asked this directly, and at the knowledge that apparently Mr. Richards had been inside the Swan's Tooth since they'd arrived. She gave a quick nod, and once the barman's back was turned, she reached for another sip of the fortifying fire liquid in her glass.

The second gulp went down much smoother, and the blossom of warmth in her center was expected this time, and most welcome. She wanted to ask Kit to describe their approaching third, but when she looked to him after enjoying the flush of warmth from the gin, she found him rather fixated on her veiled personage, rather than anticipating the arrival of Mr. Richards.

It made her very much want another drink, though she could not posit why that might be. She knew she should not, that she must keep a clear enough head to have the impending conversation, but even with the veil between them, meeting Kit Cooper's sharp blue eyes across the hazy candlelight of the table made her feel quite intoxicated all on its own.

He blinked, seemingly realizing the intensity of his stare, and quickly reached for his ale, keeping it firmly in hand when he stood to usher a nervous and reluctant-looking Mr. Richards into the booth, under the watchful eye of the barman.

He was not at all what Gigi had imagined.

Here was not a greasy and slinking purveyor of the dead, but a very neatly turned out little man, with a soft build and carefully combed brown hair, clutching his hat to his chest in utter respect for the woman in silver. He whispered thanks to Kit for making room for him, and slid quickly into the booth with the manner of someone who does his utmost to avoid inconveniencing others.

"Drink?" the barman barked.

"Oh. No. I-I. No," stammered Mr. Richards. "I do not imbibe."

"Tea?" suggested Gigi, turning her veiled head carefully to face the barman.

"No tea," the man responded, looking for the first time something less than formidable, perhaps in amusement at the suggestion. "Milk?"

"Milk would be fine, yes, thank you," Mr. Richards said with immediate gratitude, which only made the barman shake his head in wonder as he stalked away and Kit slid back into the bench, trapping Mr. Richards against the wall.

"Thank you for meeting with us so immediately," Gigi began, assuming Zelda Smith's Winchester clip, without going so far as to entirely impersonate her.

"Of course, of course," Mr. Richards said, straightening his back. "Anything for the Silver Leaf. It has been so very long since I met with anyone other than Mathias, and I was never able to properly thank you for all you did for my family. All you've done for me."

"It is nothing at all," Gigi said, casting a quick look at an equally baffled Kit, whose top lip was firmly planted in the foam of his ale, his eyes cut to the side to examine Mr. Richards from his periphery.

All of that rehearsal they'd done in his jagged cockney had not prepared them at all for this polite and diminutive man.

Unable to help herself, Gigi said, "Mr. Richards, I imagine you are a very comforting presence for those whose loved ones you put to rest."

He blinked at her, clearly just as surprised by this outburst as Gigi herself was. "I thank you kindly for saying so," he replied after a moment of careful consideration. "After what I saw on the Continent, it seemed to me the most important thing a man could do with his life, to show respect to those who have passed. I consider it a most humbling and gratifying profession."

"It doesn't frighten you at all?" Gigi asked, leaning forward. She was certain that it was the gin having this conversation, as her sensible, clear-thinking self sat by and watched in awe.

Had she not been taught to be silent and let others speak first? Yes, it must have been the gin.

"Oh, not at all, no," Mr. Richards said, his round face brightening at the inquiry. "As you know, my parlor is also my home. There is nothing to fear from those who have gone. If anything, it is much scarier to consider how they might be discarded and forgotten were I not there to intervene."

"Is, um," Kit said, startling both Gigi and Mr. Richards, "is that how you came to service the prison?"

"Beg pardon." Mr. Richards cleared his throat, squinting at Kit. "We have not been introduced."

"This is Mr. Cooper," Gigi put in quickly. "He is assisting me in a current Silver Leaf undertaking. You may speak freely with him."

"Well, Lady Silver here arranged for my life to begin again in Hackney," he said, sniffing as though this were a story Kit should well know. "Because the prison itself is an important link in the chain of Silver Leaf operations. I was as surprised as anyone else when our agreement with the warden was violated."

Gigi inhaled sharply through her nose, then quickly exhaled again because she had not accounted for the way the veil would adhere to her face. Truly, it was very inconvenient.

"You must forgive our ignorance, Mr. Richards," she said. "But we believe Silver Leaf operations were undertaken by an imposter, and we are now scrambling to assemble the relevant information before more damage is done. Am I to understand that you were involved in the disappearance of Mr. Randall Ferris from his imprisonment?"

At this moment, the barman returned to their table with a mug filled with lukewarm milk, which he slid across to Mr. Richards before vanishing again.

Mr. Richards considered this unappetizing offering, perhaps particularly offensive as he was already being forced to digest unpleasant information.

"Of course I did not know," he said thinly, making to reach for the mug, but losing his gall and allowing his hand to collapse uselessly on the table. "I would never have ... You must know I never ..."

"We know very well, Mr. Richards, that you would never

betray us," Gigi assured him, reaching past the mug of milk to touch his hand. "We simply must know what occurred so that we may take steps to rectify the trouble it has caused."

He swallowed with some effort, staring down at the gray gloved hand sitting atop his.

"The warden was so very upset," he told her, sounding on the brink between hysteria and relief, "he will be overjoyed to know it was not truly your work. I would not have agreed to it, you know. Not after all these years. I was just as surprised as anyone else when Mr. Ferris popped out of that casket, shouting for his wife. I thought I was picking up the usual cargo, correspondences and the like, and that he was one of three actual dead that needed to be put to rest.

"I had to return two days later to retrieve the third body, after Mr. Ferris had finally left my home. I felt we were put into great danger harboring him for as long as we did, you understand. I have two young daughters and another child on the way."

"Of course, Mr. Richards. You must know we would never compromise your safety in that way," Gigi murmured as she pulled away, leaning back against the bench. To her own ear, she sounded completely certain of this statement, which was, in reality, only an optimistic assumption. "Where did Mr. Ferris go?"

"He went with the French gentleman. Older fellow. Oliver, I think it was?"

"Olivier," Kit corrected. "Mr. Olivier came into London to retrieve Mr. Ferris?"

"Well, into London so far as an outer rung such as Hackney

is concerned, yes. Mr. Ferris was none too happy to see him, and kept demanding over and over that the French gentleman produce Mrs. Ferris immediately. They were still arguing as they left, and I know not where they went. I was so relieved to see the back of him that I did not think to inquire further."

"This is very good information, Mr. Richards," Gigi told him, hoping to appeal to his eagerness to please in order to override his obvious disquiet. "Did Mr. Ferris say anything about his escape while he was in your care? Did he indicate how it was planned or why he expected his wife to be present?"

"He did not," Mr. Richards answered, finally steeling himself enough to take a sip of the milk he'd been brought. He wrinkled his nose, clearly regretting the decision, and sighed. "If the wife hasn't vanished yet, I'd suggest you speak with her. Mr. Ferris wrote her three letters a week, every week, for many years."

Gigi nodded, glancing at Kit, whose ale had apparently evaporated during the short space of this enlightening conversation.

"We thank you, Mr. Richards," Kit said to the man. "Is there anything else you can recall that might aid us?"

"Well, the coach was odd, that brought the French gentleman. Glossy and crested, from some country estate. It was much finer than any horse and cart you'd usually see in Hackney."

"What was the crest?" Gigi asked.

"I cannot say with certainty," he admitted sheepishly. "I

believe it was a pair of fish, but I was not committed to studying the details at the time. My most sincere apologies for that."

"A pair of fish," Kit repeated, shaking his head in wonder.

It was at this juncture that Gigi felt it was appropriate to partake in another gulp of the gin.

It might alarm her later, but in the moment, she found she liked the taste of gin quite a lot, after all.

CHAPTER 13

*K*it had expected Gigi to initiate their departure the instant they saw the back of Mr. Richards, but to his surprise, she lingered over her glass, gazing down at it with an expression he could not see from behind her silver veil.

"Don't tell me you want another!" he teased, grinning at her.

"It's just ... a novel experience," she replied with a dreamy sort of lilt. "I feel rather free just now. Free and strong."

"Yes, that particular drink has been known to make a person or two believe they've inhuman strength," he replied with amusement. "Go on, then. I'll have another glass as well, hm? We've earned it, haven't we?"

"We surely have," she replied with a dramatic little gasp. "Oh, Kit! It went splendidly, didn't it? Mr. Richards was exactly the right person to speak to, and we found him straightaway. Well, Mathias helped, but we did the true work!"

Her excitement was contagious, and Kit felt an answering jolt in his belly. It was pride, certainly, over the surprising amount of information they'd gathered tonight. But it was also a little zap of electricity that sparked when she called him, so casually, by his Christian name.

He motioned from where he sat to the barman, who hadn't looked away from them for more than a handful of seconds since they'd arrived. He held up two fingers and the barman nodded, moving to prepare two new glasses with haste.

It was impossible not to wonder what sort of rapport Mrs. Smith had built up in this place over the years, and exactly how she'd gone about doing it. Whatever had passed here over the years had resulted in exactly the type of quick and uncomplaining service someone like Zelda Smith likely expected from any and all experiences she undertook.

He wasn't sure if the thought was droll or galling, but either way, they were currently benefiting from her particularly strong personality. Their drinks arrived on the table before he'd had time to knock back the final dregs of his first glass, which the barman swiped from between his hands without a word, leaving a gently foaming, full glass in its place.

He wanted to ask if Gigi had seen this trick too, but when he looked up from the ale, he found she was on her feet, leaning precariously forward in that wide, heavy brocade gown, to unhook the curtain that offered a bit of privacy in this little nook. It wasn't exactly that he wanted to stop her from doing this.

No, quite the contrary. He felt rather eager at the idea of seclusion with Gigi Dempierre and a selection of spirits, which was all the reason in the world why he should have prevented it from happening.

Alas, it was too late, and what could a man do when it was already too late? It was clear for any angel on his shoulder to see that the curtain was already shut, and the lovely Lady Silver was settling back into her seat with a relieved sigh, reaching immediately to the pearl-lined clasps by her dainty ears where she could rid herself of the cumbersome veil.

It would be downright rude for Kit to interrupt.

There was something strangely forbidden about watching her remove that veil. Her face had been a secret all evening, and though he knew it very well by now for as much time as they had spent together (and as often as he'd conjured her image in his mind), there was still something thrilling about being witness to the transformation. Lady Silver was whisked away and in her place was that visiting queen he had joked about some hours earlier, on their ride to Seven Dials.

Her face was flushed, a little pink from the trapped heat beneath the fabric, and there were faint lines etched into her hairline where the ornamental anchor of the veil had sat. It did nothing to detract from her allure as she broke immediately into a toothy smile, her dimples springing to life in her round cheeks.

"*Salut!*" she chirped, giving his glass a delicate tap with her own and bringing the gin to her lips again with giddy anticipation.

It was, he thought, exactly what her mother had been imagining when she begged Gigi to stay safely at home.

"I think I might be a little bit in love," she said dreamily, propping her chin on her hand, oblivious to the way his heart had slammed to a halt with that statement. "With London."

He exhaled, his heart resuming its business. What had he thought she was going to say? What had he *wanted* her to say?

Get a grip, Cooper.

"They say it was built by giants," he told her, lifting his ale to his lips. "Do you believe it?"

"I do not. A giant would have no eye for detail, and would never think to let a place like this thrive only a stone's throw from a place like Zelda's shop. Mr. Richards was an odd little fellow, wasn't he? You never meet people like that in Dover."

"Undertakers?"

"You know very well I do not mean undertakers," she scolded playfully. "What about Mrs. Goode? The only spinsters I ever knew coming up were said to have been prematurely widowed by the war. Mrs. Goode is the opposite of everything I ever believed a spinster to be! She seems positively chuffed just to wake up every morning and go about the business of being herself. It makes the whole business seem a lot less dire."

"It is an enviable quality, to be sure."

Kit steepled his fingers, peering at the way Gigi cradled the glass of gin against her lips, as though she had to coax it into submission. She was a curious little bird, wasn't she? He had started this trip thinking he couldn't quite get the measure of her, and now, several days in, he simply believed she had endless facets, all working in tandem to showcase her light in a variety of ways.

"It does indeed have a smell," she confessed, taking a dainty sip. "I can't tell you what a joy it is to smell anything other than lavender for a few moments."

He chuckled. "Even if the replacement smell is of a distillery?"

"Especially then. Does my company shame you?"

"Never."

She smiled at him for a moment, taking another sip, and then her head came up, as though struck by revelation from the ether. "Are you afraid someone will recognize you?" she asked, suddenly breathless. "You did say you conduct quite a lot of business in London, didn't you? Oh, won't it get you in trouble if someone does?"

He couldn't help but to give a short, dry laugh. "Gigi, to tell you the truth, I have to remind my own solicitor who I am with a series of mnemonics and anecdotes every time I walk into his office. There is no better place to be anonymous than a large city."

She thought about this, her moss-green eyes going a bit starry as she gazed into the air, imagining it. "Yes, how utterly delightful, to simply go wherever you wish, doing whatever you like, and rarely having to worry about being bothered or recognized. I did notice that when I was here in the spring, even if I didn't put it to words. I crossed a long bridge over the Thames, steps behind my chaperones, and for a moment, it truly was like I was alone in the universe, and could be anyone or anything I liked."

"Why would you wish to be anyone other than Gigi Dempierre?" he asked without thinking, bafflement clear in his voice.

She blushed, taken aback by the reaction, and blinked at him for a moment while she conjured a response. "Perhaps I don't truly wish to be someone else," she said, after considering it, "but it's fun to pretend for a moment or two, isn't it?"

"Like tonight," he supplied, giving her foot a playful nudge with his own.

She brightened, nodding with enough enthusiasm to make her curls bounce. "Yes, exactly! Tonight I was someone else, and it was great fun, but I am also very relieved to close that curtain and be myself again."

"Tonight is the first time I've seen you without feathers in your hair," he told her, gesturing at her hair, which had been disrupted by the removal of the veil and left rather lopsided and messy.

"I have one in my sleeve," she told him immediately, producing from thin air a small, sky-blue feather with a black tip. "One of Pip's. For good luck."

"I stand corrected," he said, reaching for the feather with a chuckle. "Is this an enduring superstition of yours?"

"We're all entitled to one or two eccentricities, Kit Cooper," she said with a lift of her chin. "I'm sure you've got a few."

"You'll have to find them and point them out to me, in that case," he told her, thumbing the soft edge of the feather. "I confess, however, that it seems your good luck charm was effective, so I've no right to condemn it."

"That's right," she replied triumphantly. "Besides, you *have* seen me without a feather before, and it certainly wasn't a moment of good luck!"

"I have?"

"You *have*," she drawled, twirling her fingers on the rim of her glass. She turned those enchanting green eyes up to meet his and said, lower, "Or don't you recall?"

It hit him like a punch to the gut, the realization of what she was referring to. He couldn't help but see it again in his mind's eye, those thin, white undergarments soaked through and clinging to her salt-kissed skin. He had truly thought they would simply never speak of it, as though it hadn't happened at all. Now that the issue had been acknowledged, he had no idea how to proceed.

"I ... erm," he said with a little cough. "I recall very well."

Her lips curled up in a slow, feline smile, evidently in amusement at his discomfort. "Are you blushing?"

"Men don't blush."

"Hm," she murmured, averting her eyes to sip at her gin, as though granting him a moment to compose himself. "I thought, afterward, that it wasn't a bad thing after all, and that since we'd shared such a startling introduction, it might pave the way for true friendship. I haven't had many friends in my life, and so I set my cap at you."

"Is that what we are?" he asked her, waiting for her eyes to turn back to his. "Friends?"

It was her turn to be flustered, her eyes narrowing and lips pressing shut. "Well," she said, tilting her head, "perhaps not quite yet, but ... well, I thought ... presumed, I suppose ..."

"I would be honored to have you as a friend, Gigi," he said, keeping his voice low, lest anyone walk too near their little curtained alcove, "but I must confess that other possibilities have crossed my mind."

"Possibilities?" she whispered, her cheeks flushed. She reached again for her gin, but it was empty, and she stared into the hollow glass with an expression of distress.

He suddenly regretted his forwardness, wondering if he had just botched things completely and made the lady uncomfortable.

He straightened his shoulders and, determined to remedy his error, spoke with the same teasing lightness he had used earlier, "Yes, of course," he said with a smile, "we are partners in mystery and intrigue, are we not? I'd say that's a good step or two beyond simple friendship."

"Oh!" She released a pent-up burst of nervous air and a strained little laugh. "Yes, of course, you are quite right. Still, I'd say it was an unorthodox, but auspicious beginning. It certainly cleared the way for a bit of familiarity, anyhow. A shared embarrassing secret will do that."

"I suppose it will," he agreed, raising his eyebrows. "I hadn't thought of it that way."

"Well, then I am pleased to provide new viewpoints," she returned with a little smirk. "Shall we head back to the hansom? I fear if I have another gin, you will have to carry me out of here."

He chuckled, watching her reach for the veil and begin the process of jamming it back onto her head over the mess she'd made of her hair. "We need to get some food in your belly, I think."

"Probably so," she agreed. "Though I admit freely that having just the gin in there is truly lovely."

"For the moment. You might change that stance tomorrow."

"Well, you shall have to disregard me tomorrow, then," she quipped, wiggling the final pin into place to hold her veil steady with her tongue caught between her teeth.

He chuckled, draining the last of his ale. "I don't find the idea of carrying you out of here entirely objectionable," he confessed, "You seem like a pleasant enough load."

"Do I?" She was using her Lady Silver voice again, smoothing the fabric as the veil swished back into place. "I rather think I'd enjoy being carried about by you, Mr. Cooper, and you'd have to do it forevermore."

"There are worse fates."

"Mm," she agreed, pulling the curtain back so that they might step out again into the great, wide world. "It sounds like one of those *possibilities* you mentioned, doesn't it?"

He hesitated, uncertain if the brashly flirtatious comment had been intentional. He realized he was utterly unprepared for an actual romantic confrontation from the woman he had been lusting over for the last week.

"Does it?" he decided to ask. It was noncommittal, but easy to interpret either as flirtatious or friendly, depending on her perception. He did his utmost to keep his voice neutral in delivery and punctuated the question with a polite offering of his arm as they prepared to navigate through the pub.

For a moment, she did not answer. She curled her fingers into the crook of her elbow and appeared to savor this question, all the while with her own visage safe and unobserved behind her veil.

The silence was deafening.

Just as Kit opened his mouth to apologize, she turned her head, giving his arm a little squeeze, and said, "I very much hope so."

CHAPTER 14

Gigi could not say whether the panic had caused the hiccups, or the hiccups had caused the panic. Whichever started first, they were playing off one another like a harmonic duet, each squeak from her chest causing another spike of *oh no!,* which in turn conjured another hiccup.

Kit, for his part, was doing a very good job of not laughing at her, for Gigi knew that if she were in his place, she would be doubled over in amusement.

"It's only—*hic*—that I know I would get in the wor—*hic*—worst trouble if my mother found me smelling—*hic*—of an ... of a ... where do they make—*hic*—gin?"

"A distillery," he supplied graciously, all whilst maintaining control over his features while she squeaked and startled like a church mouse across from him in the carriage.

"Smelling of a distillery!" she managed, only to punctuate the end with another hiccup.

"Surely Mrs. Goode is not so stringent," Kit said gently. "She seems more a friend than a chaperone, after all."

Gigi nodded, unable to speak just now as she yet again attempted to hold her breath to the count of twenty. Yes, she had already tried this thrice, but she was a desperate woman and needed this ailment to cease. She could not fathom the words to describe the distress she felt when the hiccups managed to happen in her air-filled lungs, even as she fought them, eventually forcing her to sputter out all of the oxygen she'd been holding in in a less-than-dignified fashion.

"That trick has never worked for me," Kit said, observing her with that carefully contained amusement. "Nate and I would scare one another. A good scare will make your soul jump through your bones for a moment and set everything to rights again."

Gigi gave him a look. "It's not as though you can—*hic*—hop out of a dark corner just now."

"I could tell you a ghost story," he suggested, as though it were the most serious of matters. "Are you afraid of ghosts?"

"I am not," she lied. She twisted the veil around in her hands, pressing the metal points painfully into her fingers in the hopes that perhaps a distracting sensation would solve the issue. It hadn't yet, but Gigi was willing to persevere.

"I could talk to you about the orchard business," he suggested with a wry twist of his lips. "Are you afraid of boredom, Gigi Dempierre?"

She shook her head, pressing her lips together uselessly against the next outburst.

"Well, how do you scare a fearless person?" he teased. "Aren't you afraid of anything at all?"

She blinked at him. What *was* she afraid of?

Worms were a lifelong aversion, but she would rather avoid an encounter with them. Her mother's disapproval obviously disquieted her, but that is what had caused this mess in the first place.

The last time she had felt truly startled was the day of Isabelle's wedding, and Kit had been the culprit of that surprise, after all. Was she afraid of him? No, definitely not.

She stole a glance at his face across from her, her body still warm from the gin, and her head spinning pleasantly, even in the wake of the hiccups. It had been a bit scary to flirt so directly with him at the pub, but she had been bolstered by the armor of the veil and the power of liquid courage. She wasn't certain she could replicate that moment of bravery anyhow, unveiled and vulnerable, across from him looking so very, very composed.

She made a helpless little whimper, tossing the useless veil to the side. "Scare me, then. Just ... go on. Do it," she begged, eyes brimming with distress. It was embarrassing enough to be going through this in front of Kit himself, but combining the distillery smell and the indignity of the hiccups with her return from her first mission would just not do. "Please!"

"Are you sure?" he asked, his lips twisting in a half smile.

"I am perfectly—*hic*—certain!"

"Hmm," he replied, tapping his chin as he considered what manner of fright would work best. "Are you ready?"

"No, I'm not rea—" She found herself cut off as Kit Cooper leaned, fast as a snap of lightning, across the space between them, cupping his big hand around the curve of her neck, and drawing her lips to his.

Her mind went momentarily blank.

His mouth was so warm and so soft, evidently taking great pleasure in its sampling of hers. She could taste the ale on his lips and something else that she could not quite define. It was impossible to do anything but fall into it, to reach for more, but he was already pulling back, his fingers lingering for just a moment on the column of her neck before he returned to his place on the opposite bench.

She stared at him in disbelief, frozen in the posture he'd pulled her toward until she could regain her wits. If she was expecting him to say something, she was clearly bound for disappointment, as he had resumed his polite posture of observation, and his earlier countenance of light amusement.

She cleared her throat, pressing herself back against the cushions and making a business of smoothing imagined lines in her skirt. What was there to say after that? *Please do it again*, she thought, and her mind answered, *He only did it to startle you.*

She blinked, her eyes widening as she gazed up at him in wonder. "It worked!" she realized, raising a hand to rest over her throat. She waited, anticipating the next spasm and gasp, but it did not come. "It actually worked!" she repeated in wonder.

"I am pleased to hear it," he replied, his voice low and soft, giving nothing at all away.

She thought that, if not for the gin, she might have been able to quickly formulate a clever rejoinder, but as it was, any solid remnants of her mind this evening had been reduced to mush by that kiss, and so she had no wit to speak of in the moment when she needed it most. She held his eye, able to manage at least that much, and attempted to commit his expression to memory so that she might dissect it in the morning.

She didn't have much time. The coach was already slowing on the cobbles outside of the print shop, and here was the door being pulled open by the cheery driver.

Kit followed her out onto the street, taking care to remember the veil and hand it to her discreetly. Fog was beginning to build on the darkened streets, and Gigi thought it unlikely anyone would have noticed such a thing anyhow, but it was likely the correct thing to exercise caution at all times. She took his arm, reflecting again on how warm he was, as though vitality and life were just radiating off him, curling around her and tugging her into his orbit.

He stopped at the doorway and gave her a little bow, evidently bidding her good night.

"You aren't coming up?" she asked with some surprise. "I believe Mrs. Goode kept a plate of dinner for you."

"I cannot," he said regretfully. "It is already late, and I must arrive at Marylebone before the staff has all retired. I think I am soon for slumber myself, as it is."

"Oh," she said, forcing herself to swallow her disappointment. "Shall I see you on the morrow?"

"Undoubtedly," he assured her. "We must make for Mrs. Ferris's home tomorrow, I would think. Shall I call in the late morning? We may decide our plan of attack on the trip to her home."

She nodded in agreement, her heart giving a rather pitiful flutter in her chest. Were they really not going to speak of it?

"Until morning, then," she heard herself saying.

Kit smiled at her, lifting her hand to his lips. He pressed a sweet, lingering kiss onto her knuckles, those clear blue eyes turned up to meet hers, full of things that went unspoken. "Good night, Gigi," he said as he straightened, his voice in such a low timbre that it strummed the chords in her chest.

"Good night, Kit," she replied, her voice breathy and thin.

They stared at one another for a moment in silence, and then, just as the last thread of Gigi's nerve began to fray, she spun on her heel and slipped through the door of the shop.

Once inside, she rushed through the dark room, feeling her way for the doorway that led to the little flat above. She found herself almost running, climbing the stairs as though they would vanish beneath her feet at any moment. It felt, in that moment, as though she might never think clearly again.

When she burst into the antechamber of the flat, it was dark and still, with a single candle burning next to two covered plates of food, where she had served tea some hours earlier. She used her body to lean the door shut and sank down onto the floor in the ornate silver dress, which puddled dramatically around her legs.

She stared across the room at the simplicity that awaited her at the end of such an unpredictable evening. It seemed to Gigi that the flames jumped a bit at her attention, as though they knew what wild airs she had brought in on her back.

Still, it was a peaceful scene, a still life of quiet and repast.

Finally, she thought, *I can catch my breath.*

CHAPTER 15

*K*it awoke feeling unusually buoyant.

He sprang from the sheets, energized for the day before even his ritual cup of coffee, and found himself whistling as he dressed. Whether this was the gift of the indulgent bedding in Marylebone or the aftershocks of finally having kissed Gigi Dempierre, he could not say for certain, nor would he admit that the answer was obvious, even to himself.

When was the last time he'd considered truly courting a girl? So long ago that Kit didn't recognize himself in those far-flung memories. It had been before the war, before university—hell, maybe it was before he could grow a respectable beard. It had been a consideration only in a time when it couldn't have ever resulted in true action. Thus is the privilege of youth.

Growing up, he'd been dead set on marrying the daughter of one of the orchard foremen, a fantasy his parents had mostly ignored with the odd pat on the head and shared glances of amusement between them. She had been an older girl and obviously a pretty one, with long legs and shiny brown hair.

She likely had never noticed Kit as anything more than a hovering child, and certainly didn't wait around for him to reach his majority and propose to her, as was her unwitting destiny to his young mind. He couldn't remember her features beyond those two things, though he was reasonably certain she hadn't had dimples in her cheeks, and more's the pity for her.

He'd had flirtations as a young man, certainly, but none that involved what he would consider courtship. None that even came close.

Since returning from the war, there had been some interest from plotting mamas in London, especially those with an excess of debutantes to offload. Luckily, his sparse attendance to much in the way of social leisure had made him a difficult target.

He suspected that he wouldn't have been a desirable marriage target at all if not for his relation to Nathaniel.

Often, when these conniving mamas found out that Kit had very little in common with his distinguished cousin, they lost interest and retreated back to their dens to amend their battle plans to more suitable targets.

It was just as well to him. Those debutantes would have been mightily disappointed by Kit's hands-on approach to such a lowly vocation, and likely deeply disturbed by the state of his family name.

As far as Kit was concerned, repairing all mistakes his father had made was a necessary first step before he could think about carving out something new for himself. Archie Cooper hadn't been a bad man, just a gullible one, with a tenuous grasp on what was real and what wasn't. His father's wandering mind had been scary at times when he was a lad, and certainly infuriating as he got older.

Now, with his father some years dead and with the knowledge that Archie had not always been addled, Kit mostly felt pity for the man.

Madness is rarely an earned curse, after all. Madness can strike anyone.

He tossed his straight razor into a bowl of water and toweled his face off, recalling again that quick, chaste little kiss he'd won in the carriage. Well, he had taken it, he reckoned, though she had given unwitting permission. He thought that she hadn't minded it, though she had certainly been surprised.

Adorably so.

Gigi Dempierre was not a Society miss, trained from birth to navigate the *ton,* nor was she a sturdy country rose, bred for the practical demands of home and hearth. She was something else entirely, and Kit did not think he could confidently define it just yet. So, why on earth was he flitting around his bedroom like a wee hummingbird in anticipation of spending another day with her? Why was he seriously considering a formal courtship? What sort of wife would a woman like that make with a man like him?

Maybe he was mad too.

His mother would certainly think so.

He chuckled to himself, whipping a neatly folded shirt out of his valise and tugging it on over his head. His mother, for all her bluster about the French, had proven herself a hypocrite when confronted with the charm of a Frenchman, hadn't she?

He wondered if she was behaving herself in his absence.

If his mother were to remarry, it would certainly change things. Perhaps it was simply the effects of a giddy mood, or perhaps he was thinking about it more reasonably after a few days of pondering, but he hoped she did find happiness with someone new. He hoped she had another chance at love and life.

Susan Cooper had known too much pain, and some of it, Kit knew very well, was his fault. Perhaps salvation was closer than he realized. It was a hopeful thought for a hopeful sort of morning, and his mood was good enough that he could acknowledge these things, these very real things about his life, without feeling even a dent in his cheer.

He dressed carefully, ensuring his hair was neat and his cravat was straight, wishing to cut a dapper figure this morning in contrast to his rather rumpled presentation during the previous few days. He had truly felt like a servant attending a queen last night, with her in that ridiculously ornate silver gown. It had been *fun*, he realized.

When was the last time he had prioritized the simple pleasure of having fun?

He smiled to himself all the way to the carriage.

∽

Mrs. Smith's Fine Prints was already open and in bustling operation when Kit arrived at Bond Street.

Apparently, the business of buying illustrated gossip was a task best reserved for the morning hours.

He shouldered his way past a trio of tittering gentlemen considering a board of new arrivals and tipped his hat in greeting to Harriet Goode, who gave him a cheery wave as he made his way toward the staircase at the rear of the shop. She returned to her task before he could give an answering wave, evidently unconcerned with his intent to climb to the flat unaccompanied, in the task of locating Miss Dempierre.

He announced himself as he scaled the steps and pushed the door open, struck immediately by the smell of tea and the sweet notes of pastry and chocolate. He cast a quick look into the mirror by the door, tucking away a wayward strand of his sandy hair, just as the sound of footsteps began to click on the hardwood floors.

She rounded the corner in a prim pink gown, with freshly starched lace at her collar and a fluffy white feather in her hair. She blushed the instant she came into view, ducking her head with a warm smile, and bade him, "Good morning!"

"Good morning," he returned with a grin. "Did you sleep well?"

"After a fashion," she replied with a little giggle, folding her hands in front of her. "I confess my head was a bit sore on waking, but Mrs. Goode prescribed a copious amount of tea, which did help, in the end."

"Wise guidance," he said, leaning against the door. "I am in no great rush if you wish to have more tea."

"Oh, no, no," she demurred. "I've had more than enough and am rather eager to be off. Unless you would like a cup? Oh, of course I should have offered straightaway. Will you have some tea?"

He opened his mouth to answer but she waved him off, clearly flustered at her oversight of good manners.

"I shall pour you a cup of tea. Do not argue. I insist. Sit!"

"It is really no—"

"Sit!"

He obeyed, holding up his hands in surrender and crossing the room to the floral couch. "Yes, Mistress," he teased as she poured him a cup of tea and pointedly dropped in a copious amount of sugar.

"Ah, a woman after my own heart," he said gratefully, accepting the cup and basking in yet another lovely blush upon her cheeks. He waited for her to situate herself opposite him, spreading her striped pink skirt around her legs, and asked, "Are you feeling quite prepared to meet Mrs. Ferris?"

"I suppose as prepared as I can be to meet a total stranger," she said with a little sigh. "I confess I rather wish I could wear the costume and veil again. I think it was easier to assume an air of competence when I could pretend to be someone else."

"I daresay there's no better person to be than yourself, Gigi."

"Oh, stop it," she tutted, squirming in her seat at the unexpected compliment. "Besides, Zelda implied that the only reason we'll be able to have an audience with Mrs. Ferris is because of *your* connection with her. I imagine that means you will be doing the lion's share of the talking."

He took another sip of his tea and swallowed it as he digested this statement. "Yes, I suppose you are right," he realized with a little frown. "I was so looking forward to just watching you do everything."

"It's a true partnership after all," she said with a little curve of her lips. "She knows my mother, so at least that will endear me to her in some fashion, I hope. We must be very careful not to alert any of her keepers to our affiliation with her erstwhile charges of espionage. I reviewed the notes Zelda left us this morning over breakfast, but beyond a carefully crafted series of directions for the driver, I found the rest of the information rather useless."

"What sort of information?"

"Just things like the year she married her husband, her favorite literature to perhaps employ in building a rapport, and that sort of thing. I do not even have a clear understanding of how her arrest came to happen."

"My father said something he oughtn't have in mixed company, I think." Kit sighed, shaking his head. "Aunt Mary must have still been alive when it happened, if he was privy to sensitive information, which means this woman has been locked in her home for twenty years at least."

Gigi gave him a sympathetic look, lacing her fingers together in her lap. She considered her words before speaking, and then said, carefully, "I'm sure it was an accident, Kit, on your father's part."

He nodded, setting his cup on his knee and taking a deep breath. The topic of his father felt as though it had sucked the warmth out of the room, leaving only the unpleasant necessity of explanation behind. He gave her a bland smile and agreed with her, hoping it would soften the subject of Archibald Cooper. "Oh, it likely was an accident, yes ... in one fashion or another."

She waited patiently for him to elaborate, and he nodded, resigned to the fact that she was entitled to know the information that informed their mission today.

"My father died some years ago," he began. "He had been sent to debtor's jail and then sold on indenture to a plantation in Jamaica. I was still at war at the time, having fled Kent the instant I reached my majority, so it was left only to my mother and Nathaniel to attempt to rescue him, and by the time they were able, it was already too late."

"Oh, how terrible!" She leaned forward, as though she wished to reach out and touch him, to comfort him in some way.

"It is all right. It was terrible, but not surprising. You must understand that my father was already beginning to lose his grasp on reality all those years ago, at the time when the Atlases died and Nathaniel came to live with us. My father was always eccentric, but it seemed to worsen with every year of his advancing age, turning him extremely susceptible and erratic. It is easy to believe he would get confused and say the wrong things to the worst possible people without realizing the damage he was doing. For years, he ranted to us about the Silver Leaf spies responsible for his sister's execution—a twisted misunderstanding of the reality of her death. It sent Nathaniel on a wayward, resentful path that could have prevented his potential for happiness, had he not found Nell when he did, and had she not been the key to what truly happened.

"My father didn't intend malice, but he sowed it all the same."

There was a beat of silence, the two of them just looking at one another for a moment, as the gravity of this information took hold. She seemed to wait deliberately, to ensure he was finished with all he wanted to say, before she stepped into the conversation or interrupted his flow of thought.

"My own father seems to live in another world as well," Gigi said after a moment, with a gleam of understanding in her eye rather than the shadow of abject pity he had anticipated. "I would not call it madness, just ... vacancy. There is nothing behind his eyes.

"I have tried so very many times to find some subject with which to engage him, to pull him into the same time and place with me, so that we may see each other for even a second, but I have never succeeded. I realized at some point that it is no use. He is as much as he will ever be."

"It is maddening to feel so powerless," Kit said, registering a gentle release in his chest, as though a knot of anxious anticipation had been tugged loose into flowing, gentle ribbons.

"It's impossible to resist trying, though, every now and then, to reach them."

She nodded in what appeared to be perfect understanding. "Do you think Mrs. Ferris knows that your father was not always in control of his actions? Do you think anyone attempted to apologize or explain matters to her after her arrest?"

"I seriously doubt it," he said, considering it. "Once she was put in house arrest, it would have been difficult to offer either apology or explanation without incriminating themselves. I can't imagine what she has believed all this time, but perhaps I can give her some measure of peace."

"I wish we knew more about this whole blasted situation," Gigi said impatiently. "It is just like Zelda to withhold pertinent information."

"She hasn't been able to speak to this woman since her arrest, from what I gathered," Kit pointed out, rubbing his thumb on the edge of the teacup as he pondered refilling it. "It might simply be that Zelda has no further information to give us."

Gigi leveled him in her soft green gaze, her mouth a flat line punctuated by skeptical dimples.

It immediately made him laugh, a lovely shattering of the brittle tension that had formed over discussion of his father. Better still, it made her laugh, too, a gentle tinkling titter as she shook her head in wonder at the situation they had found themselves in.

"Yes, yes," he admitted. "You are right. Mrs. Smith derives

her joy in life by making us poor mortals grope about in the dark."

"Ha," she replied with a lift of her chin. "Until you've got an opaque silver veil obstructing your vision and filling your nostrils with a decade of lavender oil, you haven't experienced groping around in the dark."

"I'll wear the veil," he told her in mock somberness. "Don't think I won't."

"I'll keep it under advisement," she said, her eyes sparkling at him. "More tea?"

"Please," he said, and noted with pleasure that she poured herself a cup as well.

CHAPTER 16

What sort of home could double as a prison? What sort of prison could pass for a home?

Gigi was unsure what to expect when they reached the dwelling that had contained Mrs. Ferris for most of the time she herself had been alive. She supposed any sort of place, no matter how opulent, would become unbearable if she were trapped there for twenty-odd years.

In some small way, any girl with a worrying mother and a country home she'd never left for more than a few hours likely understood to a point what it felt like to be on house arrest. *La Falaise*, Gigi's family home, had been such a consistent container for her entire life. From the moment she'd drawn breath until just a few months ago, when she visited London for the first time, Gigi had never spent more than a day away from the "safety" of its walls. She thought perhaps she could sympathize with Mrs. Ferris, in some small way.

She knew it wasn't *really* the same, though. Not when she truly considered it. Not even a little bit.

There had been a surprising burst of briskness in the air today, a first whisper of autumn rolling out over London in a fine, misty fog. It had made the ride to the outer edges of the city slower than it would have been otherwise, and far more riddled with unexpected lurches and bumps along the way.

Kit had said, with the complete confidence of a soothsayer, "It's going to rain."

"How do you know?"

"You can't smell it?" He seemed genuinely surprised, motioning to the air around them as though it came with weather signage. "It's like iron on the wind."

"I smell only the carriage—lemon oil on the wood, dust in the cushions, and you, Mr. Cooper."

"Me?" He laughed, nervously scratching at his ear. "I hope I do not smell objectionable."

Gigi considered him, pausing only to make him laugh, for he must know that he smelled absolutely divine. She gave him a cryptic little grin and said, "Oh, I do not mind it. You smell very ... masculine."

He raised his eyebrows. "What does that mean? Dirty?"

She shook her head. *Strong,* she thought, *vital.*

She cleared her throat, a blush rising on her cheeks. "No, I ... you know that everyone has a scent all their own, yes? Yours is just very ... male. I would know from the scent of you that you were a man. There's something ... dark about it. Oh, I don't know! Do not look at me!"

He did not obey this order, watching her with a strange expression, somewhere between intensity and bemusement. "And you?" he asked. "Do you smell like a woman?"

"I haven't the faintest idea!" she replied, her throat dry and heartbeat fluttering with agitation. "I cannot detect my own scent any more than I can see myself from across a room. You will have to determine the answer to that question yourself."

"Is that an invitation?" He was beginning to grin, clearly enjoying how flustered she had become.

"You hardly need an invitation to employ your nose." She had been resisting the urge to fidget, but the shrillness of her voice, of course, gave her away.

"Well, in that case," he said, casual as you please, and flung himself across the coach into the bench next to her.

She squeaked in surprise at the sudden warmth radiating off his body, of the closeness of him, that male scent she had just described winding around her. He leaned toward her, his breath warm and light on her neck as he took the liberty of inhaling the smell of her hair, so close he was almost touching her, so close she could feel the tip of his nose, a breath away from the curve of her ear.

"Yes," he decided, his voice gone husky as he lingered in this task. "I see what you mean. You smell very much like a woman."

She felt as though a thousand little pinpricks had exploded over her flesh, each one generating its own heat. She felt just a little paralyzed, frozen in place for fear that if she moved even slightly, he would pull away from her. She did *not* want him to pull away from her, and when she felt he was beginning to do so, her hand shot out and landed on his thigh, wordlessly beseeching him to stay.

He released a sharp breath in surprise, the warmth of it spreading down the column of her throat and blossoming throughout her body. For a moment, he did nothing at all, staying frozen in place as she had bade, and then, slowly and with great deliberation, he lowered his lips to the surface of her skin, just behind her ear, where her curling golden hair met the soft flesh of her neck.

She shivered, warmth exploding through her arms and out of her fingertips, and she found herself leaning into the sensation, the delicious friction of his lips on her body. He was clearly enjoying the taste of her, his tongue darting out now and then as he made his way down the line of her throat and to her shoulders, his teeth nipping at her collarbone. It was that moment of liberty that finally won a gasp from Gigi's throat.

He came away, raising those clear blue eyes to meet hers in askance, perhaps concerned that he had gone too far. It was devastating, the sudden absence of his touch, and she found herself leaning into him, her hands reaching up to press into his chest, her fingers curling around the lines of his cravat.

It was answer enough, she supposed, for his expression had changed from one of caution to one of hunger, deepening to ravenousness when she touched his chest.

"Gigi," he said, low and dangerous, and used the considerable strength in his arms to pull her into his lap, her skirts falling around them like a silk coverlet. He did not hesitate again, wrapping those big, warm hands around her neck, his thumbs tracing the twin rivets of her throat as he claimed her mouth with his own.

It was not like the kiss he'd given her last night. It was not fleeting and soft and oh-so-dry. This kiss was lingering and demanding. It was hot and wet. She felt his tongue brushing against her lips, sending the same ripples of delicious shock through her body that had happened when he tasted her neck.

She opened her mouth and tasted him too, curious and just as hungry as he was; hungry for more of this feeling. She wanted more of *him*. She wanted this exactly, and somehow hadn't known until it had been given to her. She wanted to claw under the cravat and the waistcoat and touch his bare skin, she wanted to do to him what he'd done to her.

His hands had fallen to her waist, gripping her with an intensity that suggested, perhaps, that he was afraid to let his hands roam freely. Her waist was an anchor, something satisfying enough to wrap his hands around without straying even farther off the trail of propriety.

He had looked so neat and presentable this morning, when he came into the flat, that she had been momentarily struck still by it. His presentation during the trip from Kent had been a man completely at ease with himself, slouchy and casual, and that in itself had been very attractive. It was confidence and masculinity embodied, as far as she was concerned, the way he rolled his sleeves up over his strong forearms, smiled easily, sat with no concern other than comfort.

However.

Seeing him fresh-faced and buttoned up in a well-tailored

suit had immediately awakened something new in her. There was something about Kit Cooper that compelled her to misbehavior. He was a bit more broad-shouldered than the usual gentleman, a bit more quick to smile. It was something that might simply have been a desire to return him to that easy, rumpled state, all on her own.

She wished her legs were not trapped in layers of skirts, that she could move and twist more comfortably here, so close to him that he almost seemed a part of her. It was a quarrel of sudden, wild freedom while still being too restricted to fully lose herself. She thought about the careful combing of his sandy hair and could not resist raising her hands from his chest and sinking her fingers into it, feeling the carefully oiled shape give in between her fingers and savoring the surprised moan that he fed her as they kissed.

She took an odd pleasure in the strength of his grip on her, the way his fingers dug into the flesh beneath her stays, pulling her so firmly into his thrall that she could feel the muscles of his thighs beneath her own. Realizing that made her keenly aware of the possibilities of male arousal, and unable to resist, she sank her weight deeper into him, curious if she could feel that forbidden indication that he truly, sincerely wanted her.

He cursed, seemingly enjoying the sensation of her search, and she was rewarded with a distinct hardness against the curve of her bum, a clear answer to questions that she knew she should be afraid to ask. It made her thoughts spark, like the fizzling ends of burning embers, crackling and bright and totally incomprehensible.

Was she imagining it or was he now pulling her downward, pressing his arousal into her flesh through the inconvenience of the skirts? It emptied the breath from her lungs, filling her with nothing but heat and desire, and leaving her gasping for breath in the sparse moments when she could bear to breathe in anything but Kit Cooper.

It was so overwhelming, so completely intoxicating, that neither of them realized right away that the carriage had come to a stop. Even as they gradually began to realize the conundrum, they took their time separating, their kisses softening, their grip on one another sliding every so slowly away, until Gigi found herself deposited back on her bench, her cheeks red and her lips swollen, as Kit scrambled to find his place on the other side before the driver could open the door.

She watched him through hooded eyes as he patted uselessly at his hair, which was sticking up in several directions where her fingers had clutched into it. There was something immensely satisfying in knowing that this disarray was her doing. And there was something deliciously painful about being forced to stop … for now.

She had kissed men before. She had kissed Kit before! If last night could be called a true kiss. This had still felt like something entirely new, something unexpected and exotic and *dangerous*.

He looked so unsettled, considering he had initiated this, and his hurried attempts to straighten his clothes and restore his neatness made a slow, curling smile blossom on her lips. He gave her an exasperated look, as though she were making this much harder than it ought to be, but he did not have time to speak.

The door was pulled open, allowing a cloud of brisk fog to

roll in and disperse over their heated skin. The driver was uninterested in peering into the carriage. If he suspected anything was amiss, it was not a suspicion that awoke any manner of curiosity or scandal in him.

Beyond the foggy drive there was a wrought iron gate on a pebbled path, and somewhere in the distance was the skeleton of a house, neither grand nor modest, looming in wait.

They had arrived.

CHAPTER 17

The rain began almost the instant they had crossed the threshold into the house, a light tapping patter sounding on the windows as they managed to talk their way past the keeper at the door.

Gigi ducked in under his arm as Kit argued their case, unwilling to wait for permission with the incoming rain at their heels. It was that more than any of Kit's oratory talent that likely secured their entry, in the end. She stood, innocently batting her eyes at the outraged man, and suggested that he announce them to his mistress.

Once he was gone, Kit allowed himself to snort, cutting her a look across the marble entryway. "You do know that he is very likely her jailor, not her servant?"

"Oh, yes," Gigi confirmed. "I am well aware."

"Delightful."

She threw him a little smirk, reaching up to adjust the

feather in her hair and smoothing down her lace collar in anticipation of their presentation.

He wouldn't say it, of course, but he was the one who'd been disheveled in their melee. He had taken extreme care to mind his hands from all the damage they had wanted to do to her prim presentation. He cleared his throat, giving his head a little shake to dispel any particularly tantalizing memories of what had just transpired in the carriage from claiming his better senses.

It would not do to go through this entire interlude in a state of arousal. How embarrassing.

Mercifully, his youthful strategy of reciting arithmetic problems in his head until his libido was quelled had begun to work fairly quickly upon the opening of that carriage door. It had taken him only a moment to catch his breath and fling himself out into the cool, misty air, which had also had a nice, calming effect on his ardor.

There was nothing quite so ridiculous in the world as a man inflamed with desire.

Gigi, for her part, seemed utterly composed, as though he had fabricated everything and was simply losing his grip on separating fantasy from reality. The way she hummed under her breath, patiently awaiting their entry to the inner sanctum of the house, seemed not at all the actions of a girl who had just come so close to full ravishment.

He stared at her for a moment, and despite himself, felt a niggle of doubt regarding reality itself.

The clip of a door being snatched open as a different man

appeared in the foyer at least drew his attention away from this slightly alarming train of thought.

The man frowned at both of them, drawing his dark eyebrows together into a flat line over his eyes. "You were not expected," he said, his words echoing through the empty stone around them.

Gigi glanced at Kit, giving an almost imperceptible nod to indicate that it was he who should speak.

"I acted in haste," he said, wincing at how loud his voice seemed in this marble cavern. "Mrs. Ferris was made known to me by an acquaintance in London, and her connection to my late father bade me to act immediately. I would very much like to speak with her, if she will receive me."

"Yes, she recognized your name," the man said with distaste. "Very well, then. Come along. You have come at a most chaotic time, sir. Is your wife coming as well?"

"Yes," Gigi answered for him, immediately closing the space between them to take his arm. "I attend my husband in all matters of great importance."

"Oh, fine," the man huffed, turning on his heel and jerking his index finger over his shoulder in what appeared to be a command to follow.

Kit did so, trying his hardest to not think about the way her scent had woven itself back around him and just how much he liked it. He also made a point of *not* thinking about the fact that she had just called herself his wife. Yes, he decided so resolutely to *not* think about it, that his mind certainly wouldn't dwell on it for the next several hours.

He focused on the simmering hostility of the man in front of them as they were led through a poorly lit hallway and into a large sitting area, framed by opaque, beveled windows. It was clean and thoroughly decorated, but Kit could see immediately that most of the things in this room had fallen into disrepair some time ago.

There were badly worn patches on the furniture, he noticed once they were invited to sit. Several threadbare sections showed where the stuffing was almost bursting through the upholstery. The low central table was scuffed in several places and had a visible crack down one leg. The carpet beneath them had once had flowers on it, though they were all but invisible now.

Despite it all, the woman who awaited them looked cheery as could be, seated in the center of a large sofa, hands clasped together in anticipation. Her dress was in better shape than her furnishings, reasonably bright and new, cut to fit her slight frame in a flattering way. She had dark hair piled up on her head, with streaks of gray throughout, and fine lines around her eyes and mouth that crinkled pleasantly when she smiled.

She waited for them to situate themselves, asking the surly gentleman to pour her guests cups of tea.

Kit did not typically make a habit of accepting food and beverage from someone who so clearly disliked him, but he decided that it was necessary to make an exception, given the current atmosphere in the room.

He glanced around as he sipped his woefully under-sweetened brew, taking note of two more men in the doorways, likely eavesdropping on their conversation, and a maid with frizzy, waist-length hair worn in a loose ribbon at her nape, who appeared to be attending to household accounts at a nearby secretary desk.

Quite a few monitors for such a harmless-looking lady, he thought, frowning at the injustice of it all. Diane Ferris looked so fragile to him, barely weighing enough for a grown person, the corners of her smile trembling in uncertainty.

"You are Archie's boy?" the lady said, her soft voice cutting so suddenly through his thoughts that he gave a slight jump.

"Yes," he confirmed, snapping back to reality with a quick nod. "Yes, my name is Kit."

She nodded at him, as though she approved of his name, and simply smiled at him for a moment.

Her eyes moved over to Gigi, sliding around the room with the languid ease of one who has seen this room far too many times. She took in this new person, seated opposite her, and tilted her head, a dreamy quality coming over her face. "Hullo," she said to Gigi, with all the familiarity of an old friend.

"Hello, Mrs. Ferris," Gigi answered, raising her arched brows in surprise. "Thank you kindly for seeing us."

"When have I ever turned you away, Therese?" the woman asked, blinking slowly and gazing off over their shoulders for a moment, as if caught in a reverie. She frowned suddenly, shaking her head, and looked back at Gigi a little harder. "No," she realized. "You are not Therese."

"I am her daughter," Gigi explained, a note of apology in her voice. "She sends her love and best wishes to you."

"She ought to send herself to me," Diane Ferris snapped,

almost petulant. She crossed her thin arms over her chest and complained, "I never have callers anymore. Tell her to come."

The maid glanced up from her papers, casting a concerned look at her mistress, a faint frown on her lips, but she did not move to intervene.

Outside, the rain persisted, brushing lazily against the windows in large droplets. Kit thought that it would be a long storm, but not a harsh one.

"I will tell my mother you are missing her company," Gigi said carefully, tossing a questioning glance to the maid, who nodded. "She misses you too."

This seemed to mollify Mrs. Ferris, who smiled again, slumping back in her chair. She sipped at her tea and observed off-handedly to Kit, "I heard that Archie is dead."

"Mama!" the maid—whom Kit immediately realized was *not* a maid—hissed, coming to her feet and crossing the room. "You mustn't say things like that to people! Apologize to the gentleman!"

Mrs. Ferris looked up at the girl who was apparently her daughter with a wan look of patience. "There's nothing rude about being dead, Jade," she told the frizzy-haired girl. "We all will be eventually, no matter how polite we are about it."

Gigi coughed a little in what Kit suspected was the attempt of hiding either a gasp or a titter of uncomfortable laughter.

The girl cast an apologetic look at both of them with her big, round eyes and gave a short curtsey. "My mother is sometimes confused," she said, her consternation deepening as her mother replied "Nonsense!" in an unbothered, singsong voice.

"We are not here to upset her," Kit assured the girl, realizing that she was older than he first imagined, likely close to Gigi's age, despite the primness of her dress and the loose mass of hair down her back. "She is correct that my father has passed away. When I heard that he had some small part in your mother's misfortune, I wished to come and offer an apology on his behalf. It is important to me to do so."

"Poor Archie," crooned Mrs. Ferris. "He was much more confused than I am."

"Mama!" Jade choked, her cheeks flaming red.

"It's all right," Kit assured her, holding a hand up with a helpless little chuckle. "She is quite right. My father often seemed in another world entirely."

"I can't imagine what that must be like," Jade muttered, immediately flushing at the inappropriateness of what she'd said. She cut her eyes up to Kit, but he shook his head, refusing to accept an apology for feelings he knew all too well.

"He was quite hopeless without his sister," Mrs. Ferris continued, staring down at the milk swirling in her teacup, as though she could see her old life and all her lost friends within it. "Mary was his anchor in the storm, you know. When she died, his last tether to the world died with her. I know he never intended us harm."

"No, I don't think he did," Kit agreed, surprised at how relieved he felt to hear her say it. "He wasn't a bad man," he added, hoping dearly that this woman would agree with him.

"No, not bad," she concurred, looking up to meet Kit's eyes. "I'm not bad either, Mr. Cooper."

"Of course you're not, Mama," Jade assured her, patting her shoulder.

"I have recently seen Zelda Smith as well," Gigi said, her voice light in an attempt to cut through the heaviness of the room. "And she, too, sends her love."

"To me or to Therese?" Mrs. Ferris asked with a sudden, bright chuckle, as though she'd made a fine joke. "Ah, I do miss them. I miss them all. My friends."

"My mother too often speaks fondly of her girlhood companions," Gigi told her. "Of you, of course, and Zelda, and Mary, and Pauline. She misses them all terribly and does not speak to those who remain as often as she would like. I believe she has even lost an address for Pauline, and no longer knows a way to reach her."

"Pauline got married," Mrs. Ferris said decisively. "And moved to France."

This clearly piqued the interest of the two men by the door, who exchanged a rather conspicuous look between them.

It sent a warning shot through Kit, but Gigi did not hesitate, keeping her eyes on Mrs. Ferris and her smile soft. "Yes, I believe she returned to the city of her birth," she said, this information pointedly directed at their eavesdroppers, who would take far less interest in a Frenchwoman's moving to France than an English one. "But she has since moved on from there as well."

A change came over Mrs. Ferris at this information, her teacup lowering into her lap and her dark, green eyes sharpening as they brought Gigi into keener focus. "Is that so?" she asked, with great interest.

"It is the rumor we've heard," Gigi replied easily, as though they were exchanging pleasant gossip. "She and her husband have been seen touring their favorite spots in London, I believe, with a fondness for the northern boroughs especially."

Yes, Mrs. Ferris was listening now. Her spine had straightened and her narrow shoulders had aligned, clearly baffling her daughter.

"We thought they might be staying with friends, and my mother hoped to catch them," Gigi continued. "Do you happen to have a mutual friend with a family crest depicting a pair of fish?"

This question made the color drain from Jade Ferris's face, and conjured a curling, almost conniving smile on the face of her mother.

"I do, as a matter of fact," Mrs. Ferris said, a sheen like flint sparks in her eyes. "That is my family crest, once used by my parents, and of course, now belonging to my brother. Jade shall give you the address to pass along to your mother, hm?"

There was a beat of baffled silence, which may have drawn the attention of their monitors again if Mrs. Ferris had not jumped to the rescue with a bit more chatter.

"I *do* hope Pauline is taking the utmost advantage of my brother's hospitality while in London," she said, her expression now canny rather than dreamlike. "How *heartening* to know he is welcoming to my friends still, after all these years. You must pass along my well wishes to him, when you can. Perhaps someday soon, we might all meet for a tea party or the like."

"I would enjoy that very much," Gigi said, her tone light and gracious, despite the gravity of what they had just been told.

"Yes," replied Mrs. Ferris, leaning back into her seat, her sharp expression beginning to soften again as she gazed out the window to the gray sky beyond. "I think we all would."

CHAPTER 18

They stayed for another hour, allowing Mrs. Ferris to fall into a pattern of nostalgic storytelling.

While Gigi thought it charming to hear about her mother as a young woman, it clearly did not come anywhere near the experience Kit was having. He leaned forward, eyes locked on Diane Ferris, determined to soak up every word about Mary Atlas and Archie Cooper from a time before sadness touched their lives.

Jade Ferris sat with them, but wore the face of someone who had heard every one of these tales, countless times. When she stood and went to write her uncle's London address down for them, one of the men from the doorways went with her, carefully observing what she wrote and reading it over before allowing her to pass it to Kit.

Gigi realized, in slow measures, that these two women had no inkling of the jailbreak that had occurred. Mrs. Ferris spoke of her husband, Randall, only in the past tense, as though he had died or left for good, and Jade did not react at all to these mentions of her father. Gigi thought it strangely tragic, that they were not only prevented from stepping into the world outside, but also knowing its workings entirely.

She had kept a careful eye on the men in the doorway when she had mentioned Pauline Olivier. They had not seemed interested beyond a cursory reference to France, which Gigi found as much of a relief as she did a surprise. She would not have mentioned the name at all if there had been a way around it, and she had been careful to never mention a surname. Still, she had assumed Pauline Olivier had been a known accomplice of the Ferrises, and as such, the mention of her would have piqued their suspicions.

Evidently, this was not the case.

The more she dwelled upon it, the more sense it made. If both women had been tied to wartime espionage and possible treason, it very likely would have also implicated those in their intimate social circle, which would have drawn attention to Zelda, Mary Atlas, and Gigi's mother. The very fact of the Silver Leaf's continued existence should have told her that, though both were implicated around the same time and possibly even during the same mission, no one outside of the Silver Leaf had ever tied them together.

It was a question she would ponder more on her own, when she had the time, and she would ask questions when Zelda returned from her mysterious business in Guildford.

This was the enduring problem with all of the Silver Leaf founders, Gigi thought with a little frown. They never gave answers to the questions asked, only snippets of information that bred triple the questions one had to begin with.

Jade insisted on walking them back to their carriage, and when one of the men moved to follow them on their exit, she spun around with fire in her big, round eyes and a flash of anger streaking her cheeks. "I have committed no crime," she reminded him. "You have no leave to observe *me.*"

"I beg to differ, you little wretch," the man said with a threatening step toward Jade.

Kit was having none of it. He moved so quickly that it startled Gigi, his body appearing between Miss Ferris and the man like an armored sentinel. His face was hard and unmoving, and his voice had the cool firmness of stone. He stood so close that their noses almost touched. "All here are familiar with the law," he said softly to the man, "including you."

The man did not like it, but he did take a step backward, his arrogant expression flickering.

Once Kit had turned his back, the man threw Jade one more angry glance, leering at her in a way that made Gigi think she might regret this assertion later, when the protection of an audience was no longer available. It chilled her, and she found herself reaching for the other girl's arm, her brows knitted together in concern as she searched her profile for any clues about what sort of abuse she might suffer under this roof.

"He will do nothing," Jade said, avoiding their eyes and unspoken questions. She stopped just short of the front door and turned to Gigi, squeezing her hand in thanks for the touch of support she had provided. "These men thrive on threats and feelings of power, but they do not dare to take it any farther."

Kit was frowning too, his clear blue eyes fixed over Jade's shoulder to the hallway where those power-hungry men waited for her return. "They clearly overstep," he said unhappily. "All the same, I hope we have not caused trouble for you, Miss Ferris."

She sighed in response, reaching up to rub the bridge of her nose. "I'd rather trouble than boredom," she confessed, though she sounded miserable about it. "I wanted only to warn you that seeking out my uncle in London will be fruitless. Your information cannot be correct. There is absolutely no chance that my mother's family would give shelter to one-time intimates of the disgraced Diane. They would not even allow me to visit, tainted as I am by my relation to her. This was true even when I was nothing but a child."

"But the crest," Kit protested.

"I cannot explain the crest," Jade told him, her voice hushed and urgent, "I only know that anyone connected to my mother would be unwelcome in the Benton estate. Their final act as her family was securing her eternal house arrest. They have not even written since then."

Gigi wanted to ask Jade if she knew anything at all about her father, but the suspicious looming of shadows in the corners of the big, empty foyer gave her pause. The first man might have retreated after being chastised, but it was very likely that there were others, listening, just out of sight.

"Are you trapped here?" Kit asked, a brewing outrage darkening the fringes of his voice. "As you rightly said, you have committed no crime of your own. If you wish to come with us right now, they cannot stop you."

Jade considered him and, to Gigi's surprise, the corners of

her lips ticked up for the briefest moment. "We women are all trapped somewhere," she told him. "I would never leave my mother here alone. Never."

"Is there anything we can do?" Gigi persisted, feeling rather helpless in the light of this poor girl's lot.

"You could visit again," she suggested in a tone that did not suggest she had much hope of such a thing happening. "Or write to us. All of our letters are read by others, of course, but they are still a comfort."

"I will write to you," Gigi promised her, squeezing her hands in an effort to belay her sincerity. "You may write to me too, at Mrs. Smith's Fine Prints on Bond Street."

Jade gave another of her little smiles, a shadow of happiness that flickered away almost as soon as it appeared on her face. "I would like that."

"Keep yourself safe," Kit told her, very obviously still disturbed by the atmosphere here. "If ever you wish to leave this place, call upon us. We will take you to safety."

Jade nodded, extending her hand to shake Kit's. Gigi thought her eyes looked like they almost pitied him, for having such fruitless hope in her future. It was an image that made her heart hurt, even after they had turned and left the Ferris house behind.

The home was swallowed up so quickly into the mist at their heels that Gigi felt doubtful that it had remained where it was. Certainly if they could, the jailors would whisk the whole structure away to ensure no letters or visitors found their way back to the Ferris women.

What would they find at the Benton estate?

"Shall we go directly to Islington?" Gigi suggested. "If it is indeed a fruitless lead, we might as well rule it out quickly."

Kit agreed and handed the address Jade had written down to the driver. The tendril of nervousness that awoke in Gigi's belly was enough to set her heart to beating again, encouraging her blood to flow in her veins once more, pushing out the chill of the Ferris house.

Kit helped her into the dry and familiar confines of the coach, and as he settled in across from her, she began to feel a little more herself. The door clicked shut, the weight of the driver gave the interior a telltale sway in either direction, and Gigi Dempierre allowed herself to sigh.

After a truly harrowing morning, all they had come away with was the likely useless address in Islington and a permanent, haunting impression of two women in captivity.

It was as frustrating as it was disheartening.

"Seeing them like that ... It is enough for me to hope we fail," she said to Kit. "I would hate to be the reason that those two women never see freedom."

"I feel the same," he agreed, and heaved a sigh of his own. He dug his fingers into his hair in a gesture of practiced agitation, unaware that he was once again damaging the careful combing he'd been so desperate to restore after their arrival at the Ferris house.

It was exactly the sort of reminder Gigi needed to lighten her spirits, bringing to the forefront of her mind exactly how that hair had become ruffled the first time.

They were alone again, she realized. And there would be

endless time to brood in the future, when such opportunities to be unobserved had fled them.

"How long do you think it will be to Islington?" Gigi asked, batting her lashes innocently.

"An hour," he answered, oblivious to her motives, "maybe more. It's well past Bond Street, so longer than it took to get out here."

"Likely even more, with the rain and fog," Gigi suggested, amused at how the hopeful note in her voice appeared to evade him completely.

"Probably right," he said, glancing out the window, his sandy hair still sticking up in various directions.

Gigi licked her lips, her heart beginning to skip in her chest. Had he already recovered himself entirely from what had happened before? Had he already forgotten it, even? Or could it be that he was avoiding her eye ever so carefully because he remembered it all too well?

She began to gather her skirts between her fingers, bunching up the yards of striped pink silk until she had enough of the garment in her fists to exert control over it, and before she could talk herself out of it, she mimicked the quick tilt of momentum that Kit had used on the way out to move herself from her bench to his, though unlike Kit, she had aimed directly for the other person.

Not wanting her legs trapped in a useless dangle to the side this time, she opted to straddle him, flinging the skirt out around them to get it out of the way. He managed to react with only wide, blue eyes and a strangled "Gigi!" before she had reclaimed his mouth, sinking her fingers back to their proper place between the strands of his hair.

Whatever resistance he may have been contemplating appeared to dissolve in quick order. He said something, but it was muffled under her zealous attempts to master the art of kissing. He had his big hands on her waist and he was receptive enough to the attentions of her mouth and tongue, but Gigi realized, a moment into her plan, that he had begun to laugh.

She pulled back, using her grip on his hair to gently tilt his head back, looking hard into those clear blue eyes. "What is funny?" she asked sharply.

"Ah," he said sheepishly, stroking at her hips and waist, "not *funny*, per se. Just ... surprising."

"Oh?" She tightened her hand in his hair and gave him a sharp, feline smile. She did not pull hard enough to cause pain, but enough to make his chuckle give way into a little groan. She felt strong in this moment, powerful, the muscles of her thighs holding him still under her skirts. "What is surprising, Mr. Cooper?"

"*You* are surprising, Miss Dempierre," he replied, a darkness creeping into his voice. "So repeatedly and consistently surprising."

"Was I mistaken in thinking you enjoyed having me in your lap?" she asked, with all the patience of a stern governess. She noted the stirring of his body between her thighs and inhaled sharply, pleasure curling into her stomach. She was not particularly well versed in the ways of men and women, but she knew enough to recognize his arousal.

She leaned forward and whispered into his ear, "I already know I was not."

"Oh, Christ," he breathed, his eyelids flickering shut. "Gigi, I am trying to behave myself."

"Why?" She pulled back and looked into his face, genuinely puzzled. "No one can see us."

"I am no longer capable of answering that question," he said, exasperated and looking at her through eyelash-fringed slits. "You must know all the things I wish to do to you."

Gigi sighed, releasing her grip on his hair and stroking at his neck and throat. "I have hopes," she confessed, her heart thudding against her ribs, heat flashing through her at the way his arousal flexed against her thighs. The sensation was silky against the thin film of her stockings, and she felt her own playful authority beginning to dissolve away under the demands of her body.

"I promised not to compromise you," he reminded her, though he was already pulling her forward again, tasting the line of her throat, working his way down to the swell of her breasts at her neckline. "Don't you recall?"

"You promised to keep me safe," she corrected, letting her head fall back as he progressed on this tantalizing journey.

"This is *not* keeping you safe," he told her, tasting the dip between her breasts, his hands sliding up her sides, curling around her shoulder blades. "And if you don't stop me, it will only get worse."

"I am not going to stop you," she managed, her voice gone breathy and thin. She could not strictly describe her thoughts as clear anymore, but she had no doubt at all that she wanted this to continue.

"This ought to be done in a bed," he said, hooking his thumbs around the lace in her collar and inching it down, revealing more of the swell of bosom to his attentions. "You deserve a bed."

"Then we will simply have to repeat the experience when one is available." She moaned, arching her back as his tongue found the crest of her nipple, her stays creaking against her ribcage, the lace of her chemise's sleeves pulling its patterns into the soft flesh of her shoulders.

She dug her fingertips into the muscle at his shoulders, dragging them down the fascinating contours of his chest. He was so solid, so strong and warm, and his very particular scent, which had been the catalyst of all of this madness, was woven around her, urging her further and further into madness.

He held the center of her back with the flat of his hand, supporting her weight as his tongue flicked over her breasts, lingering on the sweetness of her nipples as they stiffened against his tongue. His other hand was finding its way under her skirt, palms sliding over her knees and teasing at her thighs.

"I am going to touch you," he told her, his fingertips tracing higher.

"You are already touching me," she said, lost in her own haze of sensation. When his fingers brushed over the bare softness between her legs, she realized what he had meant, and said nothing but a throaty, epiphanic, "Oh!"

She could feel a slickness to his fingertips, stroking at a part of her she had only rarely dared touch herself. His touch was torturously light, careful, and rhythmically matched to the path of his mouth on her breasts. He did not rush to entry, lingering on all of the surprising jolts of sensation and pleasure that hid within the velvet-soft flesh in this forbidden place.

His cheeks were free of stubble and smooth against the tender swell of her breasts. His lips were firm and persistent, no longer withholding from going where they wished. He came away from her breasts only to reclaim her mouth, flicking his tongue against hers as he slid the tip of his finger into her body.

Her mouth opened, a surprised gasp escaping her as his lips curved into a wicked grin against her own.

"You're going to touch me too," he told her, nipping at the lobe of her ear as he inhaled the scent of her hair and pressed his fingers deeper inside of her. "Not today. Not now. Soon."

The pad of his thumb, slightly calloused from his work in the orchards, ran lazy circles over the most powerful of the places he'd discovered before penetrating her, while he lingered in the forbidden sensation of coaxing more wetness from her, and using it to press a sensual path in and out of her entrance.

He whispered into her ear, his breath hot and slow, spreading waves of tingling excitement over her skin. "I wish I could taste you right now," he confessed. "I've wanted to taste you since that day at Meridian."

She knew she could not answer. She was too overwhelmed

with the way she was feeling, too carried away by bliss. She could manage only a sound of what she hoped was approval at this concept, which made his breath quicken and his touch on her gain intensity.

He returned to her breasts, allowing her to collapse forward and rest her forehead on the crown of his tousled hair. She breathed in the scent of his hair, her hips seeming to move of their own accord as pressure within her built and built, far more effectively than she had ever managed to awaken with her own touch, in moments of dark desire and keen curiosity.

She whimpered, the muscles in her legs tensing. Her thoughts spun, each coherent thought or sensible word beginning to crackle and fray and smoke. She held her breath, attempting to control the noises she was making, but it was no use, he was drawing something wild out of her, and she had no power to stop it or even to slow it down.

She was completely in his control, and knowing that only made her hungrier for more.

The first wave of relief came with a crashing violence, startling her into a straightened spine and gripping hands at his shoulders. It was not a sudden experience, nor an isolated one. It felt as though her whole being was opening and closing, her skin bursting into a thousand tiny fires as the last fragments of her ability to think splintered into a thousand glittering shards.

He caught her, otherwise she might very well have tumbled backward, a helpless heap on the floor.

He pulled her forward, where she clung to him, gasping for breath, dizzy with it all. She could hear the speed of his breathing as well, could feel the thundering of his heart. But he demanded nothing of her.

He held her safe, firm and gentle, against the strong column of his body. After a moment, he dropped a wordless kiss into her hair.

CHAPTER 19

The expectation for such an encounter, where only one party has found release, would have always struck Kit as discontent and frustration for the other party. Why, then, was he filled with such a sense of peace, ungratified as he was, and with Gigi Dempierre all but asleep in the crook of his arm?

The feather in her hair rested against his cheek, fluttering now and then with the pace of his breath. Her own breathing had gone slow and steady, her head heavy on his shoulder and her hand resting softly on his chest.

If ever there was a feeling completely to the contrary of frustration, it was this. He felt immensely satisfied at his success in pleasuring her. Yes, there was the chest-puffing boost to his ego, of course, but it was something more. Something just a little bit more complicated, lingering like a mysterious, unborn beast beneath the warm protection of its thinning eggshell.

He could feel it, fighting to hatch, just beneath the ivory of his own ribs, while somewhere, deep inside him, a frantic voice begged for more time. He had not yet finished his work. He had not yet repaired the damage his father had done. He was not yet allowed to live strictly for himself.

It was not a thing he was willing to dwell upon just now. It was not a thing he would let pollute this one stolen moment of stillness and peace.

He rested his chin in her hair, and inhaled the scent of her. This was enough for the moment. Sometimes the moment was all one had.

He knew they would reach their destination soon. Dirt roads had already given way to cobble, and the trilling of birds had been overtaken by the rumbling of man.

Soon, the fantasy would be shattered, so Kit listened hard to the patter of rain on the windows and memorized the warmth of her skin against his body. He carved it into his soul so that he would always be able to return here, in spirit.

When the carriage began to slow, making its turns more carefully, Kit knew the driver had begun to scan the numbers on the townhouses of Islington.

It was time to wake her.

He did it softly, with gentle strokes to her arms and a shower of little kisses to her head, whispering that she must rise now, if only for a little while.

Her eyelids were heavy, those pale lashes fluttering against one another as she came to, giving him a sleepy smile and a stifled yawn behind her slender fingers.

"I fell asleep," she observed, seemingly rather pleased about it. She leaned away from him only to stretch her arms out, wiggling her fingers. "Mm, I feel much restored!"

"Do you indeed?" he asked with some amusement, twirling her fluffy white feather between his fingers.

She giggled and dropped a kiss on his cheek before fleeing back to her side of the carriage, arranging herself most properly before they could be again exposed to the outside world.

"What shall we say to Lord Benton?" she asked him, tilting her head with a little smile. "Or am I to do the bulk of the talking again?"

"Now, now," he said with mock sternness. "You mustn't point out my tendency to be completely eclipsed by you. It is immodest."

"Ah, modesty." She lowered her eyes, a smile hovering over her dimpled cheeks. "Key amongst my virtues."

The townhouse was one of many stark white homes of status along the curved line of Islington's high street, each a miniature castle for a miniature monarch to reign supreme. The Benton house was the largest of them all. Kit wished dearly that he had thought to bring calling cards along with him today, though of course they had not anticipated at the outset that such a thing would be necessary.

There was nothing to be done for it but to hope the Bentons would be willing to receive them with no warning or introduction. Upon approaching the door, Kit took note, with a small lurch of his heart, of the design of the door knocker: two plump fish, curled around one another in opposing arcs.

He exchanged a significant look with Gigi before reaching forward to make use of it.

For a moment, it seemed no one would answer. They stood surrounded by stark, white marble in the gray drizzle with nothing to answer them but their own echoes.

What sort of people abandoned their flesh and blood to the conditions he had just witnessed? What sort of man blames his infant niece for the sins of her parents, and offers her no protection as she comes of age? Young, innocent Jade Ferris had never known any life but being her mother's protector.

It made his blood boil.

It was not an auspicious way to begin an acquaintance, he knew. Resenting a man before you even acquire an introduction is less than ideal, but how else was he to feel?

That girl had acted so bravely, had such anger in her eyes, but still trembled on her feet. It was something he had seen in captured prisoners, those who kept their pride, but knew they had no power to stop their inevitable torment; with narrowed eyes and firmly set jaws, but hands that shook and posture that swayed.

He pressed his thumb against the palm of his hand, willing himself to be cordial, until the door finally swung open, revealing a harassed-looking butler adjusting his spectacles, as though he had just been roused from a nap.

"We are hoping for an audience with Lord Benton," he said immediately, "and his guests, if they are in house. I am Mr. Kit Cooper and this is Gigi Dempierre. We are known to the Benton family."

The butler blinked at them, requiring a moment to absorb

this onslaught of information. When he spoke, it was with strained patience. "Lord Benton retired to the country well over a month ago, my good man."

Kit and Gigi exchanged a glance.

"Are visitors making use of his townhouse?" he pressed. "It is only that we saw the Benton carriage in London some days past and thought he had returned."

This got the man's attention. His bleary eyes seemed to clear and his posture straightened, his brows arching in surprise. "We have recently been victim to a theft. It is not information I would otherwise share with callers, but if you caught sight of our stolen property, I must implore you to make a report for our investigator. The thieves must be punished!"

"Someone stole a carriage?" Gigi repeated, bafflement clear in her voice. "Isn't that an odd thing for a thief to take?"

"Not if it was attached to stolen horses," Kit replied, glancing at the butler for a quick nod of confirmation. "Did they take anything else?"

"I am not at liberty to say," the butler replied, sniffing in what appeared to be genuine distress. "I had thought the matter quite hopeless. Will you make a report, sir?"

"There is not much to report upon," Kit replied, taking a tiny step backward. "We saw the carriage rounding a corner in ... erm ... Kensington, but were too far away to hail it. We assumed that the Bentons were enjoying a shopping trip, just as we were."

As far as Kit could guess, it was likely prudent to avoid

record of their comings and goings. He was new to espionage, but not to common sense.

The butler frowned. "Is that all?"

"I'm afraid so."

There was a pause while the butler considered them, his frown deepening. "What guests were you seeking, may I ask?"

"Why, those we saw in the carriage, of course," Kit replied, damning the dryness that was creeping up into his throat.

"It was too far away to signal, but close enough that we could see it housed several occupants," Gigi added quickly, spinning more yarn onto Kit's fabrication. "Women, I think. Yes, three or four ladies in hats. It was a rather colorful ensemble."

"Women!" the butler repeated, astounded. "You really must speak to the investigator. I insist. I will take your information down if you just give me a moment. Cooper, you said your name was?"

"Oh!" Gigi gasped, loud enough to interrupt the butler's rambling interrogation. Her hand snapped out to grab Kit's arm, as though she had been overcome by a sudden and violent illness. "Oh, darling, I am having another of my spells," she cried. "Oh, I am quite faint!"

He caught her against him, supporting her weight as he turned to signal their driver. "We must get you back home immediately," he tutted, patting her hair. To the butler, he said, "Good day!"

"Sir!" the butler called after them, but they hurried away,

with Gigi swaying and clinging to Kit in dramatic, limp-footed fashion until she was again safely enclosed in the carriage.

It wasn't until the horse began to move again that either of them dared to breathe, both releasing pent-up oxygen in a gale of relief. Kit jerked the curtains closed over the late-afternoon light, and opened his mouth to comment upon this most recent encounter, but no words would come.

Gigi, for her part, had doubled over and was holding her head between her knees. It took a moment for Kit to realize that she was laughing, a silent, almost wheezing episode of madness that had gripped her until her breath wore thin.

It was contagious. It was impossible to watch her without catching the strain of crazed relief, and Kit found himself laughing too, the way one laughs after a good, deep scare.

He collapsed onto his back, staring at the ceiling of the carriage as they bumped along, heading back to Bond Street none the wiser about the location of Pauline and Gerard Olivier, and potentially having incriminated themselves with that butler.

Good Lord, what had his life become?

He glanced over at Gigi, who was wiping tears from the corners of her eyes with her palms, and shook his head, the laughter rumbling deep within him, wild and primal in a way he hadn't experienced since he was a child.

She mimicked his posture, lying on the opposite bench, curled onto her side and facing him. She sighed, little hiccups of residual laughter coming and going as they settled into comfortable silence.

CHAPTER 20

The stillness of the flat above the print shop was almost surreal. She had felt strange all night, and the feeling had persisted through the morning. How was it possible that all of those things she had seen yesterday were happening at the same time as the tranquil peace of the spaces she usually occupied? What determined someone's luck, and which environment they must pass their years in, for better or worse?

Gigi poured afternoon tea and marveled at the gentle tinkling the liquid made as it splashed against the porcelain teacup. It felt like a month had passed in the last few days, and yet here was the flat on Bond Street, utterly unchanged, and here was her hand, pouring tea, as if all was just as it should be.

Kit stood at her side, freshly turned out for a new day and seemingly unfazed by all that had passed. He seemed his usual, casual self as he occupied himself in choosing the largest and most attractive sugar cubes for his own cup, which he arranged in a little cluster on his saucer.

"I confess, the more I think about it, the more I find the very concept of the theft somewhat amusing," he was saying. "Lord knows the Bentons deserve it, after how they have treated Mrs. Ferris and her daughter. A family such as that could do with a bit of humbling."

Gigi nodded without looking up. She chose a small biscuit and snapped it in half as a special treat for her birds, knowing they would love the crumbly shortcake, even if it was not strictly nutritious. They were roosting in the common room, and had trilled so sweetly when she had returned from her business in the city yesterday. She wondered if they had sung while she was out, sweet, secret arrangements of symphonies for the empty rooms. She hoped they had not missed her too badly.

She had realized last night, shortly after Kit had departed for Marylebone, that she did not know how to behave with him now, after what had happened in the carriage. It had hit her all at once, after she had brushed out her hair and tucked herself into bed, alone with nothing but the deafening silence of night. She had been almost on the cusp of dozing when her eyes had flown open, her body struck suddenly and sharply with the realization that something so intimate should and likely had fundamentally changed the dynamic between herself and Kit Cooper.

She had lain there, staring up at the uneven paint on the ceiling, bathed in moonlight, and had been wracked with the horrifying and sudden knowledge that by pushing Kit to intimacy, she had *changed* things. They would never be simply friends now.

So what were they?

What did she want them to be?

She had not slept very much.

She shivered, passing the teapot to Kit and making her way past him out to the couches and her birds, suspended in a strange, bubbling emotion between anxiety and anticipation. She knew she wanted more. She knew she had enjoyed everything about this day very much, but she also knew, with a keen and persistent awareness, that she had no idea what she was doing.

As far as the world at large was concerned, Gigi was barely as experienced as someone many years her junior. She was not completely ignorant to all the ways of the world, but she could not even guess what came next when one had crossed the threshold she and Kit had, at the behest of her own impulsiveness.

He was still chattering about their mission, about the information they had found, on ideas he'd had throughout the night, and what they might do next. Gigi tried to listen as he followed her to the chairs near her birdcage and began arranging their tea and a plate of sandwiches where they would sit. The little echoes of his sugar cubes falling into the hot liquid felt like they were happening in another world entirely, so overpowered were they by the volume of Gigi's thoughts.

She imagined the two crises grappling in her mind, with the mighty shadows of the missing Oliviers buckling under the blunt weight of her petty romantic concerns.

She clicked her tongue at her birds and slid the biscuit halves through the grates of the birdcage, doing her best to ignore this absurd mental image. She let Emerald nibble at the crumbs that clung to her fingers, hoping that maybe the sensation would snap her back to normal, rather than leaving her as she had been, staring off at nothing in particular.

So taken was she, that it took her a moment to realize she had been asked a question. She blinked, forcing herself back into the moment, and turned to meet Kit's expectant blue eyes.

"I am so sorry, I was lost in thought. What was that?"

"I was asking if you were well," he replied, his brow scrunched in concern. "You have experienced several moments in the past days that were rather intense ... erm ... intense in a great many ways. I want to ensure you are not overwhelmed."

She saw the worry in his face, the dull glint of guilt in his eye, as though he considered their interlude the key contribution to her woes. It melted some of the pressing edges that had been digging into her mind. She reached out to cover his hand with hers, and immediately, that connection of warmth made her feel better and more grounded, more a part of reality.

"I feel as though, in the last days, I have finally, truly been living my life, Kit. You are correct. It is a little overwhelming, after an entire lifetime of the uneventful, but it is by no means unwelcome. I think it is just a little ... disorientating."

"I understand," he replied, flipping his hand around so that he could wrap his fingers around hers, drawing his thumb over the soft skin at her wrist. "I truly do. When I ran off to war, it felt like I had passed into a different universe entirely, where nothing at all functioned the way

I thought it did. It wasn't bad, but it was jarring for certain."

"Well, I don't presume to compare the drama of war to our little bit of excitement around London," she said, a little flicker of sheepishness at such a comparison in her chest. "I think perhaps I just need a moment to catch up with myself, if you can imagine that. I feel as though I quite literally got away from myself and was left chasing after."

"Going mad, are you?" he teased, his voice gentle so that she would not mistake it for sincerity. "Me too, I think."

"Oh?"

"Mhm," he said, a softness teasing at the curve of his lips as he studied her face. "Almost certainly."

She gazed at him helplessly, somewhere between fleeing in a panic and melting in place. If the warning creaks of a person stomping up the staircase to the flat hadn't interrupted the moment, she could not account for how it might have unfolded from there. They withdrew to their respectively appropriate cushions and Gigi retrieved her tea so that she would be sipping it innocently as the door opened.

Zelda Smith came blowing into her flat as though propelled by the very forces of nature at her back, already barking instructions for the offloading of her valises to a thoroughly intimidated young man who followed behind her. She did not wait for him to leave to begin shaking off her jacket or untying her hat, tossing an extremely unimpressed "Good evening" to Kit and Gigi, frozen as they were just outside of her orbit.

She swept over and helped herself to the remaining dregs of

the teapot, dropping onto the free seating with all the comfort of a woman in her own home. "Dreadfully dreary out, isn't it?" she said, and then got up again to go in search of milk for her cup.

Kit threw a baffled glance at Gigi, who shrugged in response. It was the only communication they could fit into the single breath she gave them before returning, stirring her beverage, and dropping back into her seat.

"How was Guildford?" Gigi asked, aware of how awkward she sounded. "Good progress on the extraction?"

"Mm, as much as can be made before your brother returns from Lisbon," she answered. "And what about here? How have the two of you gotten along?"

Gigi froze, feeling suddenly caught in their indiscretions, but Kit answered quickly and smoothly, seemingly with no such concerns.

"We met with Mr. Richards and Mrs. Ferris," he said, drawing her sharp gray eyes to him. "The latter was a rather disturbing experience. She and her daughter are not faring well in their current conditions."

Zelda pursed her lips, taking note of the implied rebuke in this statement. She looked as though she might scold Kit for his impertinence, but after a moment, she simply replied, "It is less than ideal."

Seeing the way Kit tensed, the narrowing of his eyes, Gigi spoke quickly to prevent the outbreak of a spat. "Would you like to hear what we have found?" she asked quickly and a bit shrilly. "Or perhaps you would prefer to rest first, after your journey?"

Zelda took her time shifting her eyes from Kit's face to Gigi's, lingering for a moment on him in a way that was very clearly meant to disquiet her opponent.

"Proceed," she said once she had settled her attention on Gigi.

Gigi took a breath, bracing herself to present their findings in the least inflammatory way possible. "Mr. Ferris was smuggled out of the prison in a coffin, in place of a deceased prisoner and without the knowledge of either the warden or the mortician. I'm afraid you may have some repairing to do with the warden, and perhaps an apology to Mr. Richards would not be out of place either."

"Blast," Zelda muttered mildly.

"Mr. Ferris was retrieved a few days later, in a carriage stolen from the Benton estate in Islington. We spoke with their butler today, but he would not tell us if anything else was stolen, but we do know that no perpetuator has been caught, despite the employ of an investigator."

To Gigi's surprise, this caused Zelda to smile, a raspy chuckle escaping from her generally stern countenance. "Oh, Pauline," she said with an affectionate sigh, briefly closing her eyes. "You have not matured a single day in all this time."

"I am reasonably certain that Mrs. Ferris is not only innocent of participation in this scheme, but that she hasn't any idea that it is happening," Kit added. "She and her daughter were both clearly under the impression that Mr. Ferris was still under lock and key."

"Well, now that is most curious," Zelda said, sipping at her tea. "They must not have made any significant changes to her confines, or she would know something was amiss."

Gigi pressed her lips together at that.

She was not certain Mrs. Ferris *would* notice, to be completely honest, but Jade would have. It would only be speculation and guesswork regardless, and the mood in this room was already quite tense.

"So we have a stolen coach and an angry prison warden," Zelda observed, tapping on her teacup in consideration. "I suppose that narrows the possibilities of their safe house, as the Benton carriage would need to be concealed."

"They may have abandoned the carriage by now," Kit put in. "It seems foolish to keep it for very long, even if it was meant to humiliate Lord Benton."

"Yes, I agree," Zelda said. "But if the Oliviers have not taken custody of Diane yet, we still may have a chance in intercepting them. We will need to find more threads to tug on. I am suspicious of this seeming ignorance and non-action around Diane's confinement. It feels like a laid trap, does it not?"

"Unless she is not a real concern to the powers that be." Kit ran a hand through his hair, his brow furrowed. "She is likely not the skilled spy she once was, after a lifetime abandoned in a box."

Again Zelda pursed her lips at Kit, and again she withheld from retorting.

"Mathias did suggest one other contact," Gigi said, pushing herself to her feet and moving to retrieve the envelope her brother had given her back in Kent. "In his letter, he says that there is a woman with an acting company who assists with moving contraband and information for the Silver Leaf. He says that she undertakes hands-on missions of risk as well, and so may have gotten involved with a jailbreak, but he does not know how to contact her, as she is not tied to any particular theater or housing in London ..."

Gigi trailed off, her voice drowned out by the heavy, irritated sigh that came from Mrs. Smith.

"I take it you are familiar?" Kit asked with some amusement.

"Mm, he is talking about a Miss Liberty Lennox; scandalous star of the theater and darling of the *demi-monde*. I use her as sparingly as possible. She is rather ... unpredictable. Useful, mind, and talented, just ... well." Zelda frowned, setting her jaw at an angle. "Disobedient."

"I have heard that name!" Kit realized, perking up in his seat. "She was the one with the acrobatic show some years back, yes? Bending every which way whilst singing." He tilted his elbow over his arm as though to demonstrate a body in contortion.

Zelda narrowed her eyes at him, but did not answer. Instead, she said to Gigi, "Mathias must suspect that Miss Lennox was the port of call when Pauline landed in London, and I confess it is very likely she was. You must approach her carefully, however. She will be on the side of the jailbreaks and chaos, without any doubt."

"Do you know where to find her?" Kit pressed, leaning forward with his elbows on his knees. "I see nothing to lose in seeing what she may know."

"Of course I know where to find her," Zelda snapped, clearly affronted at the suggestion that there was any knowledge to which she was not privy.

She then sighed again, this time in a beleaguered, defeated sort of way, and rolled her eyes. "Oh, very well. The only reliable way to speak to Miss Lennox is to buy tickets to whatever new nonsense she is currently forcing upon the populace. I will see to it."

"Oh!" Gigi said, wide-eyed and filled with a burst of excitement despite herself. "I have never been to the theater!"

Both Kit and Zelda turned their eyes to her at this statement, though their expressions could not have been more different.

CHAPTER 21

The persistent fog of impending autumn had moved London into a full blown chill by midweek. With Mrs. Smith's help, they had secured two tickets to a small playhouse production in Mayfair for the following Saturday, with not much else to do in the interim but to wait and to stew upon the possible whereabouts of the Oliviers and Randall Ferris.

Kit was in from his morning ride, the tip of his nose gone red from the chilly air and his hands stiff from his tendency to hold a bit too hard to the reins first thing in the morning. It was still so early that the light was not yet entirely blue, and the fog that hung latent on the cobbles and grasses of London could still, reasonably, be called morning dew. Marylebone parish maintained a public green only a short ride from Nate's townhouse, and Kit had found it at its most beautiful just at the moment when the sun rises, and far more private and wild than the well-beaten paths of Hyde Park.

If he were to buy a property in London, it would be in one

of these quieter neighborhoods—close enough to enjoy the bounty of the city without constantly being bombarded by its chaos. London was large enough to offer variety.

If it were warmer, still summer and the height of the Season, there were at least a dozen places he'd be dragging Gigi Dempierre to see, just to watch the way her face lit up at the new and novel. As it was, his favorite natural places in the city were still hovering between summer grandeur and autumn mystique, but he had put in a request with an old friend at the British Museum, in hopes of a tour built especially for the type of woman who would most enjoy every step of the halls.

When her back was turned, during their time at Bond Street, Kit had taken to attempting to charm her birds. The green one was not impressed and often snubbed him with a flinging raise of her beaked nose. The blue one, though, little Pip, would return Kit's smiles with a little song, which Kit liked to think the bird had composed especially for him —a gift to a new friend.

Throughout his ride today, he had turned his ear out for the sounds of birdsong, none of which was quite as melodic as that of Gigi's parakeets. The birds of the green had a wild charm all their own. He had taken note of the flash of gold and silver he had seen in the trees, so that he could tell Gigi he'd spotted an early waxwing, just arrived from distant shores and enjoying the last of the warmth for the year. In the winter, they would flit and fly around the berry hedges, looking for the sweet juice of the fruit. Was there anything so beautiful as birds eating bright red berries in the snow?

By the time he had returned to the townhouse, he felt invigorated for the day ahead. To his surprise, he was told immediately upon crossing the threshold that there was mail awaiting him. He hadn't even been away from home that long, but still, somehow, the sight of an envelope with his mother's looping handwriting on the face filled him with an immediate curiosity about the happenings at home.

Though he was usually a man who took care in the neat disposal of his outerwear, Kit gave himself leave to toss his gloves and overcoat onto a chair in favor of quicker access to his letter, and the welcoming crackle of the fireplace in Nate's meticulously neat sitting room, which he had taken full ownership of during his time in Marylebone. This townhouse was a lot like Nate had been prior to his marriage—elegant and charming, but quite dark and never quite what one could describe as welcoming.

This was the only room where Kit didn't feel as though he was being rushed along and urged to go be productive elsewhere—probably because he'd been able to clutter it up a bit so it felt more human.

He settled in, taking his time to break the seal on the envelope, running his fingers along the grit of the parchment.

My Dear Son, it began, and in his mind he could hear his mother's voice, always a little bit more formal on the page than she ever would be aloud.

He only got so far as the first sentence before realizing he needed to put his coat and gloves back on and go, immediately, to Bond Street. It was only right to share this news straight away with those who could share his excitement. If he left straightaway, he could get to the shop before any customers could arrive, demanding attention.

He bounced to his feet with a jolt of giddiness and a wide grin.

At long last, Nell had given birth.

∽

"Twins!" cried Harriet Goode, her fingers curved and pressed against her ruddy cheeks in delight. "Oh, Zelda, it's *two* babies!"

"Yes, I heard," Zelda Smith responded, giving a short sniff that Kit suspected strongly was the result of suppressed emotion. She had her face turned away from them, fussing with an arrangement of flowers, so that they might not see whether or not she had tears swimming in her eyes. "Very exciting, I'm sure."

"Oh, we must send a gift, Zelda," Mrs. Goode continued, throwing a knowing smirk at the carefully managed posture of the other woman. "Something thoughtful for the babies."

"Well, how thoughtful can you be to two little girls, not even yet named, who cannot yet speak their minds?" Zelda replied. "I think something for my Nell, to simplify her new lot, would be more appropriate."

"Kit, did you read the rest of this letter?" Gigi asked, standing on the opposite end of the room with the parchment held in her gentle grip. She looked up at him, her moss-green eyes seeming particularly vibrant today against the matching hue of her dress. "There is news beyond just the babies."

He realized, with a short jolt of surprise, that he had not

read anything at all past that first sentence. "What news?" he asked with a raise of his eyebrows.

Gigi glanced at the page and then back at him, biting her lip. Rather than read it to him, she crossed the room and handed the letter back over, so that he could read Susan Cooper's words for himself.

First, she spoke of the harvest, which she was managing with the acumen of a woman who had lived among the fruit trees for most of her life. Kit had not been worried about the orchards, but reassurance was always welcome. His eyes ticked down over the sentences, taking in a request for a box from a particular chocolatier on Regent Street, noting that Isabelle and Peter Applegate had left for their honeymoon in Sherwood Forest, and the mundane observations of day-to-day life.

She had saved her most explosive news for the end, and of course it was regarding her ongoing acquaintance with Yves Monetier.

"Married?!" he exclaimed, shooting an alarmed look up over the letter to Gigi's smiling face. "Already?!"

"Well, no, not for another several months yet. She says she wants to be a springtime bride," Gigi responded, dimples flashing as she stepped closer to him to point to the part of the page where Susan specified her preferred wedding date. "How very exciting! I wonder if Isabelle knows."

"Doubtless she does," he muttered. "As though this family could get any *more* entangled."

"*Pah*," agreed Zelda. "You'd think one husband would be

more than enough for a lifetime. And here I thought your mother a sensible sort."

"I think a gift for the Atlas family is a splendid idea," Gigi said over Zelda's grousing, giving Kit a reassuring pat to the shoulder while he experienced an ongoing state of numb surprise. "Kit and I could explore some nearby shops?"

"I will come with you," Zelda said in a tone that would entertain no argument. "No one knows my niece as well as I."

Privately, Kit thought Nell's husband probably knew her plenty well, not to mention her twin brother. However, he knew better than to cross any opinion of Zelda Smith's out loud.

No, if nothing else, Kit was a survivor.

~

IF KIT HAD BEEN EXPECTING Zelda to perform the duties of a chaperone on this outing, he would have been sorely disappointed. She charged ahead of them, peering into this shop window and that, sometimes getting so far ahead that they would momentarily lose sight of her.

It felt rather more like being a queen's attendant than participating in a group outing.

"I do not mean to sound overly wild," Gigi whispered to him, "but I suspect she does not need us here."

He laughed, drawing her a little closer on his arm. The sun had risen higher, softening the edge on the early autumn chill, and to Kit's delight, the sky had cleared itself of fog and clouds for the first time in days, presenting them with a lovely setting for wandering the streets of London.

"What sort of gift do you get for a new mother, anyhow? Nate and Nell already have all the obvious things, cradles and blankets and so on."

"I think a gift is always better when it is not a strict necessity, but rather a luxury one would not have thought to get for herself," Gigi said, considering. "But I have no idea what sorts of tools you need to rear a baby, especially when you're surprised with a second one in the critical moment."

"I suppose twins must run in the blood," he said. "I wonder if the girls will be impossible to tell apart or if they will be as different as can be."

"Oh, it's hard to decide which would be more delightful," Gigi said on a wistful sigh. "Do you want children, Kit?"

He startled, glancing down at her innocent, curious gaze in surprise. "Yes, I suppose so," he said. "Eventually. I've much to accomplish before I can consider such things."

Her brow wrinkled, as though this were a very strange thing to say. "Finding a wife, you mean?"

This time, he nearly choked on his surprise. Granted, he suspected she did not realize how bold such questions were. That didn't make them any less unsettling. He could feel the heat climbing his throat and clawing at his cheeks as he attempted to find an answer.

"Well, yes, I suppose that is the most necessary step," he managed to say, "and a house, now that my mother will no longer be alone in her own home. The orchard business is not fully restored to what it once was, just yet. And I am rather committed to making amends to everyone my father unwittingly harmed in his life."

"A house in Kent?" she pressed. "Will you stay there, near your orchards?"

"I haven't thought about it. I only got the news this morning."

She nudged him, giggling under her breath. "Of course, but we all think about the future," she said, turning her face up to the streaming sunlight that lit their path, closing her eyes for a moment to soak up the warmth. "London could not be more different than the countryside in Kent."

Kit was not so sure that he had thought about the future. He didn't say that, naturally, for it would have been a rather strange and embarrassing confession. The question was acting as a firm nudge on his inner self, solidifying this idea that he would now need to find a place to live, lest he infringe upon his mother's newlywed bliss.

Did he want to stay in Kent? Did he prefer London instead? Was he going to miss his childhood home, or did he thrill at the idea of making one of his own?

These were not questions he had ever thought to ask himself. There had always been bridges to mend and assets to rebuild, tasks so monumental that they stretched endlessly past the horizon, beyond any time when he could possibly make choices of his own.

"Do *you* want to stay in Kent?" he asked her.

"Perhaps," she answered, a dreamy timbre in her voice, "so long as my whole life is not lived at *La Falaise*. I don't think

I could bear it, not after seeing a glimpse of something else. Not after seeing London."

He could feel the thought settling into his mind, hooking into place where it would no doubt tug at him now endlessly. Forever. Or at least until he satisfied it.

He did not know *where* he pictured his future, but he realized, with a strong and resounding stroke of epiphany, that he certainly did know *who* he pictured.

She had gone silent, her eyes scanning shop windows and gazing up at awnings and eaves.

Yes, he was certain. Whether here or there, the future he wanted was whichever one meant he could keep Gigi Dempierre as his own.

CHAPTER 22

Some days ago, she had started to make plans of her own.

Gigi was accustomed to joy being the result of impulse, as it had been thus far regarding Kit, but all his talk of planning and preparation and readiness had gotten her thinking ... about the future, about her wants and dreams and hopes, and most of all, about Kit Cooper himself.

She wanted to repeat what had happened in the carriage. She thought it would have happened again by now, all on its own. The realization that she was going to need to actively participate in the experiences she wished to have was more surprising than it ought to have been, but in Gigi's defense, she had never had much opportunity to choose her own paths in life, and the prospect was just as frightening as it was new.

She wanted whatever there was *beyond* what had happened in the carriage, of course, but so far, she was only reasonably confident about recreating that which she'd already achieved.

Besides, there was precious little time before circumstances changed again, and she ended up back in the hopeless state in which she'd started.

Was it possible to simply remind Kit that he had assured her of more dalliance without sounding utterly ridiculous? She didn't think hopping into his lap again would work like it had the first time, and she did not wish to embarrass herself.

Her attire tonight was chosen to conjure the impression he'd had of her during that first, accidental encounter. She chose a close-fitting white dress for the night of the theater, embroidered with pink ribbon, just as her underthings had been on that fateful day at Meridian. She left her hair in lax waves, catching them up with an almost haphazardness to emulate the way they'd looked after she'd been hit by that wave, though this time she was able to accent the effect with a pretty white feather and a clawed hair ornament studded with pink opals.

She hadn't lied about her excitement regarding the performance tonight. She almost wished she could separate these two events so that she might experience each one fully and individually, but this was the opportunity life had given her, and so she must make do as best as she could. Perhaps one would only enhance the other.

She powdered her face and décolletage and applied a rosy rouge to her cheeks, lips, and eyelids. She wore a pearl drop on a ribbon around her neck, angled to catch the light and draw the eye. She knew that if she continued to look at her reflection, she could find new things to fix and enhance all the night long, so she threw a shawl over the thing, just as she would to coax her birds to sleep by blocking their view of the outside world.

Zelda had only procured two tickets, claiming that she could not abide a full evening watching Miss Lennox's performance. She seemed utterly unconcerned about compromising reputations or courting scandal, likely because both Gigi and Kit were insignificant to the *ton*. Or perhaps because Zelda was personally responsible for determining which scandals mattered and which were forgotten.

Zelda's explanation when asked? "This isn't a night at the opera, dear. The people who go to these productions actually watch the show."

Whatever that meant.

She placed the backs of her hands against her throat, pushing herself to stand and willing her body to remain cool and collected. She paced in a quick circle, taking steady and deliberate breaths. It was to be an important night for her, and for Kit as well if she succeeded.

Now, where had she put her gloves?

~

SHE WAS to meet Kit at the playhouse, which was less of a formal theatrical venue, and more of a converted pub. At least, that was the impression it gave from the outside.

She held their tickets in her gloved hands, crinkled brown paper printed with proof of payment on one side, and scribbled with Zelda's distinct spiky penmanship on the back, requesting an audience with Liberty Lennox on a matter of sterling importance.

From her position in the coach, she could see the curious gathering of patrons, arriving in clusters, one colorful dollop after another. Zelda had said that this was not the same as the opera, where those of means gathered to display their wealth and exchange gossip, but to Gigi's eye, these people were also dressed to be seen. Perhaps it wasn't a matter of money, so much as eccentricity, that carried clout at a performance such as this.

Brilliant patterns and adornment caught the light as people entered, making Gigi suddenly feel rather plain, in her white dress with pink ribbon. She touched the pearl that sat between her collarbones, wondering if Kit would be distracted by these bright, unusual people. For her part, it was no contest at all for her attention when Kit's voice appeared over the din of the evening crowd.

He must have stopped to greet the driver, she realized, adjusting her skirts and patting her hair one last time. Her heart fluttered, light as a hummingbird, and he appeared a moment later to open the door for her, offering her his hand to help her down.

He had dressed for the occasion in a powder blue waistcoat that brought out the gleam of his eyes, and his silver buttons shone in the twilight. She took note of his hair, combed and stylish ... for now, and gave him a bright, dimpled smile of greeting, wondering how obviously the mischief lurked behind her own countenance, and leaned into his support as she hopped delicately to the cobbled ground.

He gave a helpless little breath, almost like a chuckle, as he took her in, his eyes lingering on the detail of her neckline and the loose arrangement of her hair. "Gigi," he began, "you look ..." He trailed off, laughing again and shaking his head. "You are a vision, Gigi Dempierre."

"So are you, Mr. Cooper," she replied with a wry smile and a tug on his arm in the direction of the makeshift theater. "I have been watching the others arrive," she told him as they walked. "What an odd bunch they are!"

"Intellectuals and artists, I'd wager," he noted, watching a white-haired man in a patched, purple suit give a deep bow to the doorman, proffering his ticket forward. "Do you think we'll stick out?"

"Very likely."

She wasn't sure what the correct greeting was, following the man in purple, so she dipped a quick curtsey and held the tickets out to the man at the door, a dark-skinned, dark-eyed wall of muscle, with a shiny bald head. She extended the tickets with Zelda's scribbles facing up, so that he would be sure to take note of them, and sure enough, there was a quick flick of his eyes to the penmanship and a raise of his thin, arched brows.

"Welcome," the man said in a deep, rich voice, giving a respectful nod of his head to Gigi and then to Kit. "It is a rare privilege. I will find you at intermission."

He shifted his attention to the guests behind them, his expression sliding back into jovial welcome, so quickly that Gigi thought for a moment that she might have imagined the verbal exchange they'd just had. If Kit hadn't urged her to move into the building, she might have stood there, questioning herself until she could get his attention again.

"Well, would you look at that?" Kit came to a halt a few feet into the big, single room that made up the ground floor. It was indeed built like a pub, with two bars on conjoining walls and a mess of tables and chairs surrounding a central, circular platform under a brightly lit chandelier. There was no curtain, no orchestra, no boxed balconies from which to perch and watch with a pair of dainty binoculars.

The tables closest to the central platform had already been claimed, with food and drink already spread out over a few of them, while those seated made lively conversation. Kit set his eye on a cluster of options near a wall that didn't have a bar, perhaps to avoid constant passersby, and guided her toward them, gesturing at a few options but deferring to Gigi to make the final choice.

She chose a small table with a tea candle in the center, its two chairs situated side-by-side so that both occupants would face the center of the room. She was careful in taking her seat, brushing her hand gratefully against his arm as he held it out for her.

This was, without a doubt, her favorite mission so far, and the show had not even begun yet.

He vanished for a moment, whispering something to a barmaid who was weaving her way through the tables, before taking his own seat.

"Look up," he whispered, leaning close to her ear. "The ceiling is painted."

She tilted her head up, unable to suppress the grin tugging at the corners of her lips at the way he continued to hover near her ear, as though he were savoring her. Above their heads was a faded mural, depicting some victorious battlefield, teeming with British standards. If it were not so old, it would have felt aggressively patriotic, but the blurred faces of the soldiers and the missing lines about the flag all lent itself to a sort of lighthearted charm.

The barmaid returned with two empty glasses and a dusty bottle of red wine, which she plopped on the table with crisp efficiency, swiping the two coins Kit held out in one smooth motion before vanishing again to her task.

"Not gin?" Gigi teased.

"Next time," he promised, tossing her a wink as he filled their glasses. "Did Zelda happen to mention what sort of performance this was going to be?"

"*Some Greek tragedy,*" Gigi quoted in her best imitation of Zelda's voice, gratified by his chuckle. "Which one, she did not say."

Two young men had approached the stage, supporting a large, rectangular frame draped in gray cloth. It swayed and shimmered in the light as they balanced it carefully between them, walking it to the center of the platform. Following them was a young girl with her arms filled with unlit lanterns.

Once the fabric frame had been positioned to their satisfaction, the men walked around the stage, lighting the lanterns as the girl placed them, and narrowing their shutters so that their light was directed onto the metallic gray shroud.

Gigi watched this curiously, noting that a hush had begun to work its way through the crowded room as this played out.

Next, a chair was carried up and positioned facing the

framework, and next to it a small bundle of cloth that clanked when it dropped to the floor. The doors leading outside were drawn shut by the man who had taken their tickets, his bald head gleaming in the abundant candlelight.

Four musicians took their places, each between two of the lanterns around the circle. A flute, a drum, a cello, and a violin were positioned. The musicians were dressed all in white, each fussing with their instrument in anticipation of the impending performance.

Every new stage of this preparation brought another wave of tension and quiet over the room. Gigi felt it, like the pull of an ocean tide drawing every face, every eye, to the stage.

An old man was the last to climb up onto the platform, his silver hair cropped in a horseshoe around his head, a sharp little goatee at his chin. He took his time, settling into the chair and reaching down for the cloth bundle, which he held in his lap. He seemed to freeze, even his eyelids going still as the candles on the walls were dimmed, leaving only the chandelier above the platform and the narrow beams of the lanterns burning high.

Gigi felt her breath catch in her throat, the anticipation of what came next prickling against her skin. She reached under the table for Kit's hand, and interlaced her gloved fingers with his bare ones, shivering as his fingers threaded between her own.

The music began with the low moan of the cello, its call drawing up the old man's head like it had come from his thoughts and not a musician just outside of his little world.

He craned his neck left and then right and opened the bundle in his lap, revealing a chisel and a hammer, and rose to his feet with the gentle grace of a dancer, circling the cloth-covered cube at the center of his imagined world. He lined his chisel up at the top of the frame, miming a knock of the hammer to its base, and the drummer struck his instrument in time.

There was a gasp of delight as a hand emerged from the cloth, as though it had been carved in perfection in that one, simple stroke.

"Ah," Kit whispered. "Pygmalion."

Gigi realized as the old man moved through his artistry, spinning and leaping lightly on his feet, that he must not be so old after all, but rather a younger man in disguise. Each drumbeat and strike of his chisel revealed more of the woman hiding within the frame, her fabrics dropping one by one to the floor as her figure came into view, held stock still in an elegant pose, with one hand turned inward and arcing up toward the ceiling.

She was painted with reflective stripes of grease paint, and appeared to have tiny, gem-like pieces of mirrored glass glued to her skin here and there, giving her the illusion of being truly made of alabaster or ivory or stone, glittering in her otherworldly way. Her hair appeared to have been dusted with flour, and it mingled in the tight, black curls she wore in a way that very much reminded Gigi of fine marble.

Her legs, such as they were visible, were bent like a dancer's, her toes pointed as though she'd been frozen halfway through taking a step. Her hair was gathered into two looping ribbons around her head, like many ancient sculptures from the Greek world. Her eyes were closed and her lips were parted. Each sheet of gray shimmered as it slid off her skin, revealing her layer by layer, as though the sculptor truly was freeing her from a block of marble.

He gazed up at his sculpted woman, his eyes glimmering with tears under the lights, and bade her to live with a series of elegant gestures. When she did not come to life, he tried again, falling to his knees to beg, gesturing to the gods above in desperation.

He did not speak, but Gigi could feel his desire all the same, radiating throughout the room.

She sipped her wine, drawing nearer to Kit, resting her cheek on his shoulder. No one cared about them, with such artistry on display, and he did not pull away from the gesture, rather resting his chin on her hair and giving her hand a lingering squeeze of affection.

They stayed like this as the goddess Aphrodite appeared, walking on bare feet into sight and up the small staircase onto the platform from the void of darkness beyond. They watched together as the sculptor begged her to make his lovely creation flesh.

The goddess glowed in quicksilver and copper. She was a force, beautiful and terrible. She paced around the sculpture with keen consideration, taking the measure of the man who had made it.

She shook her head, unimpressed, and turned her back on her penitent, whose head hung in defeat. Aphrodite bade the man to sleep, and he returned to his chair, his head drooping lifelessly onto his chest.

She tested his slumber, clapping in front of his face and twirling in place to draw his eye, neither of which roused him. Once satisfied, she turned back to the sculpture, lifting her chin in consideration, and then reached out, drawing a finger down the line of the sculpted woman's arm.

Her fingers wiggled, accompanied by high strains of the violin and deep notes from the flute. There was a murmur of delight as the sculpted woman began to come to life, twisting and bending carefully, little by little, until the goddess had released her entirely from her prison of stone. She shrugged off a final layer of glimmering cloth, her skin shining in the light, her eyes flying open for the first time with a soundless gasp of wonder.

Gigi was fascinated by the boldness of the statue's costume. She could see the lines of her abdomen and the dent of her belly button against the filmy fabric of her silver shroud. She had never seen a woman so scandalously dressed before, especially not in public. But she did not scandalize the audience, nor did she appear embarrassed of her vulnerability in a crowd, her sinuous movements catching the light as she moved and swayed.

It was impossible to look away.

Throughout the night, while the sculptor slept, the goddess bade the sculpted woman to dance, teaching her to leap and to spin and sway. When the sculptor began to stir again, the goddess sent her creature back to its pedestal and held her finger to her lips, twisting her fingers until the stone took hold again, and the sculptor's creation moved no more.

When the sculptor had woken, she made him a bargain—the surrender of his tools in exchange for her blessing. It hurt him, Gigi could see, to surrender his chisel, to sacrifice one love for another, but when he looked at his beautiful artwork, he heaved a great sigh and made his choice.

She snuggled closer to Kit, sad for the man, to have to make such a choice.

The goddess held the tools to her chest and grinned at the man, backing away with one last, elegant motion to the pedestal, where the sculpture began to wake again.

There was an interlude of dancing between the old man and his love, their bodies twisting together, colliding in lifts that looked as though they broke the very laws of nature. They caught one another in embraces that sent heat flying into Gigi's cheeks and seemed to speed Kit's breath.

The man seemed to regain his vigor in his love's embrace, his fingers stroking the lines of her jaw, dragging against the plump offerings of her lips.

His back no longer hunched, leaving him to stand taller, with shoulders that appeared broader and stronger than before. It was as though in giving life to his creation, the goddess had blessed him, too, with renewal of his youth.

He lifted from the pile a long bolt of gray cloth, which he wrapped around her shoulders like a cloak. He held her face cradled in his hands and gazed into her eyes until a shining smile formed on her mouth.

She nodded and leapt into his arms, the cloak draping around her body in beautiful lines. The old man smiled back and held her close. He seemed half the age of the man he'd been at the opening, and with the strength of a muscled youth, he carried his new bride off the stage, and into the darkness, against the rising din of applause.

CHAPTER 23

She began to pull away as the flames rose in the oil lamps around them, expanding their radius of light and bringing many a dreamy-eyed gaze blinking back into the here and now. As much as Kit wanted to tighten his grip on her, he let her slide off his shoulder and disentangle her fingers from his.

It would have been impossible to let her go, had he not believed completely that he would be able to touch her again, to hold her again, just as soon as they were alone. Even for just this moment, he felt suddenly halved by her absence. The world felt cooler and subdued.

"You know," she said, her voice soft and whispery as she turned those lovely green eyes up at him, "this would have been a worthwhile venture, all on its own."

He wanted to kiss her so badly, it almost hurt. He thought perhaps he might have thrown all caution to the wind and done it, right in view of all the people in this room, if the strong, heavy hand of the man who'd taken their tickets hadn't landed on his shoulder in exactly that moment, nearly startling him out of his skin.

"Come with me," the man rumbled, already turning to leave before they could so much as rise from their chairs.

Gigi took her glass of wine with her, sipping at it as they scaled a rickety set of wooden stairs at the rear of the room, her other hand holding her skirt out of the way of her slippered feet. Kit thought, absurdly, that he would follow her along a great number of stranger paths than the one they followed tonight.

And tonight was far from usual.

At the top of the stairs was a small foyer, surrounded by rooms for lodging. The musicians and actors were milling about between the doors, seeking refreshment or whispering critiques and the like to one another.

The goddess Aphrodite was giggling at something another woman was saying, utterly transformed when she smiled. She tugged at her hairline and slid off the long, waist-length wig she had been wearing on stage, startling Kit all the more. Underneath she had hair cropped short as a man's, which she ran a casual hand through while replying to her friend.

He was still wearing a bewildered expression, his brain unable to properly process the metamorphoses of women, when they walked into one of the lodging rooms, this one empty and situated with a narrow bed, a desk, and a washbasin.

"Soon," said the bald man, who remained in the hall as he ushered them inside. "Wait here."

The door closed and Kit found himself rooted to the spot, completely at a loss of what to do next.

Gigi approached him and handed him her glass of wine, an unspoken understanding in her eyes that he needed something to soothe his rattled disposition. He did as he had done back on Bond Street, what felt like a thousand years ago, and twisted the cup around so that his lips would meet the same place hers had been.

It made her smile.

And her smile made him calm.

There was a crisp knock to the door before it opened again, bringing their attention around to the woman who had played the ivory statue, still wearing her incredibly scant costume and fanning herself with a feathered fan. "Hello there," she said cheerfully, knocking the door shut with her rounded hip and breezing past them, chattering like an old friend. "I don't believe we've met. D'you mind if I sit? Holding that pose is hell on the legs."

"I would think the dancing to be more taxing," Gigi responded, watching wide-eyed as Liberty Lennox situated herself on the cot.

She was much different up close than Kit had expected after observing her from the audience. Even wearing layers of paint and sparkle, he could see that she had a swarthy complexion and tight, coiled ringlets of ebony hair. She had a constellation of beauty marks on the left side of her face, accenting her cheek, upper lip, and chin.

"Oh, God, no. That part is the relief! Luckily I don't spend much of the second act as a statue, hm? There, now tell me your names; I believe you already know mine."

"I am Kit, and this is Gigi," Kit said, wondering how many times he had introduced them to strangers now. He was beginning to find the sound of his own name strange in his ear. "We are here on behalf of the Silver Leaf Society."

"Yes, I know that," Liberty replied with a bright laugh. "It's a shame you didn't bring Zelda. I do so love watching her frown and squirm around the other patrons. What's this about then, hm? I don't have another shipment scheduled until summer."

"We are looking for Pauline Olivier and her husband," Gigi explained, standing at attention like a soldier in front of a lounging queen. "They likely have a fugitive prisoner in tow and are expected to be planning another jailbreak in the immediate future. They must be stopped, lest they destroy a much larger and more important mission that is occurring in tandem—one that could impact the outcome of the war."

Miss Lennox blinked her big, brown eyes at Gigi, wearing an expression of seemingly genuine surprise. One could never say with actresses, though. After a moment, she allowed her brow to wrinkle, shaking her head with an irritated sigh.

"That cannot be right," she protested. "Pauline Olivier is a founding member. Surely she would not act against the interests of the Silver Leaf itself. She is just as much its leader as Zelda Smith is, after all. Her instructions are just as valid."

"She has no way of knowing what she's compromising," Kit

explained, leaning his weight against the wall next to the washbasin. "She was forced to return to England under poor conditions some months ago and has not made her whereabouts known. Therefore, she is not up to date on the doings of her secret society, and has instead undertaken a mission all her own."

"I don't suppose you will tell me what this large, world-changing mission is about, hm?" she asked, turning those big eyes from Kit to Gigi and back again. "Ah. You can't, can you? Damn you, Zelda! Your pride is like wax wings, flapping toward the sun!"

She shoved herself off the bed and began to pace, her bare feet squeaking against the ancient beams of wood on the floor. "If that woman would just relinquish her iron grip on us all, things could operate much smoother! How was I to know I was not taking orders directly from the consensus of the Silver Leaf itself? This is Zelda's own fault. It would take little more than a courier with a single sentence on a scrap of paper to avoid this type of thing!"

"Yes," Kit agreed, tilting his head to examine the flush of outrage on this woman. "I take it that you have seen the Oliviers, then?"

"Seen them, abetted them, served them tea," Miss Lennox snapped back, stopping abruptly in her pacing to fling her head back and stare up at the rafters, as though they might deliver her from her woes. "I cannot undo it now."

"Do you know where they are staying?" Gigi asked.

"Do you have a means to contact them?" Kit said immediately after.

"Yes to both, naturally," Miss Lennox replied, her composure apparently regained as she lowered her chin and returned her eyes to the other two. "Shall I summon them here or send you to them, hm? If only they were at home just now."

Gigi cast Kit a glance, though it was impossible to say for certain what she was thinking.

"We will have to discuss our course of action," he answered, rather than deciding for them both. "If you could kindly give us an address, we will take ownership of the matter from here."

"Are you listening, Kit?" Miss Lennox asked, dropping a hand onto her waist. "They are not at home. You are too late. Why didn't you come here sooner, and so on?"

"Do you mean that they have already fled England?" Gigi asked.

"No. But they mean to as soon as tonight's business is concluded." Miss Lennox gave a weary laugh, shaking her head. "If you leave this very instant, you should be able to intervene, but it will be a close thing. I imagine that by the end of the play, Mrs. Ferris will finally be free of her prison and on her way to a new life."

In the stunned beat of silence that followed, the tinkling of a bell sounded just beyond the closed door.

"I have to return to the stage," Liberty Lennox said, in a tone that was more irritated than apologetic. "You may go after them or stay here, if you wish. Take some time to discuss between yourselves. Whatever you do, just tell Zelda Smith that this is her own doing. She should know."

Neither of them responded, sitting in the thick silence as the door clicked closed behind the retreating figure of Liberty Lennox.

CHAPTER 24

*K*it waited until they were alone again to properly breathe.

One way or another, this would be over tonight.

Either they would succeed or their mission would become obsolete, and at the break of dawn, nothing would be holding the two of them in London any longer. He had expected a jolt of adrenaline, an urgent necessity to take action. Instead, he simply felt rooted to the spot, unable to arrange his thoughts into words he might speak.

Gigi had crossed the room with a careful consideration, evidently having no issues with movement at all. She slumped onto the foot of the narrow cot, dropping her head into her hands as the musical quartet below began to weave its magic around the audience once again. She looked like a discarded doll, all porcelain and lace.

"Kit," she mumbled into her own palms. "We can't stop them."

He sighed heavily, an emotion spilling down over his shoulders, easing a weight he did not know had been sitting there all along. He paced over to her and handed her the half-consumed glass of wine, waiting for her to finish it before he sat next to her, with his legs on either side of the corner of the cot.

"She did say that if we left immediately, there was a chance," he reminded her.

She sighed, turning her head so that one green eye was peeking out at him from her fingers. "That is not what I meant. We *can't*. I do not even want to try. I certainly do not want to risk the chance we might succeed. Yes, I am perfectly aware that stopping them is the entire reason we are here in the first place, but Kit, I ... I can't."

"It might be the thing that brought us here," he corrected, reaching out to stroke the back of her hands, her words twisting through him with the clarity of birdsong. "What we are here to do is for us, and us alone, to decide."

She held still for a moment, as though she had to turn this over in her mind and ensure that she had understood it properly. She lifted her head and dropped both hands down to grasp his, searching his eyes intently. "What do *you* want?"

It was hard not to smile at the question, at the obvious answer.

You, Gigi, he thought. *I want you.*

He understood that it was not the moment for flirtatious deflection, but the instinct was too natural to ignore completely. Further, he realized that he felt just as strongly about the fate of the Ferris women as Gigi did. He told her with complete sincerity, "I could not, in good conscience, take steps to keep Mrs. Ferris and her daughter in that house. Even if you still wanted me to."

"But you fought in the war," she said, so quietly that it was almost whisked away by the music below them. Her grip on his hands tightened, her expression almost a plea to decline her, to tell her she was wrong. "Would our inaction not negate your sacrifice? Would we only be adding to the damage that your father wrought?"

He hesitated, a chord striking in his chest that sounded with the uncomfortable ring of truth. Archie Cooper had lost his wits when he did his damage. For Kit, it would be a decision.

Was it the just decision? The correct one?

Likely not.

He would be placing the good of those he knew, loved, and cared for over the good of the war effort. Strangely, no matter how hard the chord within him sang, it could not overpower his desire to do nothing at all.

"What if we damn all of Britain?" she whispered miserably.

He looked at her, her features clear and warm and more important to him in this moment than all the world and its needs.

"If Britain is damned, then it was always damned," he replied, his voice deep and steady, believing the words he spoke completely.

He did not want to be a martyr, nor did he wish to create any.

She released her breath with a shudder of emotion, sparkling teardrops gathering on her eyelashes. She released her grip on his hands and reached up to stroke her gloved fingertips along the lines of his cheeks. She pressed her lips into his with an impetuous sort of enthusiasm, as though only he could understand the things she was feeling, and only he could reflect them back to her.

It was too much to ask of him, to once again hold back everything he felt. He could not. He would not.

Enough self-control had been wrung out of Kit tonight to hold him in good standing of his moral debts for the rest of his life.

He wrapped one strong arm around her, jerking her firmly against his body, and used his other hand to draw the opal-studded comb out of her honey-blonde waves. Her hair smelled like the first gasp of fresh air, after toiling in the dark. He dug his fingers into the soft bounty of it, dragging the weight of soft, fragrant tresses down around her shoulders, free in the way it had been the first time he laid eyes on her.

It was dry now, free of the tangle of sea salt and ruined feathers. The fluffy, white feather she had been wearing tonight had tumbled down behind her ear, tickling the bare flesh on her shoulder. He plucked it from its tangle of gold, stroking its down-soft edges along the flesh of her arm, to the bend of her elbow, just above the tops of her gloves.

He grinned at the way she shivered, drawing her bottom lip between his teeth and dragging the feather back up and over the hollow between her breasts, up along the line of her throat. He pulled back from their kiss only because he needed, desperately, to look at her.

She was beautifully disheveled, her hair spilling down over her arms, her lips swollen and parted. Her chest was flushed and her eyes shone, wide and fixed upon him. He took her hand into his lap and began to slide the glove off, its silky material whispering against the softness of her skin. He draped it over his thigh and held his hand out for the other, which she readily provided, allowing him to strip the fabric away again.

"I am going to take your dress off," he told her, eyes scraping over the garment in question. "Stand up."

Her eyes widened, but she braced her hand against his for support and rose to her feet, her skirts swishing around her legs. "Here?" she asked in half a whisper. "Now?"

"Yes," he confirmed, gripping her firmly by the hips and pulling her to him, so that she was positioned between his knees. He went immediately about the business of seeking the hem at her feet, gathering the fabric up in his palms as quickly as he could without damaging it.

She lifted her arms, allowing him to pull it up and over her head in one piece, thin petticoats clinging to the delicate muslin that lay over it, leaving her in very thin chemise, held in place with ivory-white stays.

He took a moment to appreciate her like this, returned to the state in which he'd initially found her: stripped down to her last layer of feminine armor. The white fabric sculpted the shape of her breasts and revealed the hidden curves of her thighs. The stays may have been an additional layer of fabric, but they only served to emphasize the tempting offerings of her lithe little body.

She turned in place, drawing her curtain of hair over her shoulder and exposing to him the elegant line of her neck, the delicate detail of her shoulders, and—most importantly—the ties of her stays, held together with nothing more than a neat bow at the small of her back. It disintegrated to nothing but wrinkled ribbons with one flick of his wrist, and he watched the muscles in Gigi's shoulders expand as she was freed from its restriction, one tug at a time to loosen the cinching around her ribs.

The rest she did herself, freeing her arms first from the stays and then tugging off the garment and holding it out to Kit, as though it was his trophy to keep. All that was left upon her was that translucent white fabric, clinging to the curves and hollows of her body like an angel's shroud.

He took his time enjoying this development, setting aside the gloves and corset with the careful, steady hands of a man who had done such things many times before. Perhaps he had breathed in some of the talent from the actors below them. Regardless of its origin, his boldness only grew with his desire, his blood hot and insistent under the careful formality of his own clothing.

He tugged her closer with a finger hooked into her neckline, and reached up to slide his hands along the smooth, silken bounty of her shoulders and throat, urging the delicate sleeves of her chemise from her arms, and down along the swell of her breasts. He let his eyes follow the progress of her exposure, his pulse quickening in his throat as he revealed the rosy perfection of her nipples, the teardrop shape of her bare breasts. A tiny snowflake of a birthmark hid on her ribs, just above the indent of her navel. He forced himself to breathe, pulling the fabric over its last curve of resistance, revealing her hips, her pert little bottom, and the delicate, dark golden hair that curled around her sex.

She watched him, her eyes hooded with the heaviness of her golden lashes, and stepped with a sweet compliance out of the puddle created by her now entirely discarded chemise. Her legs caught the light of the single candle lighting the room, reflecting it with pale, pearl-like perfection.

He wanted to lock her in this room for a month, until he had explored every possible inch of her. He ran his hand down the curve of her waist, his thumb circling the indent of her hip. "Closer," he implored, drawing her nearer to him, until she was forced to crawl astride him on the bed, for there was no more room on the floor. Even then, it was not enough, and again, he said, "Closer."

She settled onto him, settling her hands on his shoulders and urging him onto his back, where the two of them were veiled in the curtain of her hair, and pressed her bare body into his clothed one, mouth slanting over his in a sweet, careful kiss.

He groaned, returning the attention with significantly more heat and pressure, and rolled Gigi Dempierre onto her back, allowing his weight to sink onto her delicate little body. He pressed his hips hard into hers, wanting her to know the effect she had on him, wanting her to know that her body was a thing of power. It was the first thing that drew a sound from her, a gasp, deep in her bird-like throat.

"Now, you must undress me," he whispered to her, coming

up on his arms and spiraling a tendril of her hair around his finger. "Come now. Untie my cravat."

Her lips curved, a wry sort of smile hiding somewhere beneath the demure maiden she was embodying just now. Her nimble fingers made quick work of the cloth around his neck, and her fingertips trailed down over the exposed skin there with the kind of deliberate sensuality that Gigi always seemed to hide until the most devastating moment possible.

"Are you certain?" she teased, a sparkle of mischief in her eyes as her hands lowered, flicking one silver button at a time out of its loop on his jacket. "Don't you want to know how the play ends?"

"I know how it ends," he told her, moving to allow her to pull the jacket from his body and move her attention to his waistcoat, her fingers now well adept to slipping the buttons quickly through their loops. "This story is far more interesting."

"Mm," she agreed, pulling the waistcoat from him, followed quickly by his shirt. She locked her legs around him and pushed him over, so that she was back on top, wiggling downward to free him from his boots, and then, inevitably, his trousers.

He thought perhaps he might die of heated blood and pounding heart before she could finish this task. The kiss of cool air on his skin gave rise to gooseflesh.

She revealed all of him with excruciating care, pausing only a moment when she uncovered his arousal.

It was not a suspense Kit thought he could survive for long. "Touch me," he told her. "I want you to touch me."

She did.

She rose above him again, this time with her flowing bounty of golden hair hung to one side. Her hand slid over the length of him and her soft, pouty lips dragged along the line of his throat. She took tentative little tastes of the flesh there, her slender hand exploring the length of his cock. Her touch was excruciatingly gentle and maddeningly curious.

He slid the breadth of his hand down the line of her back, filling his palm with one delightfully round cheek, which he squeezed hard enough to make her gasp. It was an immensely satisfying weight in his hand, pliant and forbidden, and something he didn't realize he'd been wanting to do quite so badly.

Her reaction set aflame blood that was already running very hot, her even white teeth grazing against the edge of his jaw, closing gently onto the lobe of his ear. It pulled a growl from his throat, primal and hungry. He pulled her with that grip on her backside to face him, her body collapsing with a bounce on the narrow mattress next to him.

"Kiss me," he told her. "Stroke me."

She obeyed with enthusiasm, her hand tightening over his shaft as she indulged him with long, slow strokes. She examined the depths of his eyes as she pleasured him, lingering close enough to tease him with short, suggestive little kisses, each one opening up just enough of her mouth to suggest the promise of more before she pulled away again.

It was almost too much. Almost.

He found her body pliable under his hands, her thigh more than willing to ride up around his hip, her breasts happy to be cupped and teased. He moved her hands away from their stroking, resting them on his bare chest, where her fingers curled against the spray of blond hair on the warm skin above his heart.

He traced the pads of his fingers along the insides of her thighs, claiming her mouth with a firmness that put an end to her teasing as he ensured that she was ready to join with him, his touch lingering on the slick heat between her legs, enjoying the knowledge that it was all for him.

He didn't have to tell her to look at him. When he drew back, adjusting their bodies so that he could enter her, her moss-green eyes were already locked on his face, her expression somewhere between trusting and challenging, as though she would have teased him just now, had she been able to speak.

He ensured that she was not able to speak.

He did not draw out the experience of deflowering her, though he was still careful not to hurt her. A quick, single stroke into her joined them and won mirrored gasps from them both. He watched her, searched her face for signs of discomfort.

He saw only pleasure, perhaps even satisfaction.

It was the leave he needed to allow himself to revel in the feel of her, slick and willing around him. He claimed her lips again, crushing their mouths together as he began to move inside her, as slowly as he could stand, with his body a pillar of heat and sensation.

His head was muddled with the feel of her, the smell of her, the sounds she was making as he claimed her in the most intimate possible way. It was impossible to grasp the passage of time. Air rushed in his ears, an enormously overwhelming crack of sensations scattering over his flesh, pulling him closer and closer into her, burying himself in the perfection she offered. He listened to her body, instinct and rhythm matching that which drove her closer to the edge of bliss, each stroke learning all the more how to make her moan.

He savored the taste of her mouth, the sweetness of her gasps and sighs as they landed on his tongue.

"Kit," she said, breathy and helpless in his ear. *"Mon Dieu."*

Her climax shook them both. It happened seemingly without warning, her moans shifting from languid indulgence to sharp and wild completion. She cried out, her body shuddering against him, her fists digging into his hair, and her legs tightening around his hips.

Below them, beyond the thin boards of the floor, music swelled to a grand final note. The audience burst into applause, their cheers and cries escaping heavenward to wrap around the lovers that tumbled together secretly overhead.

He rolled her onto her back, driving into her as she rode the final wave of her pleasure, tumbling down into oblivion. He was desperate to join her, to satisfy himself at long, long last.

It only took looking down at her beneath him, her back arched, lips parted, and cheeks pink and shiny with her lashes fluttering in helpless sensation over them.

He held her legs, his fingers digging into the plump flesh there, and finally felt the roar of climax tear through him, his vision clouding and his senses vanishing against the strength of it. He held himself aloft, only long enough to empty himself completely into her, to share with her this final and most forbidden of pleasures.

It was a miracle that he could think clearly enough to collapse to the side, rather than allowing his entire dead weight to crumple onto her sweet little body.

She held him as he caught his breath, her fingers combing through his hair as she pressed his cheek to her bosom, her own breaths coming in ragged gulps that mirrored his own. He held her, too, his arm limp but secure around the curve of her side, and he looked at her, for want of being able to do anything else.

He looked at her and knew he never, ever wanted to look away.

CHAPTER 25

How was it possible to feel so many things all at once?

Gigi's gaze was soft, her lashes creating a dreamy border around her vision as she gazed toward the ceiling of the little room. From Kit's stillness and the steady tempo of breathing, she guessed he may have drifted off to sleep for a moment, holding her close, and while she did understand the relief and exhaustion he must be feeling, there was something else happening to her. Something altogether different.

She couldn't have gone to sleep just then, no matter how hard she tried. Wrapped around the pillar of sated stillness in her body was a coil of pure electricity, cracking and spitting like a bolt of lightning held static in the sky. Part of her wanted to stay here forever, nestled into his side, smelling his skin and his hair, awash in his warmth. The other part wanted to leap from the bed and dance about the room, to throw the window open and cry out to the moon above in wordless, wild poetry.

She had felt her senses come back to her one at a time. First came touch, with the delicate ache of chilled skin under a hot cloth, then scent and taste and vision. Last of all was hearing, for it was a titanic task to overcome the cacophony of Gigi's own thoughts and emotions. When sound did begin to float around her again, it happened in layers; first Kit's breathing and the settling of the old wood in this room, then the rumble of wheels on cobblestones from beyond the window, and then finally the rumble of the festivities downstairs, a low mélange of voices and the shuffle of bodies.

It was that final sound that made her realize how vulnerable they were just now. Why they had decided to escalate their intimacy in such a volatile space, she could not say, but regardless of the risk, she did not regret it even a little. Still, she'd prefer not to be discovered completely in the nude.

She ducked out of Kit's embrace, drawing the thin blanket folded at the foot of the bed to cover him, tucking the blanket in around the center of his chest, where it might provide the most warmth. Her chemise and other particulars were in a surprisingly neat pile to the side of the bed.

He is thoughtful, she realized with a little smile, and blushed, glancing at the haphazard items of his own clothing that she had thrown in several directions.

She pulled her chemise back over her head, shaking out the fabric around her ankles, and set about gathering up his things and folding them into a pile that at least approached the presentation of her own. She hummed to herself, her bare feet sliding along the dull and well-used planks that made up the wooden floor, and twisted her wayward hair into a loose knot at the base of her neck.

She could not stop smiling.

"Come back to bed," murmured Kit from his place on the narrow cot, a dreamy expression on his face.

"That isn't our bed," Gigi reminded him. "Though I think we will be unbothered for at least a little while longer. I'll just have a peek, hm?"

"In that?" he asked, coming up to a seated position and clutching the blanket at his chest like an affronted damsel.

"Just a peek!" she giggled, crossing over to the room and leaning close to the door so that she could look out, but when she moved to turn the knob, it would not give.

She frowned. She tried again, with a little more strength, to no avail. She gave the door a jerk, her heart starting to hammer in her chest, and realized with horror that she could not make it budge.

"Kit," she said, turning to him with her eyes wide. "We are locked in."

His brows drew together and he threw his legs over the side of the bed, leaving the blanket behind to stride over to the door, utterly and completely naked.

Gigi was so stunned by this display that she momentarily forgot the problem.

It wasn't until he cursed, his own attempt to jerk the door open rebuffed by the lock, that she snapped back to reality.

"For God's sake, Kit," she said, laying a calming hand on his bare chest and drawing his outraged blue eyes down to her. "At least put on your trousers before you break the door down."

"That ... that *woman* locked us in!" he bellowed, as though she hadn't said that exact thing mere seconds ago. "We had no choice in the matter at all!"

"Then it is well that our ends ended up aligning with hers," Gigi pointed out, taking him by the well-muscled arm to walk him back over to the bed, so that he might pull on an item or two of clothing. "All things considered, I think it is best we are only discovering this trickery now."

He allowed her to lead him, but ran his free hand into his already disheveled sandy hair, his brow wrinkled in consternation. He sank down onto the edge of the mattress, wordlessly accepting his trousers as Gigi gathered them up from the floor, and raised his eyes to meet hers, bafflement swimming in the clear blue. "Do you really believe that?"

"Believe what?" She frowned, watching his face as he processed this new and unwelcome development in their mission.

"That it is better that we're only discovering it now," he replied, shaking his head sharply, as though to clear it, and beginning to pull his trousers over his bare legs. "I've a sudden flash of guilt that we haven't been trying to escape. We might have at least returned to Bond Street and given warning to Mrs. Smith."

"I regret nothing at all," she said, crossing her arms over her chest. She took a step back as he came to his feet, hitching his trousers up over his hips and securing them. She had thought his bare flesh would be less distracting once he was at least partially covered, but she realized now that this was not the case. "Do you?"

He sighed, dropping his hands on his hips and looking

around the room. "What happened here was going to happen eventually, no matter what. I only wonder if we did not choose our timing poorly."

"I see."

He hesitated, blinking several times and then turning to look at her. "I do not regret anything, Gigi."

"You don't seem particularly happy about it either," she returned, aware at the fringes of her thoughts that this was a silly, petulant thing to be doing just now. Still, it wasn't exactly the behavior a girl imagined after a first encounter with her lover.

"Happy? Happy barely describes it, but now we are awash in crisis," he said, ducking his head so that he could meet her averted eyes. "Next time we will have no other concerns plaguing us. All right?"

She gave a short nod, which seemed to satisfy him, and he went about pulling his shirt over his head with the brisk urgency of someone working against time. She did not move to gather the rest of her own clothing. She did not believe that door was going to open. Part of her even hoped it did not.

Kit strode back over to the door and pounded on it with the side of his fist.

Nothing.

"Perhaps you could use the washbasin as a battering ram," Gigi suggested primly, winning an annoyed glance over his shoulder. "Kit, unless you want to leap from the window, we are trapped. For now."

He grimaced and pounded once again on the door, though this time, he was rewarded with a response. A single, deeply voiced command. Even from across the room, Gigi could make out the word.

"Stop."

Kit released something along the lines of a laugh, though there was no humor at all to be found in it. He put his weight onto the door and threw his weight into the banging, shouting a few choice observations at the man on the other side of the door.

It achieved nothing. Not even an answer this time.

Gigi thought perhaps they might try stomping on the floor on the chance it would alert the people downstairs, but considering the volume of the revelry that was escaping heavenwards from that room, she thought she'd have to stomp awfully hard.

Instead, she sat on the bed, pulling her legs up underneath her as she watched Kit try this and that to inspire their jailor to release them. "Kit," she said, once drowned out by his own ruckus, and then again, louder, "Kit!"

He turned, looking half wild.

"Kit, we just have to wait," she said, her voice sounding just as calm as she inexplicably felt. "We can sleep, if you like."

"Sleep?" he repeated incredulously, his arms dropping at his sides as he turned completely to face her.

"Mm, or just lie together for a while," she suggested, leaning back onto the pillows as though there was nothing at all wrong in the world. "We do not have to talk."

He hesitated, scratching at his neck as though he wasn't quite sure what was happening. He tossed one last resentful glance at the door and then walked over to the bed, climbing carefully into it and sitting next to Gigi, a fair amount more rigid and tense than he had been before.

She sighed, crawling behind him and pulling him back into a recline, her fingers kneading into his shoulders until he let out a long, deep woosh of air and finally relaxed some small amount. They sat together in their little alcove of silence, serenaded by the muffled sounds of other people in their cups from below.

She rested her cheek on top of his head, her fingertips still stroking the lines of his arms and shoulders, and breathed in his particular scent, letting her eyes flicker shut.

If there was anything Gigi's life had prepared her for, it was a moment like this, in which there were a thousand things she wished to say and do, but with no choice but to sit in the silence and wait.

~

By the time a key jiggled in the lock of the heavy wooden door, both Kit and Gigi had indeed drifted off to sleep. Gigi did not immediately hear it, however, and was awakened by Kit shooting to his feet, his hand reaching for the empty space next to the bed in the half moment it took him to remember that he was not at home, nor at war, but above a converted theater in Central London.

It was Liberty Lennox who entered first, wearing a long, toga-like shift over her costume, and followed close at heel by the large, bald man who had granted them entry some hours before.

Gigi glanced at the small window on the far end of the room, opaque with years of grime and grease. Even through its significant lack of clarity, she could tell that the sun had begun to rise.

"Well?" barked Kit, clearly expecting Miss Lennox and her henchman to burst into immediate apology.

"Well," agreed Miss Lennox, glancing at the rumpled bed and the discarded clothes on the floor and raising her carefully shaped brows. "Well, well."

"Is it done?" Gigi asked, pulling herself from the tangle of blankets to sit, facing them. She stifled a yawn behind her wrist, squeezing her eyes shut a couple of times to clear her vision. She had well and truly drifted off there, for a moment.

"Signed and sealed," replied Miss Lennox, cutting her eyes to Gigi with a smile that almost looked like approval. "We only have a few final steps to complete, and we will require your assistance for them."

"Our assistance?" Kit repeated, incredulous anger building in his voice. "After you trapped us in here?"

"Oh, Mr. Cooper, leave the theatrics to me, hm?" Her smile widened, evident enjoyment writ all over her face. "Yes, I know your name. Yours too, Miss Dempierre. Or will it be Mrs. Cooper now, after such a scandalous night, hm? Do send my regards to your brother, either way."

"Mathias is the one who sent me to you," Gigi replied, still in her puddle of blankets, but her posture straight and her voice clear. "He would likely see your actions tonight as a betrayal."

"I would not be so certain of that." Liberty Lennox's smile faded, and she glanced over her shoulder at the large, bald man. "Mathias seemed a humanitarian sort, didn't he, Lem?"

"S'pose," the man replied with a shrug of his broad shoulders.

"There, see? Zelda was happy to forget her dear friends, locked away just as easily as she might have been, had fate decided differently. It was wrong, and as I said to you before, Pauline has just as much authority as Zelda ever has." She tapped at her chin, looking thoughtful for a moment. "And just as much as Mrs. Ferris, for that matter."

"Are we free to go?" Kit cut in, his eyes narrow slats of simmering blue.

"Oh, of course," replied Miss Lennox, that tone of amused satisfaction seeping back into her voice. "But I assumed you'd wish to speak to them?"

"Speak to whom?" he snapped.

"Pauline and Gerard Olivier, naturally. They are waiting for you. Downstairs."

CHAPTER 26

They dressed in haste, tugging on their wrinkled clothing, assisting one another with ties and buttons, and arranging their looks in what amounted to a fairly poor imitation of last night's elegant presentation.

Last night seemed like it had happened in another lifetime.

Kit summoned the memory of the cobbled streets at dusk, of enjoying the brisk kiss of the early autumn wind as he strolled up to the carriage. He remembered with a kind of disbelief how easy it had felt, helping Gigi down to the walkway, admiring how beautiful she looked, and exchanging playful banter as they anticipated a night at the theater. How was that only a handful of hours ago?

He glanced at her, tossing the bed sheets until she found the crushed white feather he had pulled from her hair last night. She tucked it into the shoulder of her gown, unwilling to leave it behind.

She seemed to be avoiding his eye.

Perhaps his anxiety over this situation was contagious, or perhaps she simply had other things on her mind, but Kit could not stop himself trying again and again to catch her gaze as they dressed. Each time, invariably, he felt a little tinge of disappointment that she was not looking back at him.

He wanted desperately to know what she was thinking just now, how she thought they should proceed. He wanted to peer into her mind and examine her thoughts on what had transpired between them, on how she had felt waking in his arms, and perhaps most urgently, how she had felt when Miss Lennox had implied their imminent and necessary marriage.

She hadn't reacted at all. In fact, she'd been eerily calm throughout all of this, even upon finding they were trapped in this room against their will. It was unsettling. He hadn't the faintest clue what might be brewing under her mask of placidity and silence.

He sighed, running a hand through his hair and smoothing out the front of his waistcoat as best as he could.

He had certainly felt a great deal of things, and he was reasonably certain all of them had been apparent to anyone nearby. As to that comment about marriage? What he had felt was so muddled that expressing it hadn't been an option.

He wrinkled his brow, trying to define what he had felt, beyond the simple desire to strangle Miss Lennox.

Confusion? Yes. Panic? A little. But there had also been *thrill,* lurking there at the base of it. Excitement had threaded around all of his other feelings with that familiar, soft ache he felt when tentative feelings of hope found their way into his heart. It was what he wanted, wasn't it? He'd admitted that to himself some time ago.

The Kit who had been recruited for this mission, who didn't know Gigi Dempierre, hadn't planned on marrying for another five years at least. Five years and the orchards would be reliably self-sustaining. Five years and he could think about a second home, a wife, maybe even a child.

Would Gigi Dempierre wait for five years? Could she? Time was much crueler to women. But then, what would the other option be? To marry now and have no established place in the world?

If he rushed his plans for himself, it would still take a year or two to have everything in place, to consider himself a reasonably eligible bachelor. Money wasn't the trouble. Stability was.

Would she marry the likes of him at all?

He frowned, tugging the door open and holding it as she passed.

She stopped at the head of the stairs, laying a gentle hand over her midsection as she took a stabilizing breath. She caught sight of him and flashed a quick, nervous smile, dimples hopping into her cheeks. "Ready?"

"Absolutely not," he replied, getting a snort and a nod of agreement from her. "Shall we?"

She took his arm and they descended the steps together, united as allies as they descended into hostile waters, neither of them knowing what might await them at the bottom, and neither in a great rush to find out, one way or the other.

He filled his lungs and willed the fog to clear from his thoughts, at least for the next few moments. Step by step, the lower floor came into view, sparse now and lit with burgeoning sunlight as dawn nudged at the stubborn weight of the city's horizon, ready to rise for the day.

The teeming crowd of eccentrics had mostly cleared out, leaving behind a few odds and ends—a pair of spectacles, a feathered hat, a knit shawl of eye-watering teal. The tables were still in their arrangement for the show, and the floor was free of broken glass or sticky spills that one might expect to find after such revels.

There were a few straggling merrymakers sitting among the tables in the darkened corners of the space, or perhaps these were members of the Lennox troupe, taking a moment to breathe after a long night of work. It was hard to say from a distance.

Miss Lennox was seated, alone, near the staircase with a steaming cup of something amber brown in her hands. She looked languid and unconcerned, leaning back in the chair as she watched them descend, one leg draped over the other under her toga with her ankles balanced on a second chair she was using as an ottoman. "Much better," she said with a knowing little smirk.

Behind her, two people came into view, standing and talking in hushed voices by the rear wall. A plump, middle-aged woman in a riding kit and wiry gray hair was whispering to her husband, soot smudges on her cheeks and hands. She cut herself off at the sound of Miss Lennox's comment, and turned over her shoulder, her eyes locking on Gigi and Kit with what appeared to be equal amounts of trepidation and delight.

"Oh, Gerard," the woman said, reaching blindly behind her for her companion's hand. "Oh, look at them. Fully grown."

The man behind her caught her fingers in his grasp. He was taller and leaner, with very little hair left under his cap and deep smile lines around his eyes. He did not answer; he only gave them a nod of greeting as they drew nearer.

"Little Lady Giselle," the woman sighed, tears brimming on her lashes. "My, how you have grown."

"Just Gigi, if you please," she answered quickly, a note of slight embarrassment on her voice. "And you are Pauline?"

The woman nodded vigorously. "Yes, of course ... of course you would not remember our faces. Only Mathias has been to see us in years and years. And you are Mary's little nephew, aren't you? She always said you had the most striking blue eyes."

"Kit Cooper, madam," he said with a curt bow. "How do you do?"

"We do not have time for this!" Liberty Lennox called over her shoulder. "The sun is rising as we speak."

"Leave off, Libba," Pauline Olivier said through a sniffle, squeezing her husband's hand. "We only need a moment."

"Did you know?" Kit asked her, careful to keep his tone

neutral so that he might get an honest answer. "Did you know that Zelda was trying to stop you? That we were looking for you? That you were compromising another, much larger operation?"

It was Gerard who answered. "Yes," he said. "We knew."

"We were careful," his wife cut in, her brows knit together in agitation. "Zelda has always underestimated me, and so what would have been the use of contacting her first? She'd only have put more barriers in the way than were already there. Now it is done, and she cannot undo it."

There was a beat of silence between them. Those words hung in the air.

It is done.

Kit looked again around the room, his eyes scanning those lingering shadows at the tables in the far reaches of the pub. Sure enough, his gaze landed upon Diane Ferris, also soot streaked and sitting in the lap of a man that must have been her husband, the fugitive Randall Ferris. She was leaning into him, her grip tight around his neck. Her back was to them, and the man was far too involved in whispering things to his wife to notice any onlookers.

Kit looked back at the Oliviers in bemusement. "Did you burn her house down?"

"Yes, naturally," said Pauline. "Well, I did. Gerard stayed with the horses after we got the body in place. Once they sift the rubble, they will think Diane died in the blaze. They may suspect foul play, but I doubt they will act upon it."

"'The body?" Kit repeated, horrified. "*Whose body?!*"

"Where is Jade?" Gigi said suddenly, her voice sharp as a whip cracking in the air. "I do not see her."

The Oliviers exchanged a glance, and the sound of their daughter's name drew the attention of the Ferrises as well. It had gone silent enough that Kit was hesitant to breathe, lest it draw her scrutiny onto him.

Liberty Lennox gave an impatient sigh and slapped her hands down on the table, pushing herself to her feet. "Well, there we are, it's time to act. Pauline, we really must get on."

"Where is Miss Ferris?" Kit asked, echoing Gigi's sharpness, a twist of dread clutching his gut.

Miss Lennox sighed, rolling her eyes. "She is with the authorities. She is safe, innocent, and awaiting an acceptable guardian to come retrieve her. Poor thing just lost her mother, after all. Now we really *must* get on if we are to get into position before suspicious eyes can land on us."

"Jade is playing her part. She will point to Zelda as her most viable guardian in the wake of the house fire," Mrs. Olivier explained, shooting a disapproving look at Miss Lennox. "It was imperative that she be seen as blameless in all of this, but she knows her mother is not dead. If we are to *meet* with Zelda, we must get to Bond Street before the authorities do. Giselle, I presume you have a key?"

"I do," Gigi said, though she sounded uncertain about the matter of sharing access to that key. "I am not convinced that Zelda would approve of me bringing you into her home, unannounced, at the first rays of dawn."

"Zelda doesn't approve of much of anything," Miss Lennox snapped, turning on her heel to walk toward the Ferrises.

"Which is how we got here in the first place. Diane, darling! Come here; let's get you cleaned up."

Mrs. Ferris came weakly away from her husband's embrace, her eyes puffy and wet, but her feet steady on the ground. She stood in place, rather than crossing over to Miss Lennox's summons. "I wish to go to Bond Street with Pauline," she said. "I will go. I insist."

"That would be most inadvisable, Di," Pauline replied immediately, aghast. "We must get you and Randall out of London before anyone can spot you."

Mrs. Ferris crossed her arms over her narrow chest, jutting her bottom lip out like a rebellious schoolgirl. "I have as much to say to Zelda Smith as you do, Pauline. More, I daresay, and I have kept my silence long enough."

"I would come too," came the raspy, deep voice of Mr. Ferris, who came painfully to his feet to stand beside his wife. He was shockingly thin, Kit thought, and obviously favoring one of his legs over the other. "I would see my daughter."

"Randall," Gerard Olivier replied, exasperated. "We have been through this."

Miss Lennox's foot was tapping impatiently on the soft wooden floors. "Sort it out quickly, please. It is already later than it should be, and we are still mucking about here instead of en route to Bond Street."

"I just want to see her," Randall Ferris said, the plea hanging heavy in his voice. "I have never seen her. My little girl."

"You cannot go to Bond Street," Gerard Olivier repeated. "It is too dangerous for everyone."

"You said she was with the authorities," Kit said, averting his eyes from the abject misery on Randall Ferris's face. "Do you know exactly where?"

"We do," said Pauline, turning to examine Kit. "We had someone follow them away from the fire, lest anything went awry. What difference does it make?"

Kit breathed out heavily, drawing Gigi's eyes up to him as well. "And how much time do you need with Mrs. Smith?"

"Not long. Ideally we would be gone before the authorities arrive with Miss Ferris, just in case they leave a man or two behind to watch the flat. They won't bring her around until they are certain to find people at home and about, so I imagine we have a modest but workable window."

"And is there *any* chance at all that the authorities are already watching Bond Street? Do they have any reason to suspect Zelda's involvement in either the jailbreak or the fire?" KIt pressed, taking a step toward Pauline Olivier. "Any at all?"

It was Mrs. Ferris that answered, her voice breathy and soft, delicate as a fluttering moth. She had come closer to them so quietly that it startled Kit to see her, seemingly several feet from where she ought to be, having popped out of empty air to his right. "None," she said. "I instructed Jade to withhold any idea of a potential guardian until the morning. They likely questioned her at some length before becoming concerned with the prospect of her future, in any event."

"Kit?" Gigi asked, squeezing his arm. "What are you thinking?"

He looked down at her, anchoring himself in the sweetness

of her moss-green gaze. He noted the fuzzy tip of the white feather sticking out of her neckline and felt oddly comforted by it.

Lady Giselle, he thought. Could two more different creatures exist than Kit Cooper and Gigi Dempierre?

Maybe that was why he loved her so much.

She filled all the places that were missing in his own soul. She flooded every crevice and shadow with light.

He looked around the room at the expectant faces of the rogue Silver Leaf agents assembled here. What a fine mess they'd made for themselves, wrought of stubbornness and pride and ego.

Still, a lifetime of cleaning up the messes of Archie Cooper's well-intentioned insanity had made Kit an unmatched tactician in matters of hopelessness, and he *did* have an idea.

It was not a perfect plan. It was rash and impulsive, and it would deprive Kit himself the satisfaction to be had in the room where Pauline and Diane would confront Zelda. Yes, it was less than ideal, but they hadn't time for much else.

He took in as much of Gigi as he could.

It would mean being away from her, for a time. It would mean forfeiting his opportunity to witness the scene at Bond Street, to ask his own questions, and feel satisfied with the answers. It would mean acting a little rashly for the sake of the heart. It meant taking a risk, not only with himself, but with the lives of others.

He placed his hand over hers, where it gripped his arm. The

connection was enough for him to brave the crowd of strangers, the gaggle of criminals, spies, and smugglers with whom he had found himself entangled. He met their eyes, one by one, and described his plan to them, for better or worse.

CHAPTER 27

*B*efore the ride to Bond Street that morning, Gigi would have said with confidence that silence could never make her uncomfortable. She would have believed it, too.

She had wanted to go with Kit and the men. She had even suggested it, willing to give the key to one of the women in safekeeping. Kit had said no. He had given her a hushed and urgent speech about trustworthiness, but secretly, she wondered if perhaps he just wanted some time to himself, in the company of other men.

They had stood together well in the viper's pit earlier, despite all that went unspoken between them. All that might remain unspoken.

She forced herself to swallow, her lips dry and her hands desperate to fidget as they drew to a painfully slow halt outside of Mrs. Smith's Fine Prints. It was dark in the carriage, with the curtains drawn to protect their privacy, at the expense of losing those first, tender rays of sunlight creeping over the skyline.

"I will stay here," said Liberty Lennox, who had yawned no fewer than twelve times on the drive over. "Hold down the fort, keep an eye out, and so on."

"Pull your hood up, Di," said Pauline Olivier, who was doing the same.

Gigi watched them without comment. What would be the point, after all? She very clearly had no power here. All she had was the key. She idly wondered if this was the stolen carriage from the Benton estate. The coat of paint on the doors had looked rather fresh, after all. She supposed it did not matter. Carriage theft was the least of the crimes to which she was currently playing accessory.

She stepped out of the carriage and walked quickly to the door of the shop, assuming that the other women were close at her heels. Her hands did tremor a bit as she unlocked the entry, and her heart jolted when the little bell above the door sounded as she pushed it open. Zelda was going to be furious with her.

She wanted to leave them downstairs, to provide at least a little bit of warning to Mrs. Smith, but with all the large, clean windows down here, it was simply too risky. She ushered them into the narrow staircase at the rear of the shop and followed them up to the flat, wincing at every creak and clatter of footsteps on the stairs.

The foyer of the flat was at least reasonably well lit, with all the curtains still open from the night before, casting dusty shards of orange light onto the furniture. Gigi silently motioned for the two women to take a seat and stood there until they complied. They sat near one another and Diane Ferris put her head on Pauline Olivier's shoulder.

It made Gigi feel guilty, for far too many reasons to list, and rather than ponder upon those reasons, she turned on her heel and walked down the hall to the master bedroom, her hands balled into anxious fists all the way. Even the gentlest knock she could muster sounded like the *twack* of a headman's axe on the block.

It took no time at all. Zelda Smith pulled the door open, bleary-eyed and mussed. She was wearing a man's striped pyjamas and a satin cap. It was her preferred sleepwear, but likely not what she'd prefer to receive guests in. She narrowed her eyes at Gigi, vanishing from the crack in the door for a hurried moment before returning with her half-moon glasses perched on her nose.

"What has happened?" she demanded, her whisper sharp enough to pierce the skin.

"We failed," Gigi replied, attempting to keep the cut of her honesty as bland as possible. "They knew we were coming and locked us in a room. I am sorry. They are here. They want to speak to you."

"Here?" she repeated, a shrillness invading her tone. "In my home?!"

Gigi nodded, opening her mouth to apologize again, but Zelda had already come through the doorway and shoved her aside, marching furiously toward her uninvited guests. Gigi stood frozen for a moment, unsure what to do.

Mrs. Goode appeared next, in her flowery dressing gown. She was frowning, which was most unusual. "I suppose I ought to put a kettle on, then?" she said to Gigi, placing a reassuring hand on her shoulder. "I'll just tug a frock on first, hm? Go out there and keep an eye on them, my love."

She gave her a slight nudge, without which Gigi was certain she would have just stood stock-still in the hallway for the rest of her life.

She expected to find a battle scene when she rounded the corner, with all three women rearing their claws at one another. What she found was quite the opposite.

Diane Ferris was embracing Zelda Smith with what looked like considerable strength. She was more than a head shorter than Zelda, and held her around the ribs, little hiccups of emotion sounding in her chest. Zelda, much to Gigi's surprise, was letting it happen, her hands resting awkwardly on the other woman's shoulders and a suspicious glimmering of emotion flashing behind her spectacles.

When Mrs. Ferris released Zelda, she sniffled happily and shuffled back to Pauline's side, plopping onto the settee with all the weight of a gust of wind.

"Zelda," Pauline said gently, her expression somewhere between amusement and wistfulness. "You look well."

"Oh, I do not," Zelda snapped, swiping her spectacles away so that she could rub her eyes. She dropped herself into her favorite chair, crossing her arms over her chest and frowning at her friends. "You French and your lies."

"You English and your foibles," Pauline replied, winning a begrudging twitch of the corners of Zelda's lips and another hearty sniffle.

Gigi stood a distance away, not wishing to infringe on this

reunion, nor knowing her role in it. She felt keenly sad for the sake of her mother, who really should be sat amongst her dearest friends, rather than tucked away in Kent, ignorant to all that was happening.

Mrs. Goode floated past, nodding politely to the two strange women on her furniture on her way to make tea. Gigi thought that it was amusing, that her first thought had been to make tea. Mrs. Goode had a very strict sense of proper British manners, it seemed.

"It only needed to wait another few weeks," Zelda was saying to Pauline, who was shaking her head vehemently.

"It waited twenty years, Zelda, and Gerard and I couldn't linger here any longer. It's done now. There's no taking it back, and your own plots are unaffected."

"Oh, certain about that, are you?" Zelda replied acerbically. "There is no saying what is or isn't affected yet. You realize you may have led the authorities directly to my door by coming here?"

"Yes," said Mrs. Ferris. "They will be here soon, so we cannot tarry."

"What?!"

Pauline allowed herself a chuckle at Zelda's outrage, leaning back in her chair to observe Zelda's pique. "Jade Ferris must not be implicated in her father's escape or her mother's erm ... suspicious death. She will ask the authorities to bring her here, so that you may serve as her temporary guardian."

Zelda stared at the other women, one and then the other, disbelief writ clearly on her face. "I'm no one's guardian!"

she blurted out, just as Harriet Goode rounded the corner with a tray of steaming teacups.

"That's not true, my dear," Harriet said gently, smiling to the interlopers as she handed them their saucers. "You looked after Nell more often than her own parents did coming up."

"Nell was raised in a boarding school!" Zelda retorted, staring at the teacup being offered to her like it might bite her.

"You owe it to me," Diane Ferris said, her eyes flashing with something of maternal ferocity. "All three of you do. You must protect my daughter until she is no longer in danger. You must help her acquire her inheritance, and then, when it is finally safe, you must aid her in coming to find us. I kept our secrets and endured imprisonment and now you owe it to me. All three of you, as I said."

"All three of us?" Zelda repeated, baffled.

"You. Therese. And Mar—" Mrs. Ferris hesitated, blinking rapidly and falling into silence. "No," she remembered. "Mary is gone, isn't she? Gone."

Zelda looked stunned, momentarily startled to silence as her friend struggled with the realities of the here and now.

"Poor Mary," Diane whispered to herself.

Pauline raised her eyes and burned her gaze into Zelda. It seemed to give her some vindication, to force Zelda to witness what had become of the friend they had left behind.

"I hated that you were there, Diane," Zelda confessed, her voice gone ragged. "I sent what aid I could, but it wasn't enough. It wasn't enough. I am so sorry."

"Sweet Zelda," Diane said, her gaze a little dreamy in the wake of her confusion. "Softness wrapped in iron, like I always said."

Zelda nodded, pressing her lips into a flat line.

"So you will do this for us?" Pauline pressed, wrapping her fingers around Diane's hand. "You will care for Jade, and ensure she is given what she is owed? You will assist her in finding us, when the time comes?"

Zelda inhaled deeply, her reluctance still clear on her face. She seemed to be looking for the right words to decline. She looked away from her friends only to find Mrs. Goode, standing nearby, her arms crossed and her face stony. It made all the air she'd drawn in flee her lungs in acquiescence.

"Yes," she promised, a dry, defeated chuckle sounding somewhere in the hollow of her chest. "Yes, you are right. I owe it to you, Diane. I owe it to Randall. And I owe it to Jade, too, I suppose."

Gigi felt like she might faint, like all the blood in her body had been pooled in her feet as she anticipated the outcome of this confrontation, and now it was flooding back into the rest of her far too quickly.

"There, that's nice, isn't it?" Harriet said happily. "Shall I fetch some pastries, or are you ladies on a tight schedule?"

"No pastries, I'm afraid," said Pauline Olivier, glancing gratefully first at Harriet and then again at Zelda, "but we will stay and finish our tea. For old time's sake, hm, Zelda? I have missed this. I have missed us."

For a moment, Gigi thought something had gone horribly

wrong, that Zelda's lips were pulling back in anger, that she was baring her teeth at the others, prepared to unveil some horrible *coup de grace*.

It was so strange that it took her a moment to process what she was seeing, and for years later, she would doubt she had seen it at all.

That morning was the first and only time that Gigi ever saw Zelda Smith truly smile.

~

GIGI SAT in the sun-drenched foyer, staring at those three empty cups of tea, for a long time after they departed. She fussed with the edge of the fabric covering her birdcage, but did not wish to wake them, even though she could have dearly used the company.

Zelda had accompanied the other two women downstairs, to ensure they were safely in their carriage and away. Likely there were things they wished to say to one another in privacy, as well.

They had left behind a small cloth sack, filled with some items meant for Jade. It bulged temptingly on the central table by the settee, but Gigi knew better than to open it. It wasn't for her. None of this was for her. Not anymore.

When Harriet came in to collect the teacups, and saw Gigi sitting where she was, her stare likely vacant-looking and maudlin, she stopped in her chore and immediately sat down. "Did you get any sleep at all, last night?" she asked, pulling Gigi's hands into her lap.

"Some," Gigi confessed absently. "With Kit."

Harriet raised her brows, but did not otherwise respond to this scandalous piece of information. Instead, she said, "It likely wasn't enough sleep, poppet. You ought to go get a few more hours in."

"I cannot sleep. Not until it is over..." She trailed off, raising her eyes to meet Mrs. Goode's. "Everything is so very sad."

The other woman sighed, giving a begrudging little nod. "If you live long enough, you'll have regrets too, my love. We can only hope that they won't be the same ones your elders already made."

"I haven't sent anyone to prison just yet."

Harriet chortled, giving a shake of her brassy curls. "Zelda didn't send them to prison, though, did she?"

"No. But she left them there, all the same."

"She did what she could, when she could," Harriet corrected. "The Bentons would not send money to Mrs. Ferris, so it was Zelda who did. She sent tutors for the girl, paid for a chef so that they would not go hungry. She stationed her own people on guard duty when she could, and all along she knew it was not enough. She could never bring herself to go visit, to look Diane in the eye. It was too terrifying. Too painful."

"Does Zelda feel pain?" Gigi asked, sounding hollow even to her own ear. "She seems so ... cold."

"She is anything but cold, I assure you. She laughs and cries, the same as any of us, and if you ask me, she made this whole ordeal far more difficult for herself than it needed to be, because she avoided facing it head-on."

Gigi winced, Kit's face flashing into her mind. "Sometimes it's impossible to know what to say," she countered lamely.

Harriet considered her, sitting back a bit to examine the younger woman in the brightening sunlight. Her eyes were clear and canny, as though she could see through Gigi's very skin, down to the aching in her soul.

The mission was over now. If she went to sleep, it would be more than over. She might wonder if it had ever happened at all.

"You should know that Zelda never intended to let the Ferris family's imprisonment go on for so very long," she said, tone careful and nonjudgemental. "Do you know why it happened? Because at first, it was too risky to the others, and then there was a child to think of, and then something else, and another thing, and so on. It became like a pile of dust that needs sweeping and only grows larger and larger the more one ignores it, which only makes it all the more daunting, all the more tempting to ignore."

"Are you saying Kit is my pile of dust?"

Harriet chuckled, and reached over to pat her hand. "Something like that, my dear girl. Say, do you remember, roundabout a week ago, the night we sat out here with our pudding and I read poetry to you? Do you remember the poem?"

Gigi nodded, another twang thrumming in her tired heart. It had been beautiful poetry, and she'd read it over again before sleeping that night, filled with thoughts of romance and passion. *"Someone, I tell you, will remember us,"* she quoted, *"even in another time."*

Harriet nodded. "That particular poet was remarkably wise. Another verse I think of often reads, *What cannot be said must be wept.* I have recited it to Zelda many times, and this morning, I believe I was proven correct, hm? Save yourself the tears, love. It will come out, one way or another."

Gigi glanced out the window, wondering if one of the black coaches that passed by was the one taking Pauline and Diane to their next destination, to safety. Would she be sent back *La Falaise* right away? Would she be expected to return to life the way it was?

Harriet squeezed her hands one last time before coming to her feet. "Maybe a quick wash and a new dress will perk you up, if you won't sleep," she suggested. "We should be at our best to welcome Miss Ferris when she arrives, after all."

Gigi nodded, staring out the window for a touch longer before bracing herself to act.

What can't be said must be wept, she thought.

Silence would not serve her this time.

CHAPTER 28

"Well, have you asked her to marry you?" Gerard Olivier pried, squinting at Kit in what appeared to be true bafflement. "You can't know what she'll say until you ask."

"It is not that easy for all of us, Gerard," Randall Ferris said with a wheezy laugh. "I had to write my own proposal in a letter, for fear of swallowing my tongue if I attempted to deliver it the traditional way."

"Bah," Gerard huffed in disgust.

"I can't propose until I have things in order," Kit explained, for the dozenth time this morning. "Right now, too much is in the wind, especially with my mother's impending nuptials. A man must be established to wed."

The three men were hunched in a heavily shadowed alleyway opposite a gray brick building where the authorities were holding Jade Ferris. They had waited in silence for the first hour or so, staring at the void of inactivity across the street. Randall Ferris was using the wall to support the modest weight of his body, his injured leg resting against the good one. Kit had done his best to convince Gerard to stay behind for this, but as was apparent, he had failed.

Kit wasn't certain when they had begun to ply him with questions about Gigi and their mission together, nor could he rightly account for why he'd been answering the questions with such bald-faced honesty, but to be frank, it was a relief to have it off his chest. Nate and his mother were the only people he'd ever really been able to confide in, and neither seemed rightly suited for his current conundrum.

Besides, he was reasonably certain he'd never have to face either of these men again, after this morning, so why not humiliate himself?

"Women like *big, flamboyant* declarations of affection!" Gerard was telling him, his French accent thickening with passion for this message. "No red-blooded lady is stirred by ... by words on paper."

"Oh, I beg to differ," Randall Ferris said quietly, a bit of a smirk on his sallow face. "There's a lot about women you've never understood, my friend."

"Bah," repeated Gerard, drawing his bushy eyebrows together.

"It likely very much depends on the woman in question," Kit suggested in his most calming voice.

"Precisely so," Randall agreed, "and if this is the woman for you, then you know to what she will best respond. I daresay it isn't waiting for you to secure a new townhouse, however."

"Agreed on that much," grumbled the Frenchman with a curt nod.

"You would have me bring my new bride to my mother's home?" Kit asked in disbelief. "That's hardly befitting."

"It is such a shame," mused Randall Ferris, gazing once again at the stone building across from them, "that rental properties no longer exist for exactly such purposes. Truly, the world has much changed whilst I have been locked away."

"It just hardly seems fitting," Kit muttered, "carrying your bride over the threshold of a rented property."

"If you think the girl would prefer delaying the start of her life because of escrow, I suppose you know her better than I," Randall replied, a wry smile on his tired lips.

Gerard chuckled, nudging Kit in the ribs, and seemed to be gearing up to add his own commentary when, at long last, there appeared to be movement happening across the way. It immediately cast a net of silence over the three men, tension thrumming through the space between them in the narrow stone nook.

A stout man in blue came out, blowing warm air into his hands as he made his way to a small carriage station, unlocking the paddock and setting about readying a transport for the morning.

They watched him for what must have been no more than a quarter of an hour, though Kit thought it stretched on for an eternity. Finally, a bucket-shaped carriage, pulled by two rather shoddy-looking mounts, clipped out of the paddock and came to a halt. The stout man hopped out of the interior and shuffled back into the building, likely to retrieve the others.

Beside him, Kit heard Randall Ferris draw his breath in, sharp and anxious, his knobby hands clenching the fabric of his trousers.

When the door opened again, Jade Ferris appeared, flanked on either side by dour-faced men. She was dressed in prim, pressed blue. Her head was bare, her long hair hanging loose around her arms, and though she kept her eyes lowered, her posture was not that of a woman who had been cowed. She turned to the carriage, nodding absently at something muttered to her by one of the two men.

It wasn't until they stepped in front of her, setting about the business of instructing the driver and readying the carriage for its journey, that Jade seemed to feel something in the air around her, something more than just the crisp bite of early morning. She turned, just a bit, her eyes scanning the surroundings, a curious little frown playing about her lips.

Somehow, Kit realized, she knew they were there.

He stood, motioning to the other two men that they must stay put. Gerard narrowed his eyes at him, clearly disapproving of this development, but Randall Ferris barely moved at all. His eyes were locked on his child.

Kit set his jaw, brushing the dirt and dust from his trousers and stepping out into the sunlight, striding quickly in the direction of the carriage. He tucked his hands into his pockets, forcing a light tune to the surface in a whistle as he got closer, stepping directly into Jade Ferris's line of vision.

"Mr. Cooper?" she said, bafflement on her face. Then louder, "Mr. Cooper! Hello there!"

Kit performed a double take and a swing around in his

stride that he thought would have satisfied even Miss Lennox's standard of performance. "Miss Ferris!" he called back, smiling in seeming surprise and delight as he made his way over to her. "Good morning to you! What brings you to Mayfair?"

"Ah," she replied, glancing at the carriage and the impatient faces of her companions. "I am to visit a friend of my mother's for a time. I'm afraid we are already running rather late, despite the early hour."

"Well, don't let me keep you," he demurred, nodding respectfully at the two men. He met Jade's eyes and flicked his glance quickly (and he dearly hoped, imperceptibly) to the alley where her father was hidden. "Perhaps we will cross paths again soon. Good morning to you!"

"And to you, Mr. Cooper," she replied, her voice trailing off as she gazed over his shoulder, peering into the shadows of the little nook.

Kit took his leave, making a loop around the block. When he looked back over his shoulder, the men escorting Jade Ferris were pulling her into the carriage while she continued to look at the streets in the distance. He could not see her face, only a light limpness to her posture, until she turned to step into the carriage. He thought, in that brief moment, that he spotted a quiet smile on her lips; subdued but there, all the same.

It was unlikely she had been able to clearly see her father, and even less likely that she would know that it was he who was waiting for her, there in the shadows. Wasn't it? Could she have guessed? He realized that he dearly hoped so, that perhaps there was an unspoken magic between parent and child that had transcended the need for words here this morning.

By the time Kit rounded back to the other side of the alley and hurried back to the other two men, the shabby carriage had already departed for Bond Street and presumably Jade Ferris's new life.

Gerard was leaning back against the wall, an arm slung around his old friend's shoulders, as Randall Ferris sat trembling, holding his face in his hands. Kit stood a bit away from them, uncertain if he should speak or act in any particular way. He opted to lean against the opposite wall, and allow Mr. Ferris the time he needed. The tell-tale sniffling, muffled in the other man's hands, made Kit feel curiously weepy himself. He rubbed the tip of his nose to stifle an answering sniffle and gazed up at the bright morning sky.

After all, he had no idea what it might be to see one's daughter for the very first time, especially if she had already grown to womanhood without him.

"There, now, I told you there was nothing to worry about," Gerard said with a gruff gentleness. "She looks nothing like you. Thanks be to God."

Randall gave a little tremor of laughter, coming up from his hands and wiping at his eyes. "She is perfect. Beautiful. Striking. What did you say to her?"

"I only bid her good morning," Kit told him. "I don't know if she could see you or not, but I think she knew you were there."

"She knew enough," Gerard Olivier said. "She felt your love on the wind."

Randall's lips curled into a sad smile, his eyes still swimming with emotion. "I hope she did," he confessed, heaving a deep breath and reaching up for Kit's assistance in standing. "I dearly hope she did."

"Jade is strong," Kit told him, heaving the other man to his feet and supporting him as he found his balance. Their transport was not terribly far away, but Mr. Ferris still required a bit of help in moving. "She should make you proud."

"Of course I'm proud," he replied as they began the walk back to the carriage. "I was proud of my daughter from the very moment she made herself known in the womb. You, however, Mr. Cooper, will have to prove yourself."

"Oh?" Kit glanced at Gerard, who simply grinned back at him, striding along next to them in obvious good spirits. "I rather thought this caper itself would have given me some legitimacy."

"Some," agreed Mr. Ferris with a little nod. "But you'll need to settle that business with your girl if you want our full respect."

"Agreed," said Gerard Olivier. "I'm afraid your very honor relies upon it."

Kit chuckled, maybe a little bit emboldened by the absolute certainty of these two old men. "Well, I suppose that's a challenge I can't ignore."

"Indeed not," agreed Mr. Ferris. "Godspeed, young man."

"*Bonchance*," agreed Mr. Olivier.

Kit said his good-byes and watched the carriage clip away,

taking the men to their next port. Those men, engaged in an ongoing drama of evasion and danger, had wished *him* luck.

He laughed again, turning in the direction of Bond Street.

He supposed he was going to need it.

~

Mrs. Smith's Fine Prints came into view at the end of the street, eclipsing the rising sun so that brilliant rays appeared to spray out from either side of the place. Kit had spent most of the walk over shaking a muddle of words and fragments of sentences about in his head. He had never been much of an orator, and Gigi had that way of simply waiting for a person to come up with something to say, polite and a little amused, blinking those big green eyes in expectation.

He had taken his jacket off, and had it over his arm. The air was cool, yes, but Kit found it a welcome bit of stimulation after a night of sparse sleeping and heightened emotions. Perhaps he should have gone back to Marylebone and slept. He certainly would have benefitted from approaching this task well rested and clear minded. Assuming, of course, that sleep was even possible with this task looming ahead of him. (He was reasonably certain it was not.)

He wondered, as he approached, how chaotic the atmosphere at Bond Street was, with Jade Ferris presumably arrived, and the household in the wake of Zelda's plans having gone to ash.

No one, he thought, could accuse him of waiting for the most favorable conditions. Not anymore. He was hard-pressed to imagine a worse time for what he intended, short of perhaps storming up to a woman already halfway through her vows on the altar with professions of love. Bag the matter of property, fortune, or prospects when even the basic luxuries of clean clothes, a rested body, and a welcoming family were not even available.

He couldn't suppress an ironic laugh, running a hand through his hopelessly tousled hair, and braced himself. He tugged open the door to the shop, waved at Harriet Goode, and charged his way toward the rear door. If he stopped to think, he might lose his nerve. He did not, however, have the confidence to simply burst through the front door and demand an audience with Gigi.

So he took a deep breath, and contented himself to knock.

CHAPTER 29

The bath was heaven sent.

So divine was the experience of dipping her tired bones into sweet, steaming water, that Gigi became quite insensible of the passage of time, only moving to begin the process of actual bathing once she noticed that the water was beginning to cool.

Even the sensations of lathering and the smell of lily and gardenia in the soap cake felt decadent. She massaged it into her tired muscles, sliding her fingers down the lines of her shoulders and the tender bits of her neck. She took utter luxury in the process of massaging the suds into her hair, pulling the dust and knots out, all at once, completely taken by the tiny universe she had found in a simple bathtub.

Her eyelids had grown heavier as she washed, her thoughts beginning already to drift toward the insensible clash of ideas and images that made up her dreams. She might have allowed herself to slip entirely into slumber, right there in the water, if not for the sound of voices and the clamor of heavy footsteps that made their way through the door.

She hastened through drying herself, dragging the fluffy warmth of the towels over her limbs and wrapping it tightly around the hair that hung over her shoulder. She selected a whisper-soft shift, dry and clean, to pull over her head, and wrapped her dressing gown over it for good measure, listening at the door until the sound of men's voices had gone, and the tell-tale click of the latch had confirmed that Zelda had sealed their entry behind them.

She gave it an extra moment, not wishing to interfere if Zelda and Jade were having a private exchange in their first moment alone, but as soon as she found herself dozing against the weight of the door, she forced herself alert again, and exited the room, taking up the towel over her shoulder again to continue wringing the water out of her sodden golden mane.

"Gigi!" called Miss Ferris, who came immediately to her feet from her position next to Zelda on the settee. "I was just meeting your birds. How very grand they are, and so handsome! The blue one sang me a song."

"Did he, now?" Gigi replied with amusement, reaching out to grasp Jade's hands in welcome. "Well, do not trust him. He sings for all the girls."

"I do not mind," she replied with a giggle, squeezing back with a shine in her eyes that looked to Gigi like pure and untainted happiness.

Zelda came to her feet, knocking back the final dregs in her teacup and then letting it dangle by its handle on her finger as she brushed biscuit crumbs off her morning dress. "Giselle, I am going to take Jade down for breakfast and to commission a few items of clothing. I'm afraid the majority of her belongings were destroyed in the fire, and her mother was more concerned with preserving old knickknacks than items her daughter might actually need to use."

Jade pressed her lips together, like she was stifling another giggle. On the couch, the sack that had been left for Jade was on its side, spilling out the edges of something made of fabric, and something else of gleaming brass.

"Might you lend her a frock?" Zelda continued, impatient and perhaps a little irritated that Gigi's eyes had wandered toward said knickknacks rather than tut-tutting Mrs. Ferris for her lack of pragmatism. "Just for a day or two. Poor thing is rather disheveled."

"Yes, of course, of course," Gigi agreed, clasping Jade's hand and motioning in the direction of the bedroom that they would likely be sharing from this night forward. "I'm just out of the bath if you want to rinse at all. It looks like the soot only landed on your dress, I'd say."

Jade followed, demure and appreciative, and expressed true glee in the choice of a bright, yellow dress as the one she would borrow. She was shorter than Gigi, and narrower, but the fit would be well enough for a short time, until she could have her own things made. The dress had a matching ribbon, stitched with white, but Gigi hadn't any idea how to approach the styling of Jade's wild frizz of waist-length hair, so instead, they contented to tie it at her nape, the way she had always done, which pleased Jade Ferris perfectly fine.

All the while, Gigi had to bite her tongue on the questions

brimming in her chest. She wanted every detail of what had occurred last night, to follow every moment of their grand escape. She wanted to ask questions about Jade's future and the Silver Leaf and what she knew and what she wanted, but she also knew that this was not the time to bombard the other girl. It was not the time to ask a question that could puncture her perfect optimism in this moment, and so she smiled and held her words until Jade was dressed for the day.

"Won't you come with us?" she asked Gigi, covertly glancing at her reflection, seemingly in awe of how she looked in the yellow silk.

"I cannot. I'm afraid I didn't sleep much last night and I am rather exhausted. I must catch up on sleep."

"Oh," Jade said, turning those big, round eyes onto Gigi, "I suppose I should do the same. It is strange, but I don't feel tired at all. Isn't that strange?"

Gigi laughed, assuring her that excitement can conquer many other weaknesses of the frail human body, and wished her a tasty breakfast and a thrilling trip to the modiste.

Almost the instant she was alone in the bedroom again, Gigi flung off her dressing gown and climbed into the bed, throwing the blankets up around her chin and giving a long, satisfied sigh as her tired bones sank into the mattress. She had twisted her wet hair into a sloppy braid, which would likely irk her in her waking hours, after it had dried all wrong, but in this moment, nothing at all mattered but the sweet, seductive call of slumber, and the satisfaction of letting her heavy eyelids, at long last, fall shut.

She could hear conversation between Zelda and Jade

beyond the door, not loud enough to be disruptive. It was oddly comforting, even.

She smiled into her pillow, wondering if Kit was sound asleep in the house in Marylebone, his bones toppled every which way into the bed like hers were. She wondered if he thought of her as he'd slipped into slumber, if he missed having her tucked into the crook of his arm. After last night, Gigi was certain she'd never be happy with an evening routine again, unless she could fall asleep next to Kit Cooper's warm scent, strong body, and steady breath.

She sighed, rolling onto her other side, flashes of Kit so heavy in her drowsy mind that she could swear she almost heard his voice. She loved his voice.

The front door gave its tell-tale rattle and click, its lock sliding back into place as Jade and Zelda departed for their morning errands, and for a sweet, single moment, there was nothing but the cooing of her birds and the stirring of the dust that danced in the beams of light coming in through the cracks in her curtains.

Then, so suddenly it nearly startled her out of her very flesh, she heard Kit's voice calling her name. "Gigi?" he said, uncertain. "Are you in here?"

"Kit?" she choked back, flying up to be seated and grasping the coverlet in her fists. "Is that you?"

He turned the knob of the bedroom door and pushed it open, frozen immediately in his tracks upon the realization that he had disturbed her at slumber. "Oh!" he cried, mortified. "My apologies. I can come back later."

"No, no," she insisted, flinging the blanket away and rubbing her eyes with the heels of her hands. "No, come in. Please."

He hesitated in the doorway until she shot him a look, patting the bed in obvious invitation.

Surely he could not be scandalized by her anymore? Yes, once again, he had come upon her with wet hair and a single layer of clothing, but after all this time, it hardly bore a gasp, much less any real sign of scandal. She stifled a little laugh at the thought, and said again, "Come in!"

He frowned at her and stalked in, leaving the door cracked open as though this gesture would still afford them some sliver of virtue, and perched himself on the bottom corner of the mattress, which groaned under his weight. "You must be tired," he said helplessly.

"Tired, yes, but also desperate to talk about everything that has happened! I sat here next to Jade Ferris, brimming with a thousand questions, and couldn't ask a single one of them. I stood there while three Silver Leaf founders convened, and couldn't bring myself to get a single word in. Finally, you are here and I may speak without worry."

He blinked at her, an uncertain half smile creeping onto his face. "I am pleased to be your confidant. What did you wish to discuss?"

"Oh, God, where to even start." She sighed, shaking her head in wonder. "Well, between us, I suppose. Last night."

"Yes?"

She blinked at him, impatient. "We made love."

"We did," he agreed, that faint amusement still on his face.

"I rather enjoyed it," she said, lifting her chin, even if she was making a fool of herself.

"So did I," he replied, "and I'm sorry if I gave you any impression otherwise during the chaos this morning. I'm afraid I got a little frantic."

"Hm." She considered him, pursing her lips in consideration. "Such behavior might make a girl think you do not wish to repeat the experience."

"Oh, I absolutely want to repeat the experience," he assured her. "In fact, that is why I'm here."

"What?!" she said, startled out of her coquette act. "Here? In Zelda's flat?"

At that, he did laugh, a great boom of startled amusement that vibrated in his chest.

"Good God, no!" he assured her, gasping for breath. "Well ... actually ... no. No, not now. That's not what I meant. What I was trying to say is that I very much enjoyed making love to you, and further all of the time that we've spent together, alone in one another's company over the last weeks, and I was wondering if you wouldn't want to make the whole affair a bit more respectable?"

"Respectable?" she repeated, baffled. "You think we aren't respectable?"

"Gigi," he said, scooting closer so he could reach for her hands, amusement still sparkling in his eyes but his voice deeper and more serious. "I am ... well, I suppose I am hoping you will marry me. I am *asking* you to marry me."

"Because of respectability?!" she balked.

He laughed again, leaning forward and capturing the quickest kiss from her mouth. "No, Gigi, because I am in love with you, but you have to admit that the respectability will certainly benefit us as well."

"Oh." She sat back, her hands gone limp in his. "Well, yes, I think I would like that very much."

He examined her expression, a flicker of worry flashing over his face. "I know that the question of what our lives would be is still not firmly defined, but as I saw it, on my walk over, perhaps it is better that we build it, choice by choice, together, so that it makes us both happy, rather than just me. I want to make you happy, and to be frank, I also want to hoist some of the stress of decision-making off onto another person."

She laughed, seeing by the earnestness in his expression that everything he had just said was entirely true. "We are of enough means to build a life together," she told him, "and we are in love. What more should we wait for?"

"That," he said with a sigh, "is truly the question of the day, and I've decided the answer is that we needn't wait at all."

"Well, what sort of wedding do you want to have?" she asked. "When?"

"I haven't decided that either, believe it or not," he told her, sounding just as surprised by this as she was. "We could get a license to marry here in London if you wanted to stay for a few weeks, or we could go back to Kent and marry in our home parish, I suppose."

"No," she said quickly, "no, I am not ready to go back to

Kent. I can't stand the idea of going back to the way things were."

"Well," he said thoughtfully, "we could always elope."

"Elope? To where?"

"Scotland is the usual place, I believe. That is where Nate and Nell wed, in some little hamlet just over the border from where they already were, though I think most folk head for Gretna Green. We can legally marry anywhere in Scotland on a whim, so there are many options."

"Scotland," she said, dreamy images of crumbling castles and endless vales expanding in her mind. "Have you been?"

"No, never."

This delighted her, her whole posture giving a little leap of anticipation from her seat on the bed. "Have you ever *considered* going?"

He gave a sheepish smile. "I haven't."

"Hmm." She bit down on her lip, squeezing her hands around his. "I suppose it would be *very* out of character for you to arrive in a place, and then figure out what you're doing there."

"Very," he agreed.

She gave a little squeal of delight. "Then it is perfect, isn't it? Scotland! How would we get there?"

"Well," he said, rubbing the back of her hand with the pad of his thumb as he suppressed a grin, "I've recently inherited a stolen carriage and a pair of horses. One stop to my banker here in London, and we could comfortably travel the Highlands for as long as you like, and after that ... well, I suppose we will figure it out. Together."

Gigi stared at him a moment, a burst of energy flooding through her veins that all but banished the languid, persistent need for slumber that had been plaguing her only moments ago. "I shall pack right now," she decided, flinging her legs over the side of the bed.

When she went to stand, he tugged her close once more, planting a firm kiss on her lips before he released her, a kiss that became softer for a moment, only a moment, before she forced herself to pull away.

"I shall leave a letter for Zelda," she decided, flinging open the wardrobe and tugging out her valise. "Oh, Kit, I am beside myself with excitement."

"So am I," he confessed gently.

She turned to him, holding a dress to her body with a conspiratorial little smile. "Do you recall, Kit Cooper, that when we first were acquainted, that all I wanted in the world was to make you my friend? How shortsighted I was back then!"

"We *are* friends!" he said, smiling at her.

"Are we?" she answered, a teasing lilt in her voice. "Lovers, confidantes, and friends too? My, what a complex thing we've built."

"Yes," he agreed, as though it were the simplest thing in the world. "Do you really not know how I feel?"

"I think I do," she said, pouting her lips in mock coyness. "But you might as well tell me anyhow."

Kit stood, crossing the room and cupping her cheek in his hand, gazing down at her with the sort of raw affection that nearly sent her knees buckling out from under her. "Gigi," he said, sighing. "You are my dearest friend in all the world."

EPILOGUE

Mrs. Gigi Cooper had always loved weddings. She had attended over a dozen in the last month alone.

Her husband had come to refer to their honeymoon period, spanning the months over the various moors and counties of the Scottish countryside, as "matrimonial tourism."

It seemed every town they landed in had a happy couple, all too willing to allow them to join in the day's festivities. Whether it was coincidence or some uncanny magnetism connected to their presence was a matter of some debate, but regardless, it had been a most joyful type of serendipity.

They had seen seaside weddings and vows on rolling hills, they had hiked to the peak of a small mountain to watch two people be joined, and had run from the rain into a cozy chapel in a rustic hamlet. They had sat in the pew of a grand church in Aberdeen and watched a wealthy bride take her husband, and had danced with an ancient clan whose heir had finally found his match. They had cheered through autumn leaves and drifts of snow, and headed back down through England in the first days of spring, always listening for wedding bells on the wind.

Today, though. Today's wedding was special.

Everything Gigi had learned about weddings was in motion today, from the styling of the bouquet to the arrangement of the dining chairs to the music that awaited them back in the grand ballroom at Meridian house. She stood with the groom, ensuring the spray of blossoms in his coat pocket was perfectly arranged, while his daughter looked on in amusement.

"Papa, truly," said Isabelle Applegate, "I do not think you could be in better hands."

"I look like a *croquembouche*," Yves Monetier responded with a twinkle and a wink, allowing the ladies to fuss over him to their hearts' content.

To which Isabelle responded, "Mm, delicious!"

Some might expect that Gigi's own wedding was just as meticulous and grand, but in truth, it had been rather modest, in a little church just over the border, with an array of strangers they had charmed in the local inn as witnesses. That was the thing about weddings, as Gigi would happily explain to strangers and friends alike. It was impossible to wed without charm in the air and beauty on the ground around them. Simple or elaborate, modest or lavish, each one was an exercise in joy, a moment in life that everyone would remember, always.

Gigi excused herself, hurrying to the ground level, where several guests were milling around, making conversation as they awaited the walk to the church. She spoke to the vicar and turned to scuttle over to the musicians, only to find herself halted by a strong arm around her middle and the unexpected embrace of her brother, finally returned from his business in Lisbon.

"Halt there, Mrs. Cooper," he said, giving her a tight squeeze. "At least give me a brief hello."

"Mathias!" she cried, throwing her arms around his neck. "Oh, you've arrived at exactly the right moment."

"That is what I said," agreed Therese Dempierre, appearing at their side with a glass of wine in her hand. "It is almost as though he sat just short of the shore until the latest possible moment."

"Nonsense, *Maman*," said Mathias, putting his sister down and grinning at their mother. "Business in Lisbon simply took a very, very long time."

Gigi and Therese made identical noises of skepticism, which only widened his grin. Mathias had a talent for vanishing to sunnier locales throughout the winter months, almost without fail.

"I wish to hear all about it," Gigi told him, "but it will need to wait. *Maman*, have you seen the bride? I've asked the vicar to start herding guests to the church, if you wouldn't mind assisting with that."

"She is in the master suite, fretting as brides do," Therese said with a careless shrug, followed by a grimacing glance at her own husband, drinking alone in the distance. "Some brides," she amended, making her children both stifle the impulse to laugh.

"Ah, *mes enfants*." Therese Dempierre sighed, leaning forward to embrace them both. "I love you both so very much. You make it all worthwhile, my precious ones. Never doubt it."

Meanwhile, up the stairs and beyond the door of the master chamber, Kit Cooper was standing dutifully in the corner of the room, watching as his mother frowned at herself in the large mirror, fussing at the tulle ruffles on the sleeves of her sky-blue gown.

"I am too old for this dress," she fretted. "I look ridiculous."

"You love that dress," he reminded her. "It matches your eyes."

She gave a begrudging smile, glancing over her shoulder at her son. She was glowing with happiness, white flowers woven into her golden hair and color high in her cheeks. "I do, don't I? I suppose if there's any day I'm allowed to look ridiculous, it is today."

"I could not agree more," he told her, "which means it is quite a waste that you look lovely and elegant instead."

"Oh, stop," she huffed, waving her hand and turning back to her reflection with a pleased sparkle in her eye all the same. "You know, I can't help but think about Archie today; about what he'd think of all of this."

"What do you mean?" he asked, concern creeping into his voice. "Do you think he would keep you a lonely widow for the rest of your days?"

"No, it's not that." She sighed, pressing the backs of her hands to her cheeks. "I suppose I never knew what Archie was thinking, even when he was here and I could ask."

"But you want his approval?" Kit closed the distance between them, laying a reassuring hand on her shoulder.

She gave a little smile and blinked, tilting her eyes upward to avoid the spill of tears. "Well, of course I do, silly boy. I love your father. I always will."

Kit nodded, and for a moment, he, too, felt the memory of Archie Cooper, like a light mist in the air. And, perhaps even stranger, he found the feeling reassuring. "He loved you so much," he told his mother, turning her to look at him, "and all he wanted in all the world was to make everyone happy, most of all you."

She sniffled, wiping away an errant tear that escaped down her cheek. "That's true, isn't it? He was always trying to make everyone happy."

"A losing battle if there ever was one," KIt whispered, making her laugh. "But he did try, and I think that makes his blessing for your new life implicit. You chose a good man, and you have my blessing as well."

"Imagine," she whispered, as though the powers that be might overhear, "both of us marrying French."

"Truly an outrageous scandal," he replied somberly.

A knock at the door drew their attention as Gigi poked her head through. "It is time," she said, with overt and barely contained excitement. "We must make for the church."

Susan Cooper inhaled a shaky breath and nodded, gathering the skirts of her blue wedding dress in her hands. "I am ready," she said, looking from her son to her daughter-in-law and back again, and nodded. "I am ready."

Together they followed her down the stairs and into the foyer of Meridian House, their hands linking together as though by instinct.

"Are *you* ready?" Gigi whispered to her husband, once they had fallen far enough behind to not be overheard.

"I am," he realized, turning a bright smile onto his wife. "I would say I am even happy about it, here on the morning of the event. Everything will be different now, and I suspect that will continue to be true with every year that passes."

"Mm," she agreed, "and you no longer worry about the unexpected? Fear that which has not been excessively prepared for?"

"Not so long as you're around," he told her, lifting her hand up to drop a kiss onto her knuckles as they walked out onto the lawn.

She stopped, tugging at their linked hands to have him stop as well. She turned her big green eyes up at him and flashed her dimpled smile. "Good," she said. "Because I have a surprise for you."

"Oh?"

"Mhm." She nodded, drawing his hand down to press against her abdomen, and waited, watching his face for the realization to dawn upon him. "Don't worry," she said as his eyes widened and his alarmed expression rose to meet her gaze again. "We'll have months to prepare."

He exhaled, his body deflating so quickly that it made his head spin. "Good. That's good," he said, leaning forward to press a kiss into her lips, "because we must talk about purchasing a house and decorating a nursery and discuss names. And we have to tell everyone, and find nannies and a governess and a midwife and—"

"Kit," Gigi said, rising up on her toes to kiss him once more. "Hush."

And he did. He settled for holding her instead, just long enough for the two of them to realize they'd fallen grievously behind the rest of the wedding party.

They ran, hand in hand, toward the church, toward the bells, and toward the promise of things to come. They ran toward the future.

Together.

AUTHOR'S NOTE

Thank you so much for reading!

I hope you enjoyed the adventures of Kit and Gigi as much as I did. I fell in love with London too, at the same time of year, when I was Gigi's age. For those of you wondering, Seven Dials is indeed named after literal sundials, which, by the time this book takes place, would have been moved to another location.

Jade and Mathias are next, with a book coming out in the autumn. We'll be leaving England again on *The Harpy* with a crew of characters you know and love.

As ever, I love to hear from my readers! If you have feedback, questions, or ever just want to say hi, you can reach me at Ava@AvaDevlin.com

Thanks again!

Ava

ALSO BY AVA DEVLIN:

The Somerton Scandals

The Dreamer and the Debutante (free prequel)

The Viscount and the Vixen

The Scoundrel and the Socialite

The Hero and the Hellion

The Marquis, the Minx, and the Mistletoe

The Silver Leaf Seductions

Unmasking the Silver Heiress

Unveiling the Counterfeit Bride